GW00600856

THE LIGHT THAT THAT BENDS ROUND CORNERS

Alexandra Carey

The Book Guild Ltd

First published in Great Britain in 2023 by
The Book Guild Ltd
Unit E2 Airfield Business Park,
Harrison Road, Market Harborough,
Leicestershire. LE16 7UL
Tel: 0116 2792299
www.bookguild.co.uk
Email: info@bookguild.co.uk
Twitter: @bookguild

Typeset in 11pt Minion Pro

Printed and bound in the UK by TJ Books LTD, Padstow, Cornwall

ISBN 978 1915853 639

British Library Cataloguing in Publication Data.
A catalogue record for this book is available from the British Library.

For
H + A + C + M

In memory of

Mutty
(2006-2022)
who gave us so much love

Part 1

September 2006

The arrival

Three frangipani trees lean languidly against the large white wall that guards the house, their clouds of white and yellow flowers resting on waxy green leaves. The car pulls into the driveway and almost immediately the front door opens. A short Filipina woman stands in the doorway, a shy smile on her round face. She's good-looking, a little stocky and has beautiful dark shoulder-length hair.

The family are all four squeezed into the back seat and Laura has hardly had time to open the car door before the children scramble over her lap to get out. She follows them and is immediately enveloped by the humid tropical heat but also by the soft, sweet scent of the frangipani flowers. On the journey from the airport they'd watched the sun sink with great speed, as though falling from the sky. But the cover of darkness hasn't cooled the city.

The two little girls run towards the Asian woman but

are struck dumb with shyness the moment they reach her. She smiles at them briefly then looks towards Laura and her husband, Peter, and says, "Hello, mam, sir. Welcome to Kuala Lumpur."

"Hello, Mariel, it's good to see you again. Thank you so much for being here to let us in," replies Laura, lovingly resting a beautifully manicured hand on the back of each of the children's heads. "Girls, this is Mariel. And Mariel, this is Tilly, and this is Aggie. Go on, don't be shy, say hello."

Tilly, the elder of the two, who at six is serious beyond her years, steps forwards and shakes hands solemnly with the Filipina maid. Aggie, on the other hand, normally so gutsy, hides behinds her mother's legs, overwhelmed. Mariel laughs awkwardly and suddenly Laura feels acutely aware that the girls have rarely met anyone of colour and worries that's why little Aggie is being so unusually shy.

Peter, smiling broadly, attempts to break the awkwardness by striding over and shaking hands enthusiastically with Mariel. But this seems to increase her discomfort and she's clearly relieved when he says, "Shall we go in?" Effortlessly, she picks up one of the four enormous suitcases and leads the way into the house followed by Laura and the girls. The driver brings the second and third suitcase. Peter struggles in with the fourth. They all congregate in the hall where Mariel and the driver briefly converse in rapid Malay. The driver leaves the bags and returns to the car.

"Mummy, Mummy, the house is upside down!" squeals a delighted Tilly, for the children have discovered that the bedrooms are off the entrance hall. Although, in fact, a staircase leads down to the living room as the house is built on a slope. Mariel gently herds the girls into the middle bedroom which is to be theirs. It's deliciously air-conditioned and Laura feels her senses reawaken. But it's bare, with stark white walls, large 1970s galvanised metal-framed windows and furnished with only two single pine beds. Looking towards Aggie, Mariel asks her which bed she'd like. Aggie, amazed at being offered the choice, jumps on the one in the corner whilst Tilly sits resignedly on the other. Laura finds herself charmed by Mariel's warmth yet cautious restraint towards the children – it's as if she's been handed a pair of precious stones whose beauty and value make her fearful.

There's a connecting door that leads through to the master suite, a room which Laura remembers being bright and airy but which now looks dull. It's dominated by a herringbone parquet floor made of a dark tropical hardwood that's reminiscent of a 1930s foyer in a bank. Here too the air-conditioning is whirring away and it's delightfully cool. Again, the room is unfurnished except for a large double bed which, like the children's, is beautifully well made, the sheet pulled taut and then turned back like in an elegant hotel, a careful touch which somehow accentuates the dilapidated feel of the place.

As they head downstairs, the humid heat engulfs them again for the open-plan living area is without air-conditioning – just old-fashioned wooden ceiling fans and four large French windows that open out onto a long veranda. Laura realises that the bungalow, as the estate agent had called it, is much more run-down than she'd appreciated. Its glistening brightness and historical charms have vanished into the night and the large garden that had won her over is now a dark and dangerous-looking void. A familiar knot of anxiety twists and rises up her gut. The estate agent had said there'd be enough furniture to keep them going for the six weeks it would take their possessions to arrive from England but Laura is shocked by its sparsity.

Mariel leads them through the door into the kitchen which, despite a large window opening onto the garden, feels even hotter and stuffier. It clearly hasn't been updated since the '70s – there's beige Formica everywhere. Mariel seems much more confident than when Laura had met her on her recce to KL to find a house and a school for the girls. Then, Mariel had lowered her beautiful brown eyes to the floor when asked a direct question. In fact, her reply to most enquiries had been that she'd been a maid in KL for nineteen years, which Laura took to mean she knew what she was doing. But despite such a shy response, she'd seemed perfectly happy to agree to collect the keys to the house and buy in some groceries for them. A glimmer of assertiveness had shone through when she'd said, "Mam, please, I will need take my annual leave in August so I can go back to Philippines and see my family." And of course, Laura had agreed.

Now Mariel hands over the receipt and the change from the shopping and then explains that the house had been in quite a mess and had needed a good clean when she'd arrived earlier that evening. Hearing this, Laura is embarrassed. She'd paid her in advance but only for a couple of hours' work. She'd assumed the house would've been left reasonably clean and hadn't expected Mariel to have to do so much. Perhaps she should give her more money. Mariel had clearly made a great deal of effort, turning on the air-con in the bedrooms in advance and making up the beds. Laura hesitates awkwardly, then starts to thank her profusely, but Mariel interrupts: "No problem, mam. Now I mus' go back to my boss. He want me back half hour ago." And with that she heads up the stairs towards the front door, waving goodbye to the girls, leaving Laura and Peter to fend for themselves in this land they find so foreign.

*

The driver, Prakash, a portly Indian man, is leaning against the car, still parked in front of the house, waiting for Mariel. She'd asked him to give her a lift back to her boss's apartment when they'd brought in the suitcases. It's not far but she knows it's a risk to ask. He might tell Mrs Laura and Mr Peter or, more likely, offer to keep quiet for a tip. But she doesn't have much choice. Mrs Laura hadn't offered any taxi money or called for one. She's an expat, a *mat salleh*, just arrived from England and doesn't know that the bus doesn't come up this far into Bukit Tunku. It's not the kind of neighbourhood that needs a bus. Mariel had guessed that she might have to pay for a taxi there and back, so she'd asked for nearly double the going rate for a couple of hours' work. Mrs Laura hadn't even haggled – just agreed without hesitation. *Mat salleh* – got so much money but no sense.

Mariel had been for an interview with her just over a month ago. She'd wanted a new job for some time – preferably for an expat family because they pay the highest salaries, and ideally one with little kids. So, when this friendly English woman in her fancy silk blouse and trousers had offered her a position, she'd accepted immediately. But then Mrs Laura had said, "I'm guessing you have to give your current boss a month's notice but, as it's just over a month till we move out here, that will be timed perfectly, and you can start with us the day we arrive. If you're OK with that?"

Mariel hadn't understood why she'd thought she could start in a month – it would take longer than that to transfer her work visa so, rather embarrassed, she'd just replied that she wouldn't be able to start so soon.

"But why? Is your period of notice longer than a month?"

And Mariel had felt shy, realising that Mrs Laura didn't understand about Malaysian employment visas for immigrant workers – that hers is attached to the passport of her current boss, Monsieur Duras, and that it can't be transferred until he agrees. So, she'd told her to ask Mrs Faridah at the maid agency to explain. Mrs Laura had then suggested that, if she couldn't start the job on the night of their arrival, perhaps she'd help them out for a couple of hours.

"You call my boss. Mus' ask his permission. If he say yes, then can." She'd given Mrs Laura his number – she wasn't sure that he'd agree.

But he had and now she's leaving the house, having met the whole family and carefully settled them in to their new home. She gets in the car. It's a nice Mercedes. Big in the back, more luxurious than her boss's. But a bit smelly. She leans back and buckles up her seatbelt.

"Who your boss? You want leave? You want work for Mr Peter and Mrs Laura?" The driver asks too many questions. Maybe a taxi would have been worth the fare. She feels a little nauseous as the car weaves it way down the hill.

"How long you been Malaysia? You like KL? Malaysia got good food – huh?" Mercifully they're pulling up outside the condo. She mumbles something about how much she likes Malaysian food and thanks him for the ride.

"No problem, lah! I happy help – easy, just five minute extra. No problem, any time, lah!" And she feels guilty for having found him irritating.

The condo is one of the fancy new modern ones – all glass and twinkling. She greets the security guards as she walks through the entrance gates and then through the paved courtyard with its manicured triangles of AstroTurf, towards the main foyer. She can see the swimming pool, with its subtle night lighting, to the right of the apartment block and she can hear the water cascading gently over the infinity edge. She's never been to the pool because maids are only allowed there if accompanying young children and Monsieur Duras's daughter, Amelie, is sixteen.

The apartment is on the fifteenth floor and the elevator is fast. She unlocks the front door and lets herself in as quietly as she can. She's an hour later than agreed. Her boss is a middle-aged expat from France. He's a mean man – embittered after his Malaysian wife lost a cruel battle with breast cancer. Mariel had started working for him soon after her death.

She can hear Amelie playing loud music in her

bedroom. She slips off her sandals, placing them tidily on the shoe rack, and creeps down the corridor, the cool marble soothing her bare feet. She's almost reached the kitchen when her boss emerges from his study. He follows her in.

"You are late. I said to return before 7.30."

"Sorry, sir. Flight from England delayed. Family only jus' arrive. Dinner ready soon, sir." She opens the fridge door and takes out a bowl of marinating prawns, and he returns to his study, grumbling under his breath. She knows he'd only agreed to her helping Mrs Laura out because he'd been embarrassed to say no to the polite English lady.

Piling skinny batons of freshly sliced ginger into miniature funeral pyres on the chopping board, she thinks of the English family. So very, very Western – can't see beyond their noses. Why do they want to live in that terrible old house? So many cockroaches – *aiyah!* Rich enough for a modern house. It's 2006 – plenty of modern houses in KL now. The real estate man must think Mrs Laura stupid to pay big money for such a broken old house. He hadn't even bothered to get the windows fixed and the place cleaned up before they'd arrived.

But the house had had proper 'staff accommodation' – a little separate bungalow with its own, totally independent, entrance. She'd had a good look inside before the family had arrived from the airport. The room was big – as big as the children's room in the main house – with enough space to have furniture, plenty of furniture. There'd been a built-in cupboard and a nicely sized bathroom and a lovely big window looking out onto jungle, so very private.

She's never had space like that before. Maids' bedrooms in modern condos, like her current one, are not much bigger than cupboards – only enough room for a single bed and a small side table. She must keep her clothes in storage boxes under the bed. And her window looks into the kitchen. Some maids' rooms have no window at all.

Tomorrow is Sunday, Mariel's day off, the only day of the week when she can see Vijay. She'll tell him about the house and the two little girls with their pale, pale skin and soft, tight curls. She'd been amazed by those curls – like something from a TV commercial. Vijay loves children – he would like some of his own but of course that's not likely now. He's like a child himself, simple and uncomplicated – that's why she loves him. They've been together for nearly twelve years but she's been a live-in maid that entire time with only one free day a week, so, counting the days they've actually spent together, it's more like one and a half years. She worries that she's tempting fate, but she can't help dreaming about a time when they can be together every day, can make love slowly and luxuriously – not a quick ten minutes when they're lucky enough to get some privacy.

She slices the chilli – red-hot fire waiting to light the funeral pyres of ginger. But the red chillies are actually all colour and no bite. Not so spicy, otherwise her boss will complain. He likes Asian stir-fry but French-style.

That's not the only thing he likes French-style.

Vijay's favourite is the chilli padi. He always has a little pile of them, not cooked, next to his food and every one or two mouthfuls, he pops one in. She can't take spice like that – neither her mouth nor her gut.

But in Vijay's village in Odisha, in India, even children are given chilli – so they're toughened up from a young age, ready to face the cruelties of life that are dished out to them. He grew up in Puri, a very poor region – not much food and not much education. His reading and writing skills are bad and his numbers are terrible. It makes Mariel appreciate how lucky she'd been with her school in the Philippines. She'd liked schoolwork and had always been good at it. She'd learnt her numbers well and languages came easily. Now, as well as Tagalog and her village dialect, Ilocano, she can speak English and Malay and a little bit of French. But after years in Kuala Lumpur Vijay still struggles with Malay and English, and even Manglish, the 'Malaysian English'. Sometimes she wonders how they ever manage to communicate. The rare occasions on which they've argued have always come about because of miscommunication.

The prawns sizzle and spit as she tosses them around the wok – their grey flesh pinking up gradually. When the food is almost ready, the rice cooker just rising to its climax, she places a large vase of yellow orchids on the highly polished table in the main room, and sets out cutlery for two plus taupe linen napkins with white flowers embroidered in the corner.

*

After Monsieur Duras and Amelie have eaten, Mariel clears the table. The girl, always polite and considerate, thanks her and leaves to go to her friend's house for a sleepover. The father, yet to learn from his daughter's example, says nothing and disappears behind his newspaper. Mariel, taking his plate, asks, "Will sir be requiring extra services tonight?"

There's a quiet before he replies. Even the newspaper is silent.

"Yes, I think so. Come to my room at 11.30."

She carries the plates through to the kitchen and is seized by a sudden urge to throw them crashing to the floor. It's time for something better than this.

But she must be patient and careful. If she leaves without his agreement then she risks being thrown in jail. He already knows that she'd like to work for Mrs Laura – she'd explained that it's because she wants to look after small children. He'd said that of course she's free to move jobs and he would sign the release papers. But he hasn't yet handed back her passport which, like most of her employers over the years, he'd taken for 'safe-keeping', and without it she can't apply for her visa to be transferred.

She leans over the kitchen sink and breathes deeply, calming herself. She *must* humour him. Tonight she will tie her hair the way he likes and, afterwards, ask him for her passport. Then tomorrow she will take it to the agent, Mrs Faridah, and ask her to start the transfer process.

An unexpected visitor

The roof hangs over the house but fails to protect it entirely from the strong morning light which assaults the bare windows and wakes Laura. Filled with daylight, the room is as cheerful and bright as she'd remembered. The large windows, entirely covering one side, give a panoramic view of the garden and the thick swathe of jungle that surrounds it. To the right is the swimming pool and an intense cluster of pale purple flowers that make up the crown of a fine jacaranda tree.

Laura decides to sneak down and enjoy a few moments of peace, exploring the garden, before the others wake. She's nervous about being able to keep the children fed, entertained and reassured all day as the four of them unpack and try to settle into this entirely unknown new life. Not for the first time she wishes that they'd been able to bring their wonderful South African nanny, Tracy, with them. She'd been with them since Tilly was six weeks old, had been a rock of stability during Laura's tricky patch after Aggie was born, and when Laura was working so hard she'd come home limp with exhaustion. Laura was under no illusions that Tracy knew and understood the children better than her.

"Right, my little munchkins, what shall we play?" she always used to say.

Now Laura walks down the stairs trying to recall Tracy's tactics for keeping the girls calm when anxious. At the bottom she steps into a puddle on the living-room floor and gasps. A large monkey is sitting squarely on the back of the sofa, his direct and challenging stare clearly claiming the cushioned throne as his own. She lets out a muffled squeak which her voice box had intended as a scream but her common sense had stifled. She finds she can't move, her gaze is fixed on the monkey and his is fixed on her. There's a surreal stillness, as if the frame of the movie has been frozen. His fierce eyes convey, without a doubt, that this is his home rather than hers.

Not surprisingly, a monkey in the house isn't something she'd ever encountered in her previously well-ordered life. How on earth had he got in? Last night, Peter, always the gallant protector, had carefully locked up and had mentioned a window that wouldn't shut properly because of a broken latch. Perhaps the house had been the monkey's palace for the last month and it was he that had caused all the mess that Mariel had mentioned.

The stand-off continues. Laura's always loved animals but more along the line of ponies, guinea pigs and rabbits. As a successful fashion journalist back in England, she'd occasionally encountered exotic animals on photo shoots, but she'd never had to deal with them herself. She feels vulnerable standing there in her thin silk pyjamas. She'd bought several pairs before leaving London, thinking they were pretty and would be suitable for an elegant expat life in the tropics. She certainly hadn't expected a monkey to be the first visitor to catch her in them.

Now she remembers the estate agent telling her that macaque monkeys often patrol this 'old-fashioned' neighbourhood and its surrounding jungle. He'd also said that the cooler temperatures in the hills of Bukit Tunku had been popular in colonial times. This had all appealed to Laura's romantic nature so she'd not fully absorbed his warning that monkeys can bite and sometimes carry rabies. But he'd also promised that they generally stay in the trees, too fearful to approach houses.

She's pretty certain that neither she nor the monkey has blinked yet, but she can't tell whether the impasse has lasted a minute or ten. She remembers to breathe. And wonders whether he's planning to bite her – the silk pyjamas won't be much protection. How long have you got to get to hospital if bitten by a rabid monkey? Come to that, where is the nearest hospital? Whilst wishing that Peter would wake up and come to her rescue, she thanks God that, because of the time difference, the children are still fast asleep.

She's conscious that her feet are wet and, glancing down, realises that the puddle has become a flood. Water is pouring through the skirting board onto the marble floor. But she's broken eye contact with the monkey. Panic rises through her. Is he going to pounce? Is she to die of rabies in hydrophobic agony?

In fact, the monkey doesn't move an inch but continues to stare her down. The water keeps on coming and the flood spreads across the floor. Comprehension finally dawns. Laura realises that the monkey is not courageously eyeballing her from his throne but is marooned on an island, afraid of the water. She is, in fact, entirely in command of the situation.

She takes a deep breath and readies herself to step forwards and shoo the monkey away. Sensing her intention, he bolts for the open window with the broken latch, bounding across the wet floor, lifting his feet as if the water is sticky and might trap them.

*

Peter is still fast asleep in bed, his jetlag clearly overcoming his excitement.

She shakes his shoulder. "Darling, wake up, there's water pouring all over the floor downstairs. It seems to be coming through the skirting board. And there was a monkey on the sofa giving me the evil eye."

He looks at her with a bleary, dazed and uncomprehending expression. The wrought-iron bed creaks in complaint as he sits up and rubs his hands over his eyes and through his hair in one movement.

He follows her down the stairs, calm and unflustered, stretching as he goes. Laura marvels at his steadiness and, not for the first time, thanks God she found him. After a little investigation he finds a stopcock in the downstairs bathroom, turns it off and before long the flow of water stops.

The two of them survey the expansive main room of their new home. At one end, the living-room end, is a wicker garden sofa covered with a white cushion discoloured by mildew – the monkey's sofa, as Laura now thinks of it. The floor is made of marble terrazzo and the flood is meandering towards the dining-room end of the room which is furnished with an ancient wrought-iron garden table and four equally rusty folding chairs, all of which seem to quake with fear at the sight of the approaching water.

Laura hadn't expected the first morning of their new life in Kuala Lumpur to be idyllic. Far from it: she had in fact convinced herself that the move abroad and leaving their pretty farmhouse in Suffolk was a huge mistake. But she'd looked forward to her first breakfast in the tropics – possibly enjoying a large yellow mango in the warmth of the Malaysian sun. Peter, on the other hand, had hardly been able to contain himself for the last few weeks. His adventurous nature had always yearned for the excitement of a foreign posting, especially in Asia. He'd fallen in love with the region during his 'gap' year, between Eton and Cambridge, when he'd explored it extensively. More than once he'd told the story of the time he'd been invited to dinner with a well-known British lepidopterist who had lived in an old-fashioned bungalow up in Genting Highlands, not far from Kuala Lumpur. The two of them had eaten outside, an ugly bright light above the dinner table, as his host had told him about every one of the multitude of moths that fluttered towards the light, mistaking it for the moon.

But Peter hadn't set out to be posted in Asia – things had just happened that way. He'd been 'phased out' of his well-paid job with a large consultancy firm in London and had then spent over six months getting increasingly frantic looking for a new one – with either a consultancy or venture capital firm. So, when he'd been offered a job as an associate for the successful venture capital firm Spears Anderson, he'd accepted immediately, even though the role was in Kuala Lumpur. Laura, on the other hand, hadn't accepted his decision so quickly. She'd had a very good job, as a fashion journalist for *The Sunday Times Style Magazine*, which she'd desperately not wanted to give up. She'd fought hard to get where she was, and the idea of giving up a career she loved to follow her husband halfway round the world to become an expat wife not only offended her feminist sensibilities but also filled her with a terrible fear of losing a piece of her identity. She and Peter had argued almost daily for a month, her friends and colleagues all advising her not to give in.

"Surely Peter can find another good job in London?" her best friend Sam had said over a glass of wine after work. "And he must appreciate that it's not fair to ask you to give up your career just so he can pursue his. What about a compromise? Maybe looking in Europe? That would make it much easier for you to keep your career on track." But it was Sam's final comment that really made Laura's stomach lurch: "You know what the fashion journalism world is like; if you're out of sight for too long you'll quickly be forgotten and relegated to the archives."

Now, as Laura faces the prospect of clearing up an extensive amount of water without a mop, only with a couple of old tea towels, that conversation seems like something from a different world.

And they need to find a plumber. God knows how.

Even if they had Malaysia's version of the Yellow Pages, they wouldn't be able to understand the Malay language.

They wade through the water. It's cool and calming and plays with their toes. Peter opens the four French windows that lead out to the veranda and, as he does so, the noise from the garden fills the room. Calls, squawks, clacks, clicks and critters like they've never heard before – a soundtrack to the cinematic vista of the veranda overlooking the pool and the surrounding jungle vegetation. Laura switches on the three large ceiling fans and their paddles begin to whir – laying down another music track.

The heat and the light are intense – 30°C despite it only being nine o'clock in the morning – and it dawns on Laura that perhaps there's no particular rush to clear up the gradually evaporating flood. She rummages in the kitchen for the breakfast things that Mariel had brought the night before.

After meeting her again, seeing her tenderness towards the children and the beautifully made beds, Laura is hoping that it won't be long before Mariel can move in and start work. Initially, when Peter's new boss, Jim Gilroy, had suggested they should hire a maid, saying that it was the norm – "Everyone in Malaysia who can afford a maid gets one" – Laura had recoiled, thinking it was archaic. She'd eventually come round to the idea, persuading herself that it was the Malaysian equivalent of having both a nanny and a cleaning lady. But there's a delay regarding Mariel's work permit. When she'd interviewed her, Laura hadn't appreciated that as Mariel isn't a Malaysian citizen she needs a visa to live and work in Malaysia. Mariel had seemed very uncomfortable about the whole thing and had told Laura to speak to Mrs Faridah, the Malay, *Bumiputra*, lady at the maid agency.

Mrs Faridah had said, "Yes, Mariel visa must be transferred by Immigration Office from Mr Benoit Duras employment to Mr Peter Thompson, your husband, employment. Paperwork will take some time, maybe six months."

"Six months?" Laura had been horrified.

"Yes, Mrs Laura. First Mr Benoit must agree to release Mariel. I will speak to him and ask him to revert to me." She had an obsequious and all-knowing tone to her voice which had annoyed Laura. "Then when she released, she must return to Philippines for minimum three months. If you want her start more quickly, can pay additional penalty facilitator fee to get permission for her not to return to Philippines. Shall I enquire on your behalf how much facilitator fee?"

Laura had been completely thrown by this conversation. It hadn't occurred to her that Mariel wouldn't be free to move jobs as and when she chose. The knowledge that she had to be 'released' made her skin crawl. And the 'additional penalty facilitator fee' was clearly a bung. She'd liked Mariel and was convinced that she would be a wonderful help, especially with the children. After discussing it with Peter, they'd agreed that unless the extra fee was ridiculous they'd pay it. After all, the salary that Mariel had asked for was very reasonable despite apparently being at the top level.

Laura opens the fridge and a platter of delicately cut fruit smiles back at her: papaya, mango and pineapple – Mariel had left it there last night. She finds a faded blue

21

and yellow cloth, which she spreads on the rusty table, then sets out the breakfast things and goes upstairs to wake the children. They're curled up together in Tilly's bed, both in a deep sleep – their little bodies, still on English time, thinking it's two o'clock in the morning. Tilly, shy and bookish, is fiercely protective of little Aggie, two years her junior – not that she needs protecting, for Aggie is adventurous, just like her father. Laura wonders if she should tell them about the monkey. It's rather amazing, after all, to live in a house with monkeys in the garden rather than just boring foxes and rabbits. She pictures the delight and amazement on their faces and knows that the first person they'll want to tell will be Tracy. She's clearly going to have to agree to a few expensive phone calls home.

Sunday

Mariel wakes in her own bed – thankfully Monsieur Duras has never required her to stay all night in his. She wraps her arms around her bolster cushion, hugs it like a teddy bear and dozes for a little longer. The humming of the fridge in the kitchen wakes her again and she rolls over, still in a foetal position, taking the bolster with her. Thank goodness for Sundays – one day of the week when she can rest, be lazy and just be herself. She stretches, eases herself gently out of the narrow bed and switches on the light of her little room.

There's a washroom ensuite to her bedroom – it's small with just a toilet, a basin and a handheld shower attached to the tiled wall, but it's private. She closes the toilet seat cover and sits on it, then leans forward, turns on the shower and starts to wash her thick dark hair, firmly massaging her scalp, easing the tension in her brain.

She thinks about what she should wear today and decides upon her navy-blue pencil skirt and her maroon polyester blouse with the pretty buttons. It doesn't crease so will still look smart and business-like in the afternoon when she has her meeting with Mrs Faridah. A little worm of guilt crawls its way into her consciousness – she's planning to skip church today so that she can spend the morning with Vijay as her afternoon will be taken up with Mrs Faridah. Even though she doesn't truly believe anymore she still feels guilty when she misses Mass, plus she wants to be seen as a respectable woman. And she'll miss catching up with her friends, Faye and Jenny. But she can't bear not to spend most of her day off with Vijay, and besides, she wants to tell him about the English family. She squashes the worm.

Returning to her bedroom she gets dressed and puts out her best shoes, the black ones with the bow across the front. And then she goes back to the bathroom to put on her makeup, wiping the mirror dry. She loves applying makeup, creating a better version of herself – smoother skin, longer eyelashes, more defined cheekbones and rosy-red lips. She thinks she still looks pretty good for thirty-nine despite the years of hard work. Today she'll look as lovely as she can for Vijay, and it won't hurt to look good for her meeting with Mrs Faridah.

Mariel has known Mrs Faridah at the maid agency for nineteen years – the entire time she's been in KL – and has always used her to find new positions and facilitate her visa transfers. She knows her to be a tough and greedy woman, but she's reliable and always succeeds where other agents sometimes don't. Mrs Faridah has a lot of friends at the Immigration Office.

Amelie is in the kitchen, fixing breakfast. Coming out

of her room, Mariel smiles at her; she smiles back and says, "You look nice, Mariel. Have a lovely day."

Mariel is fond of Amelie and knows it's been hard for her to deal with her father's grief as well as her own. She walks down the passageway towards the front door. As usual Monsieur Duras is sitting at the dining table reading his newspaper. She leaves the apartment, takes the elevator down and strides briskly to the bus stop two blocks away.

By the time she arrives at Megamall, a few minutes after 10am, it's already buzzing with people all enjoying their Sunday and the air-conditioned cool of the giant mall, with many preparing for the forthcoming Deepavali, otherwise known as Diwali, festival. Decorations are everywhere – on the floor of the central foyer there's a beautiful *kolam*, a huge intricate pattern of brightly coloured shapes and depictions of Diwali lamps entirely made from artificially dyed rice and grated coconut. People of all three Malaysian races – Malay, Indian and Chinese – are stopping to admire it, and Mariel smiles at the sight of two mothers firmly holding back inquisitive toddlers longing to submerge their hands into the rice. Clearly at least one captive has succeeded in overcoming their captor, for there's a patch on the edge where the colours are blurred and the pattern is lost.

Taking the escalator to the stalls in the walkway on level 6 she buys a pair of flipflops and two plain T-shirts for work, one in red and the other in green. Her current boss doesn't provide her with a uniform and she's not expecting Mrs Laura to – she certainly didn't mention a uniform at the interview. Then, she heads back down to meet Vijay in the food court.

The food court offers a wide range of different cuisines: Malaysian, Indian, Chinese, Thai, Vietnamese, Japanese, Italian and, of course, the ubiquitous American KFC. Vijay is sitting in a booth enjoying a classic Malaysian breakfast of *nasi lemak*. His entire demeanour is friendly and his seemingly ever-present bright white smile stretches across his face, contrasting with his dark skin. He has a neat moustache which curls down a little on either side of his mouth and he is short with a hint of a belly.

He greets Mariel with just a smile, careful not to embarrass her with a public display of affection, and she returns the gesture, conscious of how nice her lips are looking. Even after nearly twelve years her heart always swells at the sight of him. Sometimes she almost fears the intensity of her love for him, almost as much as she fears the thought of the sacrifices she's made to be with him coming to nothing.

Suddenly she notices that his right index finger is bandaged. She's always worried that he'll get a terrible injury at the furniture factory where he works. But he tells her that it's nothing serious; he'd just cut it slightly when he hadn't been concentrating – because he'd been dreaming of her. And she giggles and play-punches him in the shoulder. Then, without another word, he goes up to the counter to buy her some *roti canai* with dahl and she laughs at his ability to read her mind.

For a while they enjoy their food in silence and then she starts to tell him about her evening with the family, including every detail – the little girls' curly hair, Mrs Laura's long blonde hair and expensive-looking dress, Mr Peter's height and piercing blue eyes, the old-fashioned house with its veranda and terraced garden, the large separate maid's room, how they'd seemed kind and thoughtful, the little girls respectful and endearing. She talks so fast she's practically out of breath and surprises herself with her own excitement.

Fixing her with a serious gaze, Vijay says, "Sound good people – mus' get this new job." And she nods, knowing that he hates her working for Monsieur Duras. When, three years ago, Monsieur Duras had first offered her a job, she and Vijay had talked it through and agreed that, although it would be hateful to have to provide extra services, it would be worth it for the higher salary.

"Will new sir boss want extra?" Vijay asks, and she says she doesn't think so, maybe only if Mrs Laura goes away with the children on long trips.

They leave the mall together and start walking in the direction of Mrs Faridah's office until they reach a café on the corner which has a big TV showing the football. Vijay's favourite team, Manchester United, is playing. They agree to meet later in the day, back at the apartment where Vijay lives with four other men – also immigrant workers from Odisha in India, indeed from Puri, the same district as Vijay.

*

The employment agency is on the third floor of one of KL's older office blocks. The lift smells and makes an alarming groaning noise, and Mariel wishes she'd taken the stairs. The office is busy – Sundays obviously being the easiest day of the week for the agents to meet and interview maids. The corridor is packed with women, most of them young, some just girls really. Nearly all of them are Filipinas or Indonesian. In addition to Mrs Faridah there are three other agents sitting at their desks, all Malay women, talking intently to the maids, perched nervously across from them. Other than the four desks there are numerous battered filing cabinets crammed wherever they will fit with further box files stacked on top of them. This leaves only just enough wall space for a clock and the standard pictures of the current *Agong*, the king, and the prime minister.

Mrs Faridah's wearing a pistachio green *baju kurung* patterned with large pale pink flowers. Her *tudong* headscarf is in a matching pink. As usual, her manner is condescending, and Mariel is glad that she'd dressed well and worn her best shoes. She hands over her passport and tells Mrs Faridah that Monsieur Duras has agreed that she can leave his employment.

"Yes, he has told me also and asked me to find him a new maid."

Mariel is relieved to hear this.

"So is good news for you," continues Mrs Faridah, "Now I have your passport, I will arrange transfer and then ask Monsieur Duras to sign release papers." She clears her throat. "Of course, you must pay penalty fee if not returning Philippines. And I afraid my fee now double last time – prices all gone up and also this transfer very complicated. I need spend lot of time at Immigration Office."

Mariel is seething. She'd expected the price to go up but not to double. Why must these people be so greedy?

Tonight she'll have to call home to the Philippines and tell her family there'll be no money coming this month. Luckily, she's already covered her son's veterinary school tuition fees for this semester and there'll still be enough to pay the running costs of the village bakery, which she'd bought a few years ago. But her daughter and son-in-law, who run the bakery, will no doubt complain, wanting more pretty clothes and toys for the new baby, so Mariel will have to explain that it can't be helped. She'll tell them that her boss has moved away and that she's found another better job. She won't tell them the truth about Monsieur Duras.

The supermarket shop

It's their third day in Malaysia and Peter is going into his new office for the first time. He looks like a nervous schoolboy as he gets dressed and eats his breakfast. The girls give him homemade good-luck cards, a hug and a kiss, accompanied by serious 'you'll be fine' faces. The arrival of the chauffeur-driven company car rapidly brings out the executive in him and he speeds off looking distinguished and waving regally, leaving Laura feeling rather flat as she realises that she's been left alone with the children for the first time since she can remember – with no exciting fashion industry or buzzing metropolis to escape to and no nanny to entertain them.

"Run along and play," she says, at a complete loss as to what to do. Tilly, clearly sensing her awkwardness, suggests she join them for a game of cards. UNO is their current favourite – they'll teach her how to play. The situation seems almost surreal to Laura – just over a week ago she was sitting in her office in London wearing DKNY and now she's sweating in a T-shirt in KL being taught cards by her four-year-old and six-year-old. How did this happen?

When they stop the game for a snack Laura remembers that they have to make their first foray into the city to go to the supermarket. The supplies that Mariel bought have run out. Peter had said he'd ask the office driver to come back in the company car and take them to Bangsar Shopping Centre, where apparently there's a good supermarket.

They'd met the office driver, Prakash, an Indian Malaysian, on their first night when he'd collected them from the airport. He'd been extremely kind and considerate, especially towards the children, but he'd been rather flatulent, a condition which in time would become a family joke.

Laura pours the girls the last of the apple juice and is just trying to put together a shopping list when she hears the car pulling into the drive.

The three of them sit in the back, feeling a little shy and slightly giggly. Aggie had agreed to be in the middle but only on condition that they take it in turns. Laura's not entirely sure whether that includes her. She almost relaxes into the luxury of being chauffeur-driven until she remembers that once they've bought a car she'll have to navigate herself – they're not really meant to use the company car for personal journeys – so she'd better concentrate and learn the route.

The car winds down the hill, past other bungalows and patches of thick, dense jungle. And then it emerges, as though from a bygone era, into dense traffic on a six-lane highway. Malaysia proudly displays its developing status with its road networks – before long they hit a giant intersection and turn onto another highway. The stark ugliness of the roads is tempered by wide beds of vibrantly coloured flowers neatly planted between the traffic lanes, one of which Laura recognises as bougainvillea; the other, she later discovers, is hibiscus, the national flower of Malaysia.

At the front of Bangsar Shopping Centre is a drop-off point for chauffeurs to deposit their employers and a valet parking service. Clearly a shopping centre for the wealthy. The supermarket is at the far end of a large central foyer. It immediately seems foreign. Just inside the entrance are mountainous piles of unlabelled vegetables, none of which Laura recognises. And the smell of the place, a cornucopia of aromas, is completely alien to her – the bitter scent of some of the vegetables, the earthiness of others, curry powders and spices, all intermingled with a slight smell of disinfectant.

On the way Prakash had told her that this supermarket is 'good for expat, mam' because it stocks all the Western foods. But now she doubts this. The children have been surviving off pasta since they'd arrived so she's hoping to buy sausages and a chicken to roast. The three of them head down an aisle in search of the meat section. When they find it, it's so small Laura wonders if most Malaysians are vegetarian. There are no whole chickens, just packets of greying, slightly shrivelled chicken drumsticks.

"Excuse me, do you have any sausages?" she asks a man stacking the next-door fridge, and he points towards a row of cans. She gawps at them blankly, utterly confused, and assumes that he's misunderstood, until she realises that they're canned chicken frankfurters. And then, feeling an idiot, she remembers that Malaysia is a Muslim country and Muslims don't eat pork.

After settling for the frankfurters, much to the children's delight because Laura's normally very particular about them not having processed food, and grabbing a box of American-style Fruit Loops, the only vaguely recognisable cereal, they walk back towards the vegetable mountains.

"Now, which of this lot shall we try?" she asks, on the off-chance.

"None," replies Tilly with a backing chorus of "Yuck! Yuck! Yuck!" from Aggie.

Of the three types of vegetable that the girls generally agree to eat, there are no frozen peas, the cucumbers are strangely pale, and the only carrots she can find are flaccid. After paying at the checkout, getting confused with the different ringgit notes, they pop into the pharmacy next door and buy some bright orange vitamin tablets, which Laura hopes will stave off scurvy for the foreseeable future.

Prakash drops them at the house but has to head straight back to the office so the girls help Laura carry the shopping downstairs to the kitchen. The heat is beginning to debilitate them all. The 90% humidity means they're wet within five minutes of leaving the air-conditioned car. After three days Laura has realised she can't avoid sweat showing through her clothes leaving her looking like she's done a couple of rounds with Mike Tyson. What was it her grandmother used to say? 'Horses sweat, men perspire and women merely glow.' Some chance. As she struggles with the heavy bags, she feels the sweat trickling down her back and into her knickers – not sure what Grannie would have to say about that.

They start to unpack the shopping and put things into the fridge – all three of them hovering around its open door, idolising the cool. Aggie whines, "I'm sooooo hot," her tight curls plastered with sweat to her little head and suddenly Laura feels ready to explode with heat-induced irritation.

"Right, I've had enough of this! It's too hot to do anything. Let's go for a swim and we can sort this lot out later."

They leave the rest of the shopping bags and go back upstairs, deliberating which swimming costume to wear: Aggie – pink frills or yellow sunflower; Tilly – blue Speedo or Boden beach ball; Laura – elegant green and gold one piece or the rather trendy brown tankini with white spots.

*

The children splash enthusiastically in the swimming pool. Laura, drip-drying on a rickety old sun lounger in the shade of the jacaranda tree, is eyeing the pink plastic slide positioned at one end of the pool and thinks she might forgive it for being so ugly as it's kept the children entertained for well over half an hour.

She watches them play – Aggie zooming time and time again down the pink slice of delight and squealing with joy as the polystyrene floats of her swim jacket enable her almost to bounce on the water. Tilly, more cautious, having discarded her floaty jacket the previous summer, appears to be swallowing huge gulps every time the slide dumps her unceremoniously into the greenish water, and Laura tries to remember whether typhoid and cholera were included in the extensive injections that the girls were given before they left England. Despite being impractical, Peter had managed to clean the pool filter, so the colour of the water had improved marginally, or perhaps its appeal had just increased exponentially as the days passed and they'd felt stickier and stickier.

Laura scoops up a handful of the fallen jacaranda flowers, admiring their delicacy and gentle lilac colour. She'd never seen one before arriving at the house, although Peter was able to tell her what it was, and she's taken with the tree's elegance. She looks up into its skinny intertwining branches – the light so bright it seems to bounce off every flower and twig. By contrast to the dappled rays through the big beech tree at home, here the sunlight dances and twists as though it's bending round corners. It both exhilarates and frightens her – the sense that this place will bring her something new yet has torn her from her roots. She feels bereft of her home, of England. And again, angry with Peter for making her move.

She's conscious that the beauty and light conceal dangers lurking in the garden. Other than monkeys there may very well be snakes. They'd spotted a huge Jurassic-looking lizard down by the storm drain towards the bottom of the garden. It'd been at least a metre long and looked ready to take out one of the children with a quick swipe of its tail. And on their second night Peter had killed a giant centipede that was about twenty centimetres long – its legs moving in a Mexican wave as it slowly made its way across the living-room floor, apparently oblivious to Laura's screams. Later, Prakash told them its bite is as poisonous as a snake's which at least had justified her melodramatic reaction.

She'd chosen this eccentric old house because it was the only one she'd found with a large garden. She'd wanted space for the girls to play – in keeping with her belief that children should grow up in the countryside, preferably the English countryside, with space to charge around and be feral, to have pet rabbits and ride ponies and rescue hedgehogs in the summer. That's why they'd moved to Suffolk six months after Aggie was born. The commute had been hard work, especially in the winter, but it'd been worth it to enjoy, in her view, the best of both worlds – top-notch, well-paid jobs in the city and the peace of a farmhouse overlooking a river, which, in turn, had helped to shift the lingering remnants of post-natal depression.

She'd found there'd been something cathartic about leaving the city behind at the end of the working day, though she was always eager to be back the following morning, especially after she'd been given a column of her own at the magazine. She'd dreamt of having her own column for years and planned to make it one that all well-dressed women would refer to. It was called 'This Week's Fashion Must-Haves' – every Monday all the designers and brands would shower her office with samples which she and her assistant, Louise, would carefully sift through, deciding what should be included. It gave Laura a real buzz knowing that sales of a piece were likely to shoot up if included in her column. Once the list was finalised, Louise would put everything on the rails and racks in the large office storeroom and then, theoretically, the samples were shared out fairly among the departmental staff. Of course, senior staff generally got first choice, so Laura was easily able to expand her collection of designer outfits.

Commuting to and from London meant that she and Peter didn't see much of the children mid-week, but Laura had been confident that the benefits of growing up in the country outweighed this downside. Luckily, the wonderfully competent and loving Tracy had been happy to move to the country with them. And Laura had always felt that Tracy was much better with the girls than she was. So, she'd confidently left Tracy in charge whenever she had to travel for work, which she did regularly, especially to the big European fashion shows. One year, Laura was working the room at *Vogue*'s annual party during Paris Fashion Week wearing a beautiful but extremely uncomfortable pair of Jimmy Choos when Tracy rang to tell her both girls had chicken pox but that Laura wasn't to worry as she had it under control. And Laura, trusting that she did, kept networking and managed to persuade Diane von Fürstenberg to be interviewed for the magazine.

After spending several hours showing Laura properties, the estate agent in KL had clearly been amazed when she'd chosen the old house in Bukit Tunku rather than one of the newly built but, in Laura's opinion, generic and characterless ones in a gated community designed specifically for expats. These houses had had security guards, communal pools, management companies providing maintenance men such as plumbers, and ready-made social lives. But also, no charm, concrete patios instead of gardens, and nosey neighbours with twitching curtains. When she'd chosen the house, bitterness at having to uproot the children and give up her job had made her obstinately reject the advantages of an expat gated community in favour of the closest replica she could find to their house and garden in Suffolk.

Now, gazing through the purple-flowered branches, she realises that this little private jungle is not a place for children to play and that she longs for a friendly neighbour and a house with modern plumbing and air-conditioning in every room. Another wave of homesickness surges over her – if only Peter had found a job in London. The dreaded 'black dog' skirts around her perimeter. She's felt it sniffing at her ankles for the last few weeks – the sadness at having to give up her job, especially her column, and the upheaval of the move, threatening to let it overwhelm her again. With every ounce of strength she tells it to scram.

"Don't do that!" shouts Tilly as Aggie splashes water at her.

Laura thinks she'd better get them out of the pool and find a game to play. They'd only brought a few. She's not sure she can take another round of UNO – she makes a mental note to find a toy shop if sanity and harmony are to be maintained until their things arrive from England.

They head back towards the house, past the 'staff bungalow' that sits quietly behind the pool and through the side door. A burglary is apparent the moment they walk into the kitchen. The rejected contents of the shopping bags are strewn across the table and floor – the tins of frankfurters, the washing-up liquid, the loo paper. The torn cardboard cereal box lies on the floor looking violated, the inner bag and its contents nowhere to be seen. Next to it a packet of cheddar cheese with bite marks all over it has been discarded. And there's an exploded bag of flour with tell-tale footprints through the resulting dusting of snow. The bananas, mangoes, melon and even the flaccid carrots are all gone.

"Fucking monkeys!" she shouts, and the children's jaws drop.

The wet market

Laura drops the girls off at school. Prakash has driven them all in the company car – Laura's car is due to arrive next week. It's the second week of school, their third week in Kuala Lumpur and everyone is beginning to settle in. The school seems friendly despite being enormous, with seven hundred children on the primary campus alone. It describes itself as 'the British school in Kuala Lumpur' so Laura had assumed most of the pupils would be the children of British expats, but it turns out to be an international school following the British curriculum. Tilly is in fact the only child in her class of thirty for whom English is her mother tongue, which has its advantages as she's landed the part of Queen Victoria in the Year 2 play – *Queen Victoria's New Clothes* (the Empress having replaced the Emperor on this occasion). Prince Albert is played by a boy whose father is Pakistani and whose mother is Italian. There are two ladies in waiting; one is Belgian, and the other is Dutch. Other cast members are

Australian, Swedish, Danish, Indian, and there are also a few children of wealthy Malaysians who want a British education for their kids.

After the school drop-off Prakash takes her to Chow Kit wet market. Laura has finally discovered from one of the other mums at school that this type of wet market is where most Malaysians buy their fresh meat and fish, hence the paucity in the supermarket. So, she's resolved to buy a chicken to roast for dinner. Armed with her shopping bag and determination she approaches the market entrance but is immediately accosted by the stench – mainly of fish but with undertones of freshly butchered meat. It's so overwhelming that she wonders whether she has the stomach for it – perhaps she'll just buy more of the supermarket's greying drumsticks. But she steels herself and ploughs her way through aisles of wriggling glossy black eels, fish of varying sizes with varying death stares, crates of crabs and piles of prawns, and on towards the stalls with rows of hanging meat. How on earth has she ended up shopping in a place like this? It isn't the kind of retail experience she'd expected to be part of her life.

It is indeed a wet market – the floor is so wet she has to pick her way carefully through dirty puddles of water, wishing she hadn't worn her pretty Emma Hope sandals and wondering how many diseases are festering in the place. As soon as she'd entered the market she'd felt alien and conspicuously white. All three races of Malaysia are here – Malay, Chinese and Indian – the Malay ladies in their *baju kurung* and *tudong* headscarves make Laura feel exposed in her thin silk shirt and linen shorts, her blonde hair flowing loose. And the noise of the place reverberates

41

through her bones – vendors shouting in Malay, loud and repetitive, neighbouring Chinese stallholders vociferously debating in Hokkien, and the incessant scraping of knives being sharpened.

She halts in front of a stall stacked high with yellow-skinned chickens, prostrate on their backs, wrinkled legs pointing to the heavens. Her tolerance almost at its limit – *oh, to be in Waitrose.* She points at the nearest bird, hands over the money and retreats, navigating her way round the puddles and other customers as fast as her expensive sandals will allow.

*

In the kitchen that afternoon Laura stares at the chicken. It stares back at her. She'd wanted a whole chicken and it is indeed entirely whole, head and feet still firmly attached. Too firmly, she's discovering, for the feeble knives she'd found in the kitchen drawer. One, two, three – *whack* – she tries to remove the head, hoping that brute force will make up for the blunt guillotine. It now lies at an awkward angle, partially severed. The chicken looks up at her with utter contempt for the mess she's making of this simple procedure.

"You try it, mate," she growls. "Not exactly my area of expertise," and she draws back for a further attack.

Finally, the job is done, but all satisfaction is immediately obliterated by the sight of the bird's scaly feet, toes eerily curled, as though it had tried to grasp hold of its perch at the moment of death. Nausea rising and her composure beginning to waver, Laura decides that she'll just have to roast it with its feet still attached. So, she throws the bird and its unblemished limbs into a pan with some garlic and butter, savagely stuffing it with a half lemon.

"Bloody hell!" she curses on opening the oven door.

"Why are you swearing, Mummy?" Tilly asks amiably as she saunters into the kitchen carrying a colouring book carefully opened at a neatly finished page.

"I've forgotten to pre-heat the damn oven."

"Oh… right," replies Tilly, clearly unsure why that's such a serious problem. "Aggie and I have finished our colouring and are going to play tag on the lawn."

Anxiety immediately rises up Laura's spine. Even Peter, who's normally so calm, agrees that despite Laura's dream of the children having space to play, the garden is too dangerous for them to be in unattended. No secret Enid Blyton-style dens like the one under the weeping willow back home. There'd been a formal ceremony to say goodbye, an official breaking-up of camp. Tears had been shed. Although the garden in Malaysia has numerous locations perfect for dens, hidden from view by wide, dripping jungle leaves, they're already occupied by a *Secret Seven* of serpents and a *Famous Five* of monkeys. There's even a *Mallory Towers* dormitory of dusky langur monkeys at the top of the jacaranda tree.

Laura switches on the oven and, without waiting for it to heat up, shoves in the chicken and rushes out to the garden to watch the girls.

The small lawn of tough-leafed tropical grass forms a semi-circle on the upper terrace. Rough stone steps lead down to the rest of the garden through a pretty, slightly shaggy arch created from bushes with tight balls of orange flowers. The lower terraces slope down steeply to a storm drain at the bottom where there are a few clearer patches with palms, papaya and banana trees, but otherwise, especially at the perimeter, it is dense jungle, mosquito-infested and generally uninviting. The swimming pool sits to the right of the upper lawn and the main house, in front of the small separate bungalow that is the staff quarters.

There's a swing on the broad wooden veranda that leads out from the sitting room through the French windows. The roof of the veranda provides much-needed cover from the frequent tropical downpours, and a delicate but powerfully red passionflower hangs down from it, creating a perfect setting for the table which sits on the veranda overlooking the garden below. A small round pond lies to the left-hand side of the lawn, from which a cacophony of frogs detonates on a nightly basis, often drowning out all conversation at dinner.

The family had first experienced this on their second night at the house. They'd all been eating together on the veranda, the children up late with jetlag.

"Listen, girls... the frogs are farting!" Peter said, which made Aggie laugh so much she clutched at her tummy. Tilly, attempting to stay serious, tried to explain above the noise of her giggling sister and the croaking chorus that she'd learnt all about tropical frogs in her *Encyclopaedia of Animals* and that they were definitely 'calling', not farting. Unfortunately, just repeating the word set Aggie off again.

Now the little girls are racing around the lawn but already tiring of the limitations of playing tag with only two, and by the time Laura has settled herself on a chair on the veranda they've started to sing and dance at the top of their voices – one of their favourite occupations. The sight of them there, using the lawn as their stage, the green grass under their bare feet, performing with complete abandon, reminds Laura of a beautiful summer's evening in Suffolk earlier that year – the night when this whole adventure began. She and Peter had arrived back from work in London to find the children in their pyjamas begging to be allowed to do a dance for them on the lawn before going to bed.

"Absolutely fantastic!" Peter had declared once the show was over and Tilly and Aggie had gone to bed pleased as punch, with the evening call of the blackbird to sing them to sleep. Laura and Peter had returned to the lawn with a glass of wine, and Peter, grinning from ear to ear, just like the girls, had said, "You know that meeting I went to today?" He raised his glass, almost as though making a toast, and took a large, celebratory swig. "Well, I may have been out of work for six months, but it's finally happened, I've been offered a job, a really good job, by the venture capital firm Spears Anderson. The only slight issue is it's based in their office in Kuala Lumpur." His face was alight with excitement.

"Where?!" Completely thrown by this unexpected announcement, Laura gulped at her wine.

"Kuala Lumpur, in Malaysia." His childish grin morphed into an encouraging smile at the sight of her expression. "It could be really exciting, a true adventure – for us all – especially the girls." He looked up at the girls' bedroom window, his whole face now a picture of encouragement. "I know it's going to make things tricky for you and your work, but it's an amazing career opportunity for me – they want me to develop a company that's making a natural sweetener called stevia. If I make a success of it, I'll be made a partner of Spears Anderson." He stood tall and proud as he said this. "But best of all, I'm to be given shares in the stevia company, which means that when Spears Anderson sell it on, we could make *big* money."

"Tricky for my work? That's putting it mildly! Malaysia's in Southeast Asia, that's miles away. Do they even have fashion journalists in Kuala Lumpur? And it'll all be completely foreign for the children. And what about school?" Her questions pummelled him.

"There's a big expat community in KL – there'll be an international school. And I'm sure you'll be able to find something interesting to do. Asia's an amazing place."

She looked away, turning her gaze towards the river in the distance. He took her hand gently, but she snatched it from him, continuing to stare across the fields. "We've got to consider it as an option," his earlier smiles were now replaced by a clear look of disappointment, "there's no way I'm going to get offered a job like this in London, or anywhere else in Europe, for that matter."

Laura felt the foundations of her life suddenly shift, ready to slide her back into the black hole that Aggie's tricky birth had dumped her in. Her career was so important to her, Peter knew that. OK, her salary was small compared to his and he really did need to get a new job if they wanted to go on living the way they were, but surely he could find something in London. She turned back to him, anger exploding through her veins.

"So, you just expect me and the girls to give up everything and follow you halfway around the world so that *you* can advance *your* career? What about *my* career? My column? Am I supposed to just chuck it in? Have you *actually* thought this through at all?"

She stormed off. For the next month they argued more bitterly than ever before until finally the finances and the possibility of Peter being made a partner persuaded her. The salary was very generous plus they'd be able to get good rent from the house in Suffolk.

Peter said that Jim Gilroy, who would be his immediate boss at Spears Anderson, had stated quite clearly that they wanted him to develop and sell Sweet Stevia, the sweetener business, within a year. "So, that means we can come back after a year if you want to – hopefully with me as a partner and therefore able to request a role in London."

She'd spoken to her editor at *The Sunday Times Style Magazine*.

"Laura, I think you're crazy to go. But you're one of my best writers, so hopefully I'll be able to offer you freelance work in a year's time, if not a salaried position."

Laura had prayed she was being genuine and that she wouldn't be forgotten in two months' time, as her best friend had predicted.

Thunder cracks dramatically and jolts her out of her reverie. A curtain of rain falls with suddenness and weightiness onto the girls dancing on the lawn. The afternoon tropical storms are still a novelty – Tilly and Aggie run around squealing and giggling and are soaked through in a minute. But Laura anxiously tells them to come in – the strict 'lightning protocol' at the school has alerted her to its dangers. An alarm, the lightning bell, goes off the moment a storm starts, and all students have to take cover immediately. One of the other mums had told her that KL is one of the most lightning-prone cities in the world and that it isn't uncommon for residents to be struck and killed. Laura shudders at the thought of the girls being hit by lightning – she feels that every day she discovers something else frightening about their new life and she's not sure how she'll cope if the list gets any longer.

She takes the girls upstairs for their bath. They're still singing.

Mrs Faridah's phone call

The family alarm clock that takes the form of Aggie climbing into Laura and Peter's bed, cuddling up and tickling one of them, wakes Laura at 6.20am. Since those black months of post-natal depression, when she'd felt like her body and soul were being dragged through mud, sleep isn't something that Laura finds particularly easy – it often eludes her. She wraps an arm around the human alarm clock, surreptitiously pinning down the tickle-prone fingers, and calculates that she's probably had five hours of solid sleep – not too bad. Ten warm, cosy and tickle-free minutes later the digital alarm clock goes off. It's a school day.

Holding Aggie's hand, the two of them go down to the kitchen for their routine early-morning battle with the cockroaches. Today there are only six, a mid-sized battalion. The day before there'd been double that. Laura thinks they must have been there that first morning but what with the monkey and the flood she'd managed to miss the army of cockroaches. They'd certainly been out in full force on the second morning – one had even scurried across her bare foot as she'd walked into the kitchen, causing her to scream so loudly she'd woken the whole house.

For the daily battle Laura's choice of weapon is a traditional corn straw broom – its length enables her to keep a distance and she can both brush them out of awkward corners and whack them with the flat side of the broom's head. Aggie's choice of weapon is one of her father's shoes, but she only chooses to engage if she can creep up on the enemy from behind and be sure of a direct hit. Hostilities are generally over after about ten minutes, although the battle is never entirely won – the enemy just retreat behind the kitchen cabinets until the following morning.

Laura finds the whole proceedings dispiriting and wonders whether every household in Malaysia has to wage this daily war. She remembers her morning routine back in England – she'd wake up and encourage the girls to play for a bit, then cave in and let them watch TV, she'd shower and wash her hair, choose one of her many designer outfits to wear to work, return to the kitchen to find Tracy giving the children their breakfast, kiss them goodbye, and rush out of the house with Peter to drive to the train station.

Now she switches on the kettle, throws a load into the washing machine and takes Aggie back upstairs to get dressed. Tilly has already put on her school uniform and is reading a book on her bed. Peter is having a shower. Both Laura and the girls have come to appreciate the benefits of a school uniform designed for a tropical climate – one simple cotton dress in green and white gingham, white ankle socks and a pair of shoes (plus knickers, of course). No jumpers, coats, hats, scarves and gloves, all waiting to be lost, and, best of all, even though she's only four, Aggie is able to get ready for school entirely on her own, as long as someone helps her with her shoes and socks.

*

Laura drives them in her new car which they've now had for a week. It's a large automatic SUV. They were advised to get it in case of carjacking, which is not uncommon and another thing on Laura's list of anxieties. Luckily, driving in Malaysia is on the left-hand side of the road like in England, but the style of driving suggests to Laura that the highway code is a little different. And she finds the junctions on the highways confusing because, to her, they all look the same. This morning she misses the turning again so must drive to the next junction and manoeuvre around a series of complicated connecting roundabouts in order to go back in the opposite direction. Both girls stress about being late for school.

"Oh no! Have we gone the wrong way again?" asks Tilly. "I mustn't be late. We've got a spelling test in period one."

Aggie has 'Show and Tell' for the letter S for which she is taking in a half-used bar of soap. She'd only remembered just as they were leaving the house and between them it was the best they could come up with – either that or an already opened packet of spaghetti which they all agreed would make a mess in her school bag. By the time Laura gets home she feels like she's done a full day already.

The washing machine has finished its cycle, so she steels herself to hang out the clothes. She's learnt that in Malaysia they quickly smell bad if you don't hang them up immediately. In fact, the climate's 90% humidity causes all the cupboards and drawers to have a musty odour about them, and although she's put something called a 'Thirsty Hippo' in each one – a box of moisture-absorbing granules with a pink lid and a cute cartoon of a fat hippo giving a cheery thumbs-up on it – she's beginning to realise that fresh-smelling clothes are something that she'll have to learn to live without.

The washing line is in a covered area that's underneath the large front porch of the house. As the house is built into the slope of the hill, this space has the quality of part cave, part garden shed. It's dark and creepy but the clothesline is there because it's protected from the daily tropical rain. Just to enter this space requires Laura to overcome many of her childhood fears. Every few minutes there's a scuttling noise from one of the hidden nooks and crannies – she forces herself not to think of rats or snakes or tarantulas. The air is oppressive as though stored up from years and years of equatorial heat, and as she hurriedly pegs up the clothes, she feels the stinging sensation of sweat in her eyes. She longs for the gentle touch of a Suffolk breeze on her face.

Finally finished, she fixes herself a lime soda and collapses into a chair on the veranda. The ceiling fan above her makes a repetitive but strangely soothing clicking noise and she finds herself sinking into a heat-induced lethargy.

Her eyelids droop – her vision of the garden blurs into a single vibrant band of green, suddenly interrupted by a streak of yellow as a beautiful golden bird makes a fly-by, landing in the jacaranda tree. Its song is strong and lilting, and seems to pierce through the cacophony of the jungle. And much to her surprise, Laura feels a stirring of her soul.

But the moment of peace is broken by the ring of her phone. It's Mrs Faridah from the maid agency. Laura crosses her fingers and prays that she's ringing with good news regarding Mariel's work visa.

"Good morning, Mrs Laura. Thank you for penalty fee payment – transfer of Mariel's visa is nearly complete." Laura exhales a little. "Just one small delay – Mr Benoit Duras asks you pay costs incurred finding his new maid before he sign release papers."

Laura is furious – the man is effectively holding them to ransom. Not to mention the hold he has over Mariel. Her words are spluttering from anger, so she ends the conversation as fast as she can, saying that she'll discuss it with Peter and get back to her.

*

Later that night, after the children have gone to bed, Laura and Peter have dinner on the veranda. The frogs have struck up their usual chorus, but tonight their croaking just echoes Laura's irritation. She'd had to contain it because Peter had come home from work in such a good mood. One of the partners at Spears Anderson had told him about an upcoming exhibition of contemporary

Malaysian art. Peter had been passionate about modern art for years – his evident delight at discovering there's more of an art scene in KL than he'd been expecting made her feel she should at least wait a few minutes before inflicting her cross mood upon him.

When she tells him about Benoit Duras's demand he's typically phlegmatic and says that he'd been half expecting this as Jim Gilroy had suggested that this is the norm if you 'steal' a maid from someone. Jim had also said that experienced helpers who want to look after children and are able to cook Western food are not easy to find. Peter reminds Laura that they've already paid the penalty transfer fee, so they haven't got much choice.

"My hunch is that Mariel's going to be worth all this extra expenditure," he adds.

Laura looks out into the darkness and silently concedes how much she's longing for her to start work – someone to clean the house properly, someone to do the washing, someone to show her how to cook all these strange vegetables, someone to play with the girls, someone to talk to who understands this land she finds so foreign. And then perhaps she can start looking for some kind of job herself. She'd only discovered after they'd arrived that legally as an 'expat spouse' she's not allowed to work. This had caused another furious row with Peter – Laura apoplectic that he hadn't checked beforehand and a little suspicious that he had but had chosen not to tell her. And also furious with herself for not looking up the rules. But there'd been so much to organise with the move, and it hadn't even occurred to her. Now she's determined that she must be able to find something to do. Although the idea of being a lady of leisure is quite appealing – just for a bit, perhaps. Her feminist core reprimands her for these thoughts, but she *is* longing to have a rest, to give in to the overbearing heat, to go slow.

Peter tells her he'll drop into the maid agency tomorrow on his way to work, hand over the cheque and ask Mrs Faridah to 'expedite the situation as fast as possible!'. Laura laughs at the fierce facial expression he's parodying and relaxes a little.

"Thank you, darling – that would be a real help."

Dance with the broom

Mariel is doing the ironing in the utility room. It's right at the back of the apartment beyond the kitchen and her bedroom. Monsieur Duras is at work and Amelie has gone to the school swim team training session. Mariel is listening to her favourite radio station, one that plays Filipino pop – and is happily humming along to a song. She loves ironing – the satisfaction of getting round the collars and edges of her boss's shirts, of producing such a neat and perfect result, not to mention the delicious smell of the spray starch.

The song stops and the presenter announces the 5pm news headlines: "*Sixteen companies and private landowners are under investigation by the Indonesian authorities. This is in connection with the forest fires that have caused the haze that is drifting over to the Malaysian Peninsula.*" Noticing the time she realises her boss will be home soon. She must stop ironing and sweep the living-room floor before either he or Amelie get back. Carrying six ironed shirts on coat hangers in her right hand and the broom in her left, she walks through the kitchen along the corridor and into his bedroom, where she hangs up the shirts in the large built-in wardrobe. Then, crossing the corridor, she enters the large main living room where she turns off the air-con and carefully starts to sweep the marble floor. She uses an old-fashioned straw broom – she doesn't like the modern Western ones which need two hands: *No rhythm with those ones.*

Her grandmother, her *lola*, always says, "When you sweep the floor you must dance with the broom." She'd taught Mariel to place the back of her left hand against the base of her spine and to sweep with her right arm, using strong, broad strokes. Doing it that way, she'd said, protects your lower back and the gentle, lilting motion soothes your mind as well as cleans the floor. Mariel loves her grandmother. She wonders whether her mother and her children are making the effort to look after her properly. At over eighty she's the oldest woman in the village and, now that she's lost her sight to cataracts, visits from her friends and family are her only joy. Mariel hasn't seen her for nine years, and although she'd explained why she couldn't visit, she knows that the old lady is hurt and confused by her absence.

The fact is, Mariel hasn't seen any of her family for nine years. Her son, Vito, had been ten years old when she'd last returned to the Philippines – a bright kid, already obsessed with animals – always bringing the village strays back to the house, and always having to protect them from his grandmother, Mariel's mother, who was less keen to increase the size of the household. Up until that year

Mariel had been back to the Philippines every August, but she'd never really formed a proper bond with her boy. He'd remained shy around her – he was, after all, only six months old when she'd first left to work in Kuala Lumpur. Not surprisingly, all three of her children are much closer to Mariel's mother, who's had to bring them up.

Mariel's middle daughter, Mila, now twenty-one, had been twelve at the time of that last visit. She'd been a conscientious little thing but always nervous and frightened of her father and his bouts of drinking. Her elder sister, Rosa, is the strong, confident one of the three, always has been. But also, the bossy one – from a young age she'd taken on the responsibility of protecting and overseeing her siblings. Mariel had been working in the paddy field, a young wife of seventeen, when she'd gone into labour with Rosa – a wide-brimmed straw hat shading her from the sun, her bare feet in the water, little worms of mud squelching through her splayed toes. Her belly had been too large to help with the picking but her back had still been strong enough to carry the bundles of soft, hay-like grasses on her shoulders. She'd understood immediately that the pains were the baby coming and she was frightened. She'd called over to her mother, whom she could see with the other pickers, bent low in the middle of the paddy field, the backdrop of the jungle-covered mountains behind them, the sun glinting off their white shirts and hats. Together, she and her mother had walked slowly back to the village to find the midwife, stopping every ten minutes or so, waiting for the contraction to pass, her mother rubbing her back to soothe her.

The baby's arrival had been like a gift from God and had given a whole new meaning to Mariel's life. Rosa was the first ray of sunlight in her otherwise dark and oppressive marriage to her husband, Vincente. But Mariel and Rosa had only had three and a half years together before she'd left for Kuala Lumpur. Mila was born a year after Rosa and, even before Vito was born two years later, it'd been clear to Mariel that her only option was to go abroad to work. Her husband's drinking had made it harder and harder for him to hold down a steady job and support their ever-growing family, and as he had grown increasingly violent, she'd known she had to get away for her own safety. Her mother was happy to look after the kids for her; in fact, she saw that as her role in life, and thankfully Vincente was never violent towards the children. Mariel had several classmates who'd already gone abroad to work as maids in Kuala Lumpur, Singapore, Dubai and Hong Kong. At home jobs were scarce and wages were so pitifully low that Mariel wasn't alone in having few other options. She also wasn't alone in having a husband who drank too much and was willing to let his wife be the main earner. It was a classmate who had given her the contact details for the agency in KL.

The rhythmic sweep of her broom creates another little mound of dirt, adding to a gradually growing range of dust mountains across the bleached plain of the marble floor – a temporary landscape until she returns with the dustpan. She thinks of the past nine years, how long they've felt. She's spoken on the phone to her children at least once a week and they've regularly exchanged photos. She knows that even if she'd continued to go back to the Philippines once a year, she'd never have had much of a relationship with them. But it's been truly hard not being able to see them grow up and watch them with pride become such successful adults – Vito, starting this semester at veterinary school, Mila now a qualified nurse and Rosa a married woman with a baby girl of her own. But Mariel knows it'll all be worth it because once she's stayed away from her husband and her family for ten years, she'll be able to get a divorce. The lawyer in KL had told her this. Only one more year to go. Then she and Vijay will get married and be able to spend the rest of their lives together – not have to separate and return to their respective countries once their Malaysian work visas expire. As man and wife, once they decide to stop working in KL, they'll move back to her village in the Philippines. Mariel has saved her money shrewdly over the years, making her a rich woman back home, so they'll live a comfortable life. But her family don't yet know that she's planning to marry a Hindu Indian – they'll be shocked to the core. She'll have to find the right moment to tell them.

The click of the key in the front door startles her. She quickly sweeps all the little dust mountains into the pan, switches the air-conditioning back on and returns to the kitchen to start preparing the dinner. Monsieur Duras and Amelie have come home together.

Mariel is busily rummaging in the fridge for the tilapia fish she's planning to cook for dinner when her boss calls her to come through to the living room. Her heart thumps loudly against her ribcage and, under her breath, she mutters a prayer for good news. She stares at her feet as she walks into the room but then, raising her head, sees that

Monsieur Duras is beaming a smile at her. She's surprised how much it suits him – he looks kind and friendly, and for the first time she notices that he and Amelie have the same eyes.

"Mariel, I have some good news for you. I have found a new Filipina maid, so I have signed the papers releasing you from my employment. She is starting on Monday – you may leave on Sunday."

An art exhibition and cottage pie

It's Saturday and the family are driving to an art gallery through the late afternoon rainstorm. Giant raindrops are pounding the bonnet and the windscreen wipers are unable to keep up. Jim Gilroy, Peter's boss, has got them an invitation to a private view of an exhibition of contemporary art. Peter had suggested that they all went together, but Jim replied that Susan, his wife, hates modern art. Instead, he invited them to come over for an early supper afterwards.

"He wants you to meet Susan." Peter had explained to Laura. "He says she's an 'experienced expat spouse' and will help you settle in. I haven't met her, so I don't know whether she's 'friends' material. Jim's alright – bit dull but he's well meaning and he's been incredibly successful. Must have made a packet."

Laura had been pleased. She wants a friend or at least someone to talk to who understands the country. And she appreciates that it's important to be friendly with Peter's boss and his wife. She's gradually getting to know some of the mums she's met at the school drop-off but many of them are clearly new to KL as well. Plus, the school gates and the politics that so often surround them are a new experience for her, one that she's wary of.

"Do Jim and Susan realise how young the girls are and that we haven't got anyone we can leave them with yet?" Mariel's not moving in till Sunday, ready to start work on Monday.

"Yes, he said it would be a treat to have little ones in the house as their two boys are now grumpy teenagers, always out with their mates. That's why he suggested supper at 6pm."

Surprisingly, the art gallery is in a private house just outside KL. Peter is driving and Laura is directing – normally a recipe for disaster especially in such weather conditions. Clearly aware of a potential row, the two girls are sitting in the back playing quietly on their Nintendos. Luckily the invitation has easy-to-follow directions on the back and KL's motorists are driving reasonably sensibly despite the rain, so the expected marital dispute is avoided.

After about thirty minutes' drive, just as the storm is tailing off and the tarmac roads start steaming, they arrive at a large, very modern house sitting in about fourteen acres of land. As well as being a well-known art gallery, it's the home of the most eminent architect in Malaysia and his Australian wife. The house is extraordinary – it's made of steel and concrete but references the style of a traditional Malay house with a wide pitched green roof and deep overhangs. Clearly to emphasise this, there's a sweet little traditional *kampong* house sitting in the grounds. Laura wonders if it's the gardener's house or just there for show.

"Wow, what an incredible modern design." Peter's face lights up. "So original."

"It's certainly that. What date is it?" As she gets out of the car she rearranges her floaty trousers – they're sticking to the back of her legs.

"1980s, I'd guess."

The girls have put on their best dresses – for such a grown-up outing. They're matching although Tilly's has blue flowers and Aggie's pink. Laura takes them by the hand, one on either side of her, and they all four walk towards the house. She thinks the house is crazy but undoubtedly more interesting than most of the buildings she's seen in the city so far. The art gallery is attached to it by a covered loggia that overlooks a cascading water garden with vast water lily pads and spiky bamboo. It's noticeably cooler here than in the city but the mosquitoes are just as abundant, and she thanks God that she remembered to cover the girls in Mosi Guard before they left. The threat of dengue fever is no small matter – it's rife in KL and worse near building sites where mosquitoes breed in the stagnant water that collects during construction.

The exhibition is of paintings by contemporary Malaysian artists and all the proceeds are going to the Malaysian branch of the World Wildlife Fund. This had particularly appealed to Peter, who'd shown the girls a photo of the endangered Sumatran rhino, the world's smallest rhino, which was on the invitation.

The paintings are as extraordinary as the house – they're of endangered animals, although you wouldn't know it to look at them.

"Girls, come and have a look at this giant picture. What colours can you see? Can you spot any good shapes?" Laura loves the way Peter always manages to engage them. The children immediately pick up on his enthusiasm and of course are thrilled to be spending quality time with their father, whose long working hours make that a rare thing. But Laura knows that Aggie, in particular, is likely to get bored and whiney soon. Plus, they're the only children there so she feels conspicuous.

The gallery is not that crowded – the private view runs on into the evening so Laura assumes that most people will come then. It's easy to spot the artists, the more trendy and alternative-looking types, amongst the well-to-do prospective buyers. A young Chinese guy wearing a white T-shirt and baggy jeans, with shoulder-length hair and a goatee beard, is chatting to a middle-aged Malay couple. Laura moves closer to listen.

"…the heavy layers of red represent the orangutan's blood."

She and Peter know none of the other guests – that makes her uncomfortable. At private views in London they'd always bump into someone they knew. So even though it's a thrill to get away from battling the elements in the house and to find such a cultured vibe, she's relieved when Peter senses her discomfort and suggests that they leave.

"But… if it's OK with you, I'd like to buy this one?" He points to a black splodge with some green bits around it.

"Yes! Yes! Mummy, please say it's OK. That's the rhino."

"It is?" she asks, laughing.

"Yes, that's its horn there," Tilly points at a slightly spiky bit on the left of the black splodge. Looking at it Laura laughs more. She turns to Peter, who starts laughing too. Delighted, the girls join in and, within moments, the splodgy black rhino is part of the family. Luckily the painting is not expensive and despite its completely abstract depiction, Laura can see its beauty. She feels it'll be a perfect memento of their first encounter with contemporary Malaysian culture. As they drive back into the city, towards Jim and Susan's house, a comfortable sensation washes over her, a positive feeling of hope for the future.

*

Dinner with Jim and Susan is less of a success. They're both very friendly and welcoming but Susan is a matronly, no-nonsense, bossy type who wears her Scottish heritage on her sleeve, quite literally, sporting a little tartan silk scarf. Early in the evening Laura is sure that they're never going to be real friends. The look on Susan's face alone conveys that she thinks Laura's interest and career in fashion utterly frivolous. The khaki skirt and mustard blouse that form the backdrop to the tartan scarf show she clearly has no feel for fashion or understanding of the multi-million-dollar international industry that's behind it, and which filters down into all walks of life. Jim and Susan's large, ugly house, in one of the more exclusive yet characterless gated communities, is furnished like a Scottish lodge with tartan sofas and chandeliers made from antlers.

They sit down to dinner at a heavy teak dining table and the men immediately start talking about the stevia company. Tilly and Aggie are awkward and shy.

"We're having cottage pie for dinner – I thought it'd be nice to have something cosy that reminds you of home. Maria, don't stand there hovering – put the dish down on the table!" Susan's maid, Maria, carefully sets down the cottage pie in front of her mistress, keeping her eyes firmly fixed on the food, clearly not wanting to engage with any of them. Laura is cringingly embarrassed when Susan says, before Maria has even left the room, "I made this myself. Maria's a hopeless cook." And she smiles cheerfully as she dollops out a plate for everyone. But it's disgusting – the meat grey and lumpy – and the children just push it around their plates. Susan's cooking is evidently as hopeless as her maid's – Laura remembers it was Jim who'd said that maids who can cook Western food are few and far between. She also knows that Susan's lived in Asia for well over twenty years, always with a large posse of staff, and clearly hasn't got a clue how to make a good cottage pie. But she's kind to the children and settles them on one of the tartan sofas with bowls of ice-cream and a DVD of *Mary Poppins*. Aggie falls asleep the moment she finishes her ice-cream, her head gradually sliding further and further towards the bowl which she's cradling in her arms, until Laura gently removes it and lays her down on the cushion.

As she returns to her seat, Susan asks, "So, how are you settling in? I gather you've found a good maid which is no small achievement. The Filipina ones are better than the Indonesians, although more expensive. But even then, it's potluck whether they're any good or not. You must join

67

'Enjoy Malaysian Culture' – it's a group I run for expat wives. We have talks and tours on interesting cultural topics. I'll put you on the mailing list – it's a very good way to meet people and makes friends."

She hands a bowl of ice-cream to both Peter and Jim, who are still engrossed in their conversation. Laura notes that she didn't wait for an answer to her question. But, she reflects, she's obviously part of the backbone of KL expat society and a useful person to know.

*

On the way home in the car, both girls now asleep in their car seats, Peter says, "Sorry Jim and I talked so much about work. He's a total workaholic – would never think that it might be nice not to talk about it at a family supper." Taking one hand off the wheel he reaches over and holds hers. "He really wants me to get Sweet Stevia ready to sell on within a year, which we all want. But it's a tall order, even though it's a fantastic business. So apart from needing to impress him, it was a good opportunity to pick his brains about the marketing strategy."

"It was fine – I could see it gave you the chance to show him how inspired you are about the business. Susan's not really my type, though." That was an understatement – Susan had given her the heebie-jeebies. Her fast-flowing river of forceful conversation reminded Laura of Peter's mother, another matron she didn't get on well with. She was really disappointed not to have found a friend.

"Yeah, sorry about that. Maybe this Enjoy Malaysian Culture thing might be worth going to – hopefully you'll

meet some people there who are more your cup of tea."
She certainly hoped so. "But it's important that you at least
pretend to be friends with her because she *is* the boss's
wife." Peter could be so irritating sometimes – treating her
as though she has no understanding of office politics and
apparently forgetting that she'd spent ten years working
her way up the ladder of one of the most political and
back-biting industries in existence.

October 2006

The nicest room

On Sunday morning Mariel arrives by taxi at Mrs Laura's house. She has managed to fit all her possessions into two large suitcases. She feels awkward ringing the front doorbell and even more awkward when the entire family, including Mrs Laura's husband, come to the door to greet her.

"Hello, Mariel!" chorus the girls, neither of them in the least bit shy around her now.

"We've painted some pictures for you." Tilly shows her their paintings.

"Can you come meet my dollies? I've got my two most speshall ones, Lulu and Posy – my uver ones are coming on the big boat all the way from England." Aggie takes hold of Mariel's hand and leads her down the stairs towards the playroom, and Mrs Laura, smiling apologetically, follows behind with Tilly.

The playroom is a good-sized corner room with windows on two sides. It has the same beautiful wooden herringbone flooring as the bedrooms and some painted bookshelves on which the children have put the few toys they'd brought from home. On one of the lower shelves two dolls are sleeping peacefully on beds made from folded tea towels. In the corner of the room is a large metal bucket filled with a couple of inches of water. Above it there's a nasty water stain on the ceiling.

"The roof is leaking," explains Mrs Laura. "The water comes in quite fast when it's raining. I've rung the estate agent. He says we're required to do all repairs which I'm really annoyed about because he didn't explain that before. It certainly isn't clear from the contract." She suddenly looks self-conscious, as though she hadn't meant to have such an outburst. And Mariel thinks to herself that Vijay could easily fix the roof.

Against the wall adjacent to the bookshelves are two brand-new children's desks and chairs – one in yellow and the other in pale blue.

"We went to IKEA yesterday," Tilly tells her. "I've never seen such a ginormous shop in my whole life. I chose the blue desk 'cos it's my favourite colour and Aggie chose the yellow one. She's crazy about yellow." Aggie grins from ear to ear and touches her new desk as though it were sacred. Then she goes over to the bookshelf and picks up her two babies, cradling them one in each arm, and in a hushed tone introduces them to Mariel – the one with dark hair is Lulu and the blonde one is Posy. She looks dismayed when Mr Peter walks in and says in a voice loud enough to wake any sleeping baby that he's taken Mariel's suitcases to her room and that perhaps it would be nice if the girls showed her the staff bungalow.

Mariel is cringingly embarrassed that he's moved her suitcases for her. Why did he do that? She's the maid – it's her job to fetch and carry things, and she's strong, of course, perfectly capable of carrying heavy suitcases. Is he trying to shame her the day she starts? She wishes she'd just kept them with her and hadn't allowed the children to sweep her along. She drops her gaze and stares at her feet as they walk through the living room, the kitchen, the utility room and then out the back door, across a small, paved area and into the staff bungalow. To her relief Mr Peter doesn't come along – just Mrs Laura and the children.

The little bungalow consists of a small hallway, a bathroom and a big bedroom. The kids dance around the room quite freely and jump on the bed, and Mariel makes a note to herself that she will have to make it clear to them that her room is out of bounds. Apart from Monsieur Duras, who'd been married to a Malaysian woman and had lived in KL for twenty-five years, she's never worked for a European family before – she wonders if the children will be wild and badly behaved. Amelie was always sweet and kind – but she was sixteen and generally saved any 'difficult teenager' behaviour for her father. Mariel has previously looked after kids who at first had shown no respect whatsoever and who'd assumed that she'd be at their beck and call day and night. But she'd always been firm and taught them to respect her privacy. She remembers Xiu, a little boy, who'd been so naughty and rude when she'd first started looking after him, but she'd soon taught him to be nice and polite. In this new job she certainly intends to start as she means to go on.

Mrs Laura is wandering around the place as though inspecting it properly for the first time. There's a new double bed with the plastic wrapping still on it and a chest of drawers. She says, "We can also get you a little fridge if you'd like?" And Mariel wonders why on earth she thinks she'd like a fridge; she's not intending to eat in here – she'll have her meals at the table in the utility room so that she can serve and clear the family's meal. She might possibly have a snack in her room on Sunday nights – but probably just packet noodles.

"No thank you, mam, no need."

"Oh… OK. Well, you've got a kettle." It's sitting on the windowsill. "And once our stuff arrives from England you can have the TV that came with the house. What about a couple of fold-up chairs in case you want to sit on the little porch outside?"

"No thank you, mam, no need." Mariel wishes Mrs Laura would stop being so friendly – it's making her uncomfortable. After all, they're not friends – Mrs Laura is her boss. Of course Mariel won't want to sit outside, where the family can see her, when she's not working – she'll obviously want to be completely private. And, in any case, she's unlikely to be here much on Sundays because she'll spend the day with Vijay. It's clear to her that Mrs Laura has never had a maid before. At her interview Mrs Laura had asked if she'd like to have Saturdays off as well as Sundays. Mariel wasn't at all sure why she'd suggested this and worried that it would mean a reduction in salary. So, to be safe she'd replied, "Is OK, mam. I happy to work Saturdays."

"Are you sure? That'll be a very long week. The children can be quite exhausting." But Mariel had been uncomfortable and hadn't felt she could change her answer. And besides, all the maids she knows work six days a week.

"Are you going to put our paintings up on your bedroom wall?" Tilly is still holding them proudly. Mariel hesitates and then, seeing a look of hurt spread across the child's face, suggests that she'll put them up in the kitchen where she'll be able to see them when she's working. She knows better than to let affection for the children she looks after enter the privacy of her soul, into the world where she's a mother, a grandmother and Vijay's wife-to-be.

Mrs Laura gathers up the children, saying that they must leave Mariel in peace to settle in, but just as they're leaving the room Mr Peter appears and hovers in the doorway. Awkwardly he asks Mariel if she might know how to do the backwash on the main water pump for the house. He explains that the estate agent had shown them how to do it and advised them to do it monthly but now he can't remember how.

"I'm no good at these practical things – we don't have pumps like this on plumbing systems in the UK," he adds.

Mariel apologises – she has no idea.

"Oh dear, that's a shame. I was really hoping you'd know how to do it."

Mr Peter looks so disappointed that she becomes increasingly concerned that he's already dissatisfied with her – first the suitcases and now this. But why did he ask her? He should know that it's not a maid's job to do that sort of thing. Do maids in England also do maintenance work? Evidently, she's going to have to set clear boundaries with the parents as well as the children. If Mr Peter can't or won't do the practical jobs himself then he should hire a caretaker who knows how to look after an old house like this.

The family head back to the main house, leaving Mariel to her awkward and anxious thoughts. Standing on her porch she can hear them step out onto the big veranda and then the little girls playing on the swing.

They're clearly spending most of their time out on that veranda – having their meals at the round table and relaxing on the sun loungers. It seems so strange to her that they want to live in such an old-fashioned way, like in the old days in *outstation* bungalows on the rubber plantations. Nowadays wealthy KL people don't live like that – they prefer to stay indoors in the air-con, away from the humidity and the dengue-infested mosquitoes. Modern amenities enable Malaysians to get away from the discomforts of the past when the jungle was in control. And now they've got power over it, they like to show off the speedy development of the country – no one wants old-fashioned things that remind them of their previous lack of sophistication. But this crazy house has no air-con except in the bedrooms. Why does this English family want to live like that? Mariel can't understand it because she'd always thought that Western people, *mat salleh*, were very modern.

She returns to her bedroom and has another look around. It really is the nicest room she's ever had – worth working in a crazy old house for crazy *mat salleh*. She wonders why they bought her a double bed – there'd be more space if she just had a single one. She peels the plastic off the mattress and lies down on it. Tonight will be the first time since she was last in the Philippines that she's slept the night on a double mattress – on the few occasions she's stayed over at Vijay's place they've cuddled up on a couple of roll mats. Suddenly the memory of Monsieur Duras's double bed makes her shiver, and she thanks God she no longer must suffer that man.

Of course, she would never dare to bring Vijay back to the house, but that doesn't stop her dreaming about lying in this new bed with him. Her mind begins to whir. What if Vijay could live here with her? The room is big enough for the two of them. If Mr Peter can't even work the water pump the family clearly need more help with the house. Vijay could do all the maintenance and the gardening. Not only could they live together before they're married but it would be the perfect job afterwards because it'd mean they could continue earning big salaries and wouldn't have to move back to the Philippines immediately just to be able to live as man and wife – there are few jobs on offer for couples in service in KL.

But how will she persuade Mrs Laura to hire Vijay? And what if she finds out they're not yet married? Mariel has heard that some Westerners are very relaxed about this kind of thing. But if she makes that assumption and it turns out that Mrs Laura disapproves, they might both be fired and then where would they be? They'd be deported back to the Philippines and India, and her ten-year separation plan would have failed and been all for nothing. She will have to be very careful and make sure they don't get fired.

She opens her suitcases and starts to hang her clothes

in the large built-in wardrobe – there's more than enough room for his things too. Then she sets out her photo frames on the little bedside table – one of her three children taken on her last visit home nine years ago, a new one that Rosa had sent of the baby and finally one of Vijay smiling so sweetly that her resolve strengthens. No need to rush things; better to let the family struggle a bit with maintenance problems. But she must be careful not to wait so long that they hire other people to do the jobs. They've obviously already got someone doing the gardening; she'll have to find a reason why Vijay would be a better alternative.

Now her heart is beating so fast she can hear it. The idea that she and Vijay can live together in KL *like married* before she gets her divorce suddenly seems tantalisingly possible.

They'd planned to meet at his place after she'd dropped her stuff off at the house, so she sends him an SMS to say she's on her way and rings for a taxi.

Maybe this crazy old house will be their ticket to a better life in KL.

The big boat arrives all the way from England

A sense of excitement stirs Laura from her sleep and, as she dozes in the anteroom between slumber and wakefulness, she tries to remember what it is that's making her feel this way. Then it comes to her – today their belongings are arriving from England, having travelled on a container ship all the way from Felixstowe, just a few miles from their beloved Suffolk farmhouse. So now she's fully awake and sitting up in bed. It's 6.25am.

Then another gratifying thought trickles into her brain, and she leans back against the pillows, returning to a luxurious state of drowsiness. The war of attrition against the cockroaches has been won – she doesn't have to rise and take up arms. This, of course, is all thanks to the arrival of Mariel, who's only been with them a week but who's established a strict routine of washing the kitchen floor first thing in the morning and last thing at night so that there's nothing to attract even the most determined of these hardy pests. And on the odd occasion when a cockroach does venture into Mariel's domain, she catches it in her bare hand with a swift movement, crushes it and throws it in the bin. Laura and the girls had witnessed this feat of skilful heroics on Mariel's second day and all three had been awestruck.

In fact, there are already so many ways in which Mariel's arrival has transformed Laura's life in Malaysia. There's a magical quality to her ability to remove dirty clothes from wherever they may be (more often than not on the floor) and return them to the wardrobe, washed and ironed, the next day. She's rigged up a new washing line outside the back door, in the open air, and always manages to bring in the clothes, dry, just before the afternoon rain.

Thinking with relief that she no longer must go into the creepy cave-like space where the old washing line is, Laura slides further down the bed and snuggles up to Peter, who has his back to her. She presses her face between his shoulder blades, inhales his warm and comforting smell, and savours the moment. Five minutes later the alarm goes off. He stirs like a child waking from a deep slumber and then, rolling over, envelops Laura in his arms, rests his chin on her head and goes back to sleep.

"You've got to get up, lazy," she says. "Remember you said you were so busy at the office you couldn't take the day off to help with the unpacking."

"Mmm, what?" he replies sleepily. "No, I said I can't take a day off so soon after starting with the firm. And besides, you've got Mariel to help."

Laura kisses him on the chest, disentangles herself and gets out of bed. She pads downstairs to the kitchen, where she finds Aggie sitting cross-legged on the kitchen table chatting animatedly to Mariel, who's carefully listening while washing the floor. The soothing sound of the sweeping of leaves gently floats through the open window and there, in the garden, she can see the three Indian men from Shekhar's Gardening Services already hard at work. They like to arrive early in the morning to avoid the heat of the day. Mariel must have let them in the front gate.

Shekhar is an Indian Malaysian who runs a gardening company. He has a large number of men working for him who apparently maintain most of the gardens in Bukit Tunku. Laura had first come across him leaning against his red van, smoking a cigarette, outside the gates of one of the neighbouring bungalows. She'd been driving past and, noticing the sign on the side of the van, had stopped the car, wound down the window and asked him if he'd be interested in looking after their garden. She'd been immediately struck by how good-looking he was – sexy eyes and extraordinarily charming. They'd made a date for him to come round to the house two days later and give her a quote. Hardly realising what she was doing, before he'd arrived, she'd checked her hair and makeup, and put on a pair of floaty trousers that she knew were flattering and showed off her backside at its best. As they'd wandered round the garden together and she'd watched his strong, dark hands gently touching the flowers, she'd been shocked to find herself imagining what they would feel like on her naked body. Shaking off the fantasy, she'd then had to fight off the allure of his eyes and so had busily rummaged in her handbag for nothing in particular while asking, "So, how much would you charge? To do the garden, I mean," she'd added, blushing.

Now he drops three gardeners off at the house every Friday. Laura finds she's often around when he comes to collect them, and she generally pops out to say hello and thank him. Somehow, he always has time to stop and chat, causing her imaginings to become increasingly detailed, not to mention erotic. His men are undoubtedly doing a great job in the garden and have managed to tame the more jungle-like parts. They cut the grass and sweep up the endless leaves that are shed daily – there's no autumn near the equator – and they clip back the creepers and bushes so that they look beautiful rather than wild. Laura is conscious that the workers seem poor and miserable. One of them has a limp, they're all extremely thin, and they're always grumpy and scowling, except for the young one, who more than once has given her a shy little smile.

Mariel gives the children their breakfast and gets them ready for school without any bother so that all Laura must do is drive them there. Approaching the house on her return she sees a huge container lorry parked outside. Five Indian men all wearing blue boiler suits with Star Relocations emblazoned on their backs are diligently unloading numerous boxes and some extremely well-wrapped furniture. Before long there's a cardboard and cellophane mountain in the driveway, and Laura wonders how on earth she and Mariel are ever going to sort it all out. And now she's irritated with Peter for not at least taking the morning off – surely the arrival of your furniture from England is a perfectly valid excuse? Once again, the fact that Peter's job takes precedence over everything stirs up her resentment at having given up her own career for the sake of his.

One of the removal men approaches Laura. He's middle-aged, has very dark skin and equally dark hair with a touch of grey showing in his short sideburns. He's slim but sinewy and clearly very strong.

"Good morning, madam, my name is Guna. I'm team leader for Star Relocations. Please show where you want furniture – then we unpack."

"Good morning, Mr Guna, thank you so much. I'm afraid I don't think I paid for an unpacking service."

"But madam, Star Relocations service always include unpacking. It's our pleasure, madam," he replies with a slightly forced smile and a typically Indian headshake.

Approaching the cellophane parts of the mountain she recognises her elegant sofa and beautiful double bed, and is quite taken aback by how pleased she is to see these faithful old friends from home. She spends the next ten minutes showing Mr Guna around the house. There are two large contemporary paintings, part of Peter's cherished art collection, which are to go in the main living room. They're both abstract landscapes by an up-and-coming Irish artist who Peter firmly believes in. Last night he and Laura had carefully planned out where all the furniture and paintings should go, and she'd noticed the delighted excitement in his eyes when he'd realised how fantastic the artworks would look in the large, light-filled, open-plan space – in fact, how much better they'd look than they did in the Suffolk farmhouse with its low ceilings.

And so, the great unpack begins. Laura can't believe how assiduously the five removal men work. They unwrap and then she and Mariel put everything away – if it's something for the kitchen Mariel has a firm view, anything else and she says, "Up to you, mam," refusing to give her opinion for fear, apparently, of saying the wrong thing.

It's punishingly hot and more than ever before, Laura is aware of the lack of air-conditioning in the downstairs rooms. It's switched on in the bedrooms, so unpacking the clothes and assembling the double bed are more popular jobs than others, and although the ceiling fans are whirring elsewhere, Laura feels herself wilting.

After a couple of hours, she suggests a break. Luckily Mariel, in her efficiency, had reminded Laura to buy extra Nescafe 3 in 1 sachets – this is the drink that seems to be the Malaysian equivalent of the British 'builder's tea' and is what they normally offer to the gardeners. So, Laura asks Mariel to serve the coffee, together with some digestive biscuits, to the five men in the house as well as the three in the garden.

Thanking Mariel almost over-effusively for the refreshments – "*Terima kasih, terima kasih*" – Mr Guna and his team huddle uneasily at the far end of the living room. Three of them sit on unopened boxes while the other two hover awkwardly. They talk amongst themselves in muted whispers. The three gardeners are drinking their coffee silently whilst crouching on their haunches in the shade of the back door porch. Mariel brings Laura a fresh lime soda but then goes back to sit at the kitchen table, leaving her feeling like an awkward memsahib. So, she retreats to the veranda, where she sits and marvels that such a situation could still exist in 2006. Back in England, removal men would have dumped the stuff and gone, the gardener would have given her a blow-by-blow account of the damage done to the vegetable patch by the rabbits and the cleaning lady would have recounted the latest episode of her life story over a cup of tea.

By 11.30am the unpacking is all finished. As the removal men leave, Laura thanks them and gives them each a tip. Mariel had advised her to tip each man RM10, the equivalent of about £2, which Laura had thought too little, but Mariel had said it was the right amount; after all, a taxi ride across town was about RM7.

When, not long after, Shekhar arrives to collect the gardeners Laura opens the electronic front gates to let him in and enjoys a few minutes' basking in the starlight of his twinkly eyes.

After everyone has left Laura and Mariel walk around the house admiring how nice it looks. There are still things to be sorted but even Laura has to concede that with their own furniture it is starting to feel like home. The temporary furniture left by the estate agency is all in the guest room waiting to be collected.

"I was so impressed by all those hard-working Indian men. All eight of them would have worked the entire morning without stopping if we hadn't made them have a coffee break," remarks Laura as they wander back into the kitchen. "But they did look very poor and under-fed – I suppose neither job is well paid."

"Yes, mam, but Star Relocations men are Malaysian Indians – low pay but got salary. Shekhar's men are from India – very different for them, get no salary."

"What do you mean, they get no salary? Surely they get paid something?"

"No, mam, jus' food and lodging."

"But they always look so tired and hungry. And besides, why would they work for just food and lodging? Oh my goodness, look at the time! I must go and collect Aggie from school." And she rushes off, making a mental note to ask Mariel more about this later.

A kick in the face

Mariel is sitting with Mrs Laura, Tilly and Aggie in a waiting room at Gleneagles Hospital, one of the best and most expensive hospitals in Kuala Lumpur. Tilly and Aggie are both very unhappy because they're there to have a BCG jab and Mrs Laura has asked Mariel to accompany them in case she needs help keeping the children calm.

Turning her forlorn face to Mariel, Tilly says, "Before we came here, we had to have loads and loads and loads of injections. They were horrid. Aggie screamed so much she got a sore throat and her voice went all squeaky."

Mariel wonders why on earth the British doctor hadn't also given them a BCG jab. She's heard about the 'no-pay' hospitals in England – people say that they're amazing. She finds it hard to imagine a country where the hospitals are free – no need for people to die just because they're poor. Does the government really pay for everybody? Maybe they're not as good as they say.

Aggie starts to cry and wails, "I *won't* do it!"

Tilly looks down at the floor. Mariel feels for them – she remembers having a jab when she was at school. What a dramatic day that had been – she'll tell the girls about it later, make them understand that everyone must go through these tricky days.

A nurse calls them and invites them into Dr Vernon's consulting room. Aggie refuses to move and cries that she'll only come if Mariel carries her. Following them, Tilly holds Mrs Laura's hand but looks like she's ready to run.

Dr Vernon says a friendly hello to Mrs Laura and the children. Mrs Laura is unusually quiet. There's a flicker of acknowledgement in his brief smile towards Mariel – she's known him for years. He's the top paediatrician in KL and all the children she's ever looked after have been under his care. When little Jade, the daughter of the Chinese Malaysian family she'd been with for ten years, was very sick with dengue fever, Mariel had spent a lot of time with her in the hospital, even sleeping overnight on a couple of occasions. She knows Dr Vernon to be a very kind man and a good doctor. Jade and her family had been very important to Mariel. They'd treated her well, made her feel almost like part of the family and she'd been sad when she'd had to leave. The company that Jade's father worked for had posted him to a job in Sydney, Australia. But Mariel's stayed in touch – always remembering the children's birthdays especially.

Dr Vernon's shiny bald head seems to bob about as he tries to engage Tilly and Aggie in a bit of friendly talk – giving them a cheeky grin, his bright eyes sparkling. He suggests that Aggie should go first and gently explains that he'll do the jab in her backside so that it won't be painful, and she won't have an ugly scar on her arm. Mariel hands Aggie to Mrs Laura but she writhes about trying to get free, her yells getting louder. Mariel is just wondering whether she should offer to hold Aggie steady when the doctor suggests that she take Tilly to the little adjoining room where 'there are plenty of toys'. Tilly has no interest in the toys and bravely pulls her book out of her little backpack and starts to read.

The door between the two rooms is open – Mariel can see Mrs Laura sitting on the doctor's couch trying to hold Aggie securely across her lap so that the doctor can get a clear aim at her buttock. He leans across but then, suddenly, like a young foal taking aim for the first time, Aggie kicks him in the face. Luckily, she's not wearing any shoes, so her four-year-old foot doesn't do much damage to his forty-year-old nose.

Tilly and Mariel both stifle giggles. Doctor Vernon is also laughing but Mrs Laura looks painfully embarrassed. Aggie, on the other hand, appears very pleased by her surprise triumph. Taking advantage of her distraction the doctor injects her so skilfully that she hardly notices.

Then with sisterly sympathy Aggie looks towards Tilly and says, "Don't worry, didn't hurt much – promise."

But Tilly doesn't seem convinced. Looking like a courageous French countess approaching the guillotine she stands up and walks towards the couch. Bravely and modestly, she lowers her shorts and panties just enough for the doctor to have access to the top of her left buttock and within moments it's all over and done.

Later that evening Mariel is giving the children their supper – ginger chicken with plain rice and stir-fried broccoli. The three of them are sitting at the round table on the veranda and Tilly is impersonating the doctor's reaction to Aggie's kick, making the other two laugh.

Mrs Laura is still out at the supermarket. When she gets back Mariel is hoping to have a casual conversation with her while they unpack the groceries together – all part of her careful plan. She wants to tell her that the leak in the playroom ceiling is getting worse and that the backwash on the water pump needs doing again. Last month they'd finally got a plumber to come and do the backwash. Mr Peter had watched him and said that he'd do it this month, but Mariel can sense that he's hesitant to try. He really *is* impractical – she'd seen him do a terrible job of cleaning out the swimming pool filter. If Vijay was here, he could do all these chores and do them well. Mariel and Vijay have talked about it and agreed that it would be perfect if he could move in as caretaker. But they need to persuade Mrs Laura and Mr Peter, who may not be willing, especially if they find out they're not married. Mariel knows she must handle this cleverly. She thinks that the situation regarding the gardeners could be what swings it. She'd tried to start up a conversation with Mrs Laura about it the other day, after the removal men had left, but Mrs Laura had had to rush out to pick up Aggie from school, so the opportunity was lost.

Tilly is eating her supper quickly, putting everything in her mouth at once. Aggie is pushing her broccoli around her plate. The mosquitoes are biting viciously, so Mariel lights a couple of burning mosquito coils to keep them away. She remembers that she'd wanted to tell the girls about when she'd had her BCG jab.

"I remember day I got jab. *Aiyah* – was terrible day. Doctor came to my school and he got huge big needles and start sterilising them in flames—"

"What's sterwilising?" interrupts Aggie, a wide-eyed quizzical look on her face.

"It means he burn all the dirt with the hot, hot flames so needle completely clean. Everyone so scared start screaming and run away and hide."

"Did *you* hide?" asks Tilly.

"I try hide but teacher find me. She a mean bad lady and she pull me by my ear all way back to doctor. Then she hold one arm so hard and doctor hold other arm so hard and he sticks needle in. Was so so painful I can't stop crying."

The two young girls gaze at her in shock, tears of sympathy welling in their little eyes.

"Some of my classmates run far away so teachers cannot catch them. They don't come back school that day 'cos they know doctor will still be there. But next day when they come to school the teacher is so so angry. Then she tell whole class I must beat naughty ones with cane because I'm good girl who had my jab."

Aggie, struggling to follow the story, starts playing with her two dolls. She talks to them, soothingly telling them they must be brave when they have their jabs. Tilly, transfixed by Mariel's tale, asks, "But why? Why did your teacher want you to hit your friends?", her voice trembling at the injustice.

"'Cos she a bad lady – full of mean spirit. But I refuse so she cane them herself and she make me stay after school and do extra study."

"Did they get the nasty disease 'cos they didn't have the jab?"

"No, next time doctor come, parents bring them to school themselves and make them have jab. Parents scared of disease so they want children have jab even if they kick and scream. That's why Mummy hold Aggie so hard today. Now, come on – *makan, makan,* eat, eat." And Tilly turns her attention back to her supper, thoughtfully digesting Mariel's words.

Her own private jungle

After dropping the girls off at school, Laura drives to the Jalan Duta tennis courts for her second lesson with coach Rama. It's not yet 8.30am and already the temperature is 30°C. The woman with whom she's sharing her lesson has already arrived.

"Hi there, I'm Guilia," she says with a smile and a brief wave of her hand.

She's Italian, immaculately dressed in a pure white tennis dress, her silky dark hair swept back into a neat ponytail. Her air of perfection makes Laura a little nervous and relieved that before leaving England she'd had the foresight to buy most of Stella McCartney's new range of sportswear for Adidas. Today she's wearing the steel-grey tennis dress with crossover straps at the back revealing her delicate shoulder blades. At least if her tennis doesn't prove to be as good as Giulia's, she'll be able to match her on the fashion front.

Rama, the tennis coach, is a small, wiry Indian Malaysian who's full of energy and laughter. Laura's not sure he's a great tennis teacher, but he speaks good English, and she'd enjoyed her first lesson with him. He'd suggested that she share her classes with one of his other students to keep the cost down. Giulia had previously been sharing her lessons with a Dutch lady who'd just moved back to Holland, so she'd happily agreed to join up with Laura.

Giulia is exceptionally friendly and welcoming. Perhaps it's because she's Italian, but Laura is noticing an attitude amongst the other expat wives she's met, mainly through school, an attitude which seems to say, 'we're all in this together so we'd better look out for each other'. More than once she's been taken aback by the generous advice on how to survive and indeed enjoy life in KL which people have spontaneously given her.

The two women stand together at the back of the court and, in between returning shots to Rama, they chat and complain about the heat, the humidity, the insects and the lack of Western food. Giulia lives in a modern apartment block and when Laura tells her about their house, she laughs, making Laura slightly embarrassed, and says in her beautiful Italian accent that she knows another 'very English family who insist on living in the very old-fashioned bungalow'. And she promises to arrange a lunch to introduce them. Again, Laura marvels at her friendliness – in England no one asks you to lunch when they hardly know you.

By the end of the hour's lesson Laura's tennis dress is like a wet dishcloth – entirely soaked through with sweat, as is her underwear. Yet again she thinks of her grandmother telling her that ladies don't sweat. But today she finds she isn't self-conscious because both Rama and

Giulia are in the same condition. Indeed, she's learning that when there's 90% humidity in the atmosphere most things are wet nearly all of the time.

Once home she has a refreshing cold shower but afterwards her body is still so depleted of energy that she has to sit for a while, in a slightly catatonic state, under the fan on the veranda. This is becoming something of a morning routine because invariably the heat exhausts her. Lying on the lounger, she likes to watch the garden, her stillness contrasting its busy-ness. Her friend the golden oriole also seems to have a morning routine – checking out the whole garden, starting at the bottom and then working his way up, flying from side to side, ending up on his favourite perch in the jacaranda tree. He's not alone – there are other noisy tropical birds that Laura thinks she'd like to learn the names of – but the golden oriole has somehow stolen her heart.

She's starting to think of the garden as her own private jungle. From her viewpoint on the veranda, she can watch the action like a David Attenborough documentary although without his dulcet tones. Twice now she's seen a blue and black butterfly the size of her fist floating around the passionflower, its wings so large that it seems to fly in slow motion. And every day she watches with fascination the troop of monkeys that cross the bottom of the garden as they scour Bukit Tunku for food, swinging from tree to tree, the dominant male in the lead, the others following on, the young ones larking about chasing each other and the cute babies clinging on to their exhausted breast-feeding mothers. Although Laura loves to watch them, she's nevertheless grateful that Mariel is close by in the kitchen, broom near at hand. The monkeys have learnt that Mariel and her broom are not to be messed with.

Unlike her cleaning lady in England, Mariel isn't really the chatty type. On the few occasions that Laura has tried to start up a conversation, she's clammed up and been visibly uncomfortable.

"So, Mariel, tell me about yourself."

"I just regular maid, mam. Nothing interesting to tell."

So, Laura has concluded that she's a very private person. She's happy to respect her privacy but it does feel strange knowing so little about her. She knows from her interview that she's been in KL for nineteen years and that she's married with three children back in the Philippines, but she never talks about her family, at least not to Laura. She does chat to the girls especially when she's giving them their supper. Perhaps they know more about her family life – Laura thinks she might try to get some details out of Tilly.

From what she's picked up from the other mums at school it seems that a lot of Filipina maids, when they come to work in KL, leave their children behind to be brought up by extended family. She assumes that's what Mariel had to do. Laura had always been rather relieved to get away from domesticity and childcare by going to work in London, but the idea of having to move to another country to find good work and not being able to raise your own children seems a truly tough way to live your life. She admires Mariel's resilience. But she also feels guilty – the irony of the fact that Mariel must be without her children in order to work, while Laura's bitterly resentful that she's had to give up her career, is not lost on her. Nevertheless, she misses her job terribly – her column, her colleagues, the buzz of the office, the sense of independence and achievement that it gave her. At her leaving party there'd been champagne and a cake with little Malaysian flags all over it. Louise, her PA, had made them using cocktail sticks and little printed photos. Laura had cried when they'd given her a farewell card signed by the whole department and a beautiful Heidi Klein kaftan.

Looking at her watch, she realises she must get moving – at twelve o'clock she's due at a lecture on the art of ikebana organised by Susan's group, Enjoy Malaysian Culture. As Susan had said, it will hopefully be a good place for Laura to meet people.

Laura needs to make a phone call, but she'll have to do it later. The estate agent has given her the number of a handyman who'll be able to help them with the numerous things that need sorting out around the house. Apparently, he's very good and reliable but must be booked in advance as he's much in demand. She thinks she really ought to write a note to remind herself to call him this afternoon – her ability to be efficient, a skill she'd always been proud of, seems to have disappeared since she got to KL. It's as though the closeness in the air and the stifling heat have sapped her strength and made her constantly lethargic.

She opens the front door and there, waiting patiently in the office car, is Prakash, the driver. She'd asked Peter if she could borrow him because the lecture, 'followed by a light lunch', is at the Shangri-La Hotel downtown. She has no idea how to get there and can't face the idea of trying to navigate through city-centre traffic with her useless map of KL balanced precariously on the steering wheel.

She's doubly glad that Prakash is driving because he takes pleasure in pointing out the sights as they pass them and recently, she's been keen to learn more about the city.

When not in rush hour, the journey downtown is quick. Within twenty minutes they're driving past Merdeka Square. Laura knows this is where independence from British colonial rule was declared in 1957. There's a flagpole which she's been told is the tallest in the world, commemorating the moment the Malaysian flag was hoisted for the first time.

The square appears to be a huge cricket green with immaculately mown grass which Prakash tells her is called the *Padang*. Sitting somewhat incongruously on the edge of the green, with two giant skyscrapers right behind it, is a large mock-Tudor building – white stucco with black beams criss-crossing its three gables and a wide, low, strikingly red roof. The contrast between the buildings is so great it looks as though a picture postcard of a Surrey mansion has been stuck across a photo of the Manhattan skyline. From the KL guidebook that they'd brought with them, Laura knows this famous building to be a social club called the Royal Selangor Club which was founded in 1884: a place where, perhaps more than anywhere else in the city, the ghosts of the British colonials still linger, particularly on the terraces – drinking cocktails and languidly watching a game of cricket.

Opposite the *Padang* is an enormous and grand late nineteenth-century building, Neo-Mughal in style, with copper domed towers.

"Prakash, do you know what that building is?"

"Law courts, mam."

The building next to it is architecturally similar but more dilapidated. There's a cloister with Moorish-style arches covered by iron grilles running its full length and an imposing prison-like entrance gate in the centre. The traffic slows practically to a standstill just as they're level with this entrance.

"Mam, look – can see prisoners."

Shuffling up the steps into the building is a line of bedraggled-looking men – all chained together at their ankles. Gasping, Laura sits forward to see more clearly and grasps the front of her seat.

"Why are they chained together?"

"Prisoner always chained, mam, when they take them from prison to law courts."

In the cloister just to the right of the entrance she notices a Chinese man sitting at a little foldaway table frantically tapping at an old-fashioned manual typewriter, a couple of men hovering at his shoulder.

"Do you know what that man with the typewriter's doing?"

Prakash explains that, for a fee, he types out written statements for illiterate people going into the law courts.

She's absolutely astounded. KL seems such a modern city with its famous twin towers and yet here, in their shadow, are archaic activities such as these.

The traffic lights change, and Prakash drives on just as the last of the chained prisoners disappears through the massive door.

*

Laura walks into one of the conference rooms at the Shangri-La Hotel. It's an L-shaped room with about forty chairs set up in the shorter section and small round tables and a 'light buffet lunch' set up in the longer section. Women of varying nationalities are milling about, gradually taking their seats in readiness for the lecture: 'Ikebana, the Japanese art of flower-arranging'. There's not a single man in the room except for a couple of the hotel staff setting out the lunch. Laura feels shy and awkward, like a new girl on her first day at school, and wishes briefly that she hadn't come. But then Susan walks towards her.

"Laura! Hello! I'm so glad you came."

"Hi, Susan, looks like you've got a good turnout."

"Yes, it promises to be a very interesting talk. Let me introduce you to some people... Ladies, this is Laura, recently arrived from England. Laura, this is Evi," they shake hands, smiling enthusiastically, "and this is Arpana." Arpana, wearing a beautiful silk sari, is clearly rather grand, her handshake a little stiff. Susan continues, "We all know how hard it is to be a newbie so please look after her – I must go and check that our speaker has got everything she needs."

She dashes off but Evi fills the vacuum with amiable chat. She's Dutch, has ash-blonde hair and is quite a bit older than Laura – probably in her late forties. She tells Laura that her husband is in 'oil and gas' and that they've been in KL for eight years, which Laura finds surprising. It hadn't occurred to her that there were expats who stayed that long.

Arpana is Indian, about forty and her manner is slightly haughty. Early in the conversation she mentions that her son is at boarding school in England.

"He's at Eton – you may have heard of it."

"Yes, my husband was there," replies Laura.

"Oh, really? And what's he doing in KL?" Arpana's demeanour is suddenly demonstrably friendlier.

"He's with Spears Anderson, managing a company called Sweet Stevia that producers a natural sweetener."

"How interesting, my husband, Shiv, runs HSBC out here in Malaysia – we should get the two of them together. You must come to dinner."

Two invitations in one day, thinks Laura, *not bad for a newbie*. But she's painfully conscious that all three of them have described themselves in terms of their husband's careers and, not for the first time, wonders if she's stepped back into the last century.

Susan's bossy voice calls the room to attention. "Ladies, please take your seats, the lecture is about to begin." She waits as everyone shuffles through and sits down before she introduces the lecturer – a poised Japanese lady who's standing behind a large rectangular table on which there are three lovely Japanese vases together with a pile of foliage and flowers.

Flower-arranging has never been a hobby of Laura's and she wonders whether she'll be able to feign interest for the full hour. She likes the minimalist elegance of the lecturer's first arrangement – just three single-stem flowers and one branch of foliage. She's amazed by the complex symbolism and emotive thought that the speaker explains is behind the positioning of each stem. But when she says that three to five years of ikebana classes are required to acquire the full technical and expressive skills, Laura has to suppress giggles and decides that she will stick to her tried and tested method of stuffing a simple bunch into a pretty vase.

Questions are invited from the audience at the end of the talk and there's immediately a volley of serious and interested queries, leaving Laura wondering whether, like her, most of the women attending have got too much spare time on their hands. Looking around the room she sees a diverse range of nationalities – Kuala Lumpur certainly seems to attract expats from all over the world.

When the talk is finally over, Susan suggests that everyone help themselves to the buffet lunch, and as Laura is walking towards it, Evi comes over, a naughty schoolgirl look on her face, and asks quietly, "What did you think of that? Make you glad you gave up your career to follow your husband to Malaysia?"

Laura laughs. "How did you guess? Have you found something better than flower-arranging to keep you sane? If you've been here for eight years you must be quite settled."

"Yes, I've learnt to love it here, but it took some time. I'm actually a trained lawyer but I can't practise in Malaysia. As I'm sure you know, it's very difficult for expat spouses to get working visas." Her expression is thoughtful as she helps herself from the range of curries on offer. "I tried a bit of long-distance consultancy for my old firm in The Hague, but it was too complicated. So, now I help run a charity – a school for refugee children from Myanmar. It's well established – it was set up by Burmese refugees who are themselves trained teachers and then there are volunteers who help out – there are five classes with twenty to twenty-five kids in each class, ranging from age five to eighteen. I love it, every day is a joy."

"Wow, that's impressive."

Clearly Evi's not a flower-arranging housewife. Laura is taken with her feisty and capable manner, and wants to know more about her. But they've finished getting their food and Evi leads the way towards one of the small round tables where they join Susan, Arpana and two French ladies, who are all discussing the latest big scandal in the newspapers – an Indonesian maid has been found dead in her Malaysian employer's kitchen. She was chained to a pipe on the wall. Apparently, her employers had gone on holiday and had chained her up, concerned that she would 'run away'. They'd left her a bucket to use as a toilet, some food, but not enough water so she'd died of dehydration.

"This time," interjects Evi, "they're finally talking about prosecuting because the maid died. This kind of thing happens all the time in many countries around the world, but I think this is the first time anyone's been brought to trial in Malaysia."

"What do you mean it happens all the time?" Laura asks.

"Well, this is obviously an extreme example, but all types of abuse are heaped on immigrant workers. With employers controlling their passports many of them are effectively slaves." Laura remembers the prisoners in chains and once again she's shaken by the prevalence of such backwards behaviour in a country that seems so obsessed by modernisation.

Arpana looks at Evi crossly. "Keeping maids' passports safe is quite a different matter to chaining them up and letting them starve to death. Evi, you know perfectly well that maids running away can be a real problem."

With a saintly smile the French woman on Laura's left says, "We always take *our* maid on holiday with us. She has a lovely time playing with the children and that way we can be sure she doesn't leave while we're away."

"They run away because they're badly paid and over-worked."

"Rubbish," retorts Arpana. "Even if you pay top dollar, they're likely to go back to the Philippines without notice if you don't keep their passports from them."

Laura's relieved when the conversation turns to lighter subjects and the same French lady talks of her plans to have a magician at her little girl's birthday party. Evi and Arpana seem completely at ease despite the previous terse words. But Laura struggles to join in with the chat because her mind is filled with an image of the poor dead maid, chained to the wall, waiting to be found by her employers when they returned from their holiday. She wonders what kind of bosses Mariel has had over the years. Surely none that have chained or locked her up? But probably some that have taken her on their holidays purely to keep an eye on her. Of course, she and Peter will be good to Mariel and will treat her well.

Disappointed that she hadn't had more of an opportunity to chat to Evi, Laura suggests, as they're saying their goodbyes, that they meet up soon for coffee.

She takes a taxi home – Prakash had been needed back at the office. As they pass the law courts, she sees that both the typist and the prisoners are gone and wonders if she'd dreamt them.

She leans back in her seat and reflects that overall she's enjoyed her day as a typical 'expat wife' and is looking forward to spending the afternoon with the girls. Now that Mariel is working for them, not only is the house spic and span and all the washing done, but she gets the supper ready too so that Laura can focus entirely on the girls and enjoy their company – helping them with their homework and either having a swim together or playing a game. It's idyllic really. But she knows in her heart of hearts that the novelty of this new lazy life will soon wear off – she'll need more than gossip and flower-arranging to keep her mentally alive and give her a sense of purpose.

November 2006

A proposal

Shekhar's men, emaciated and bedraggled, are working in the garden. Watching them through the kitchen window, Mariel knows that today is the day she must push forward her plan. The three barefoot Indian labourers are dressed in shabby, colourless kurta pyjamas and dirty sweat-drenched vests. The younger one, with the shy smile, is squatting on the lawn cutting the grass with a pair of shears, inching forwards systematically. The small one, with the limp, is sweeping up leaves around the pool. And the one whose hunger is etched across his face is cutting back the bougainvillea around the bungalow.

Mariel is making a chicken curry for the men's lunch – Mrs Laura had asked her to earlier that morning and Mariel knows this was in response to what she'd calculatingly told her about the working conditions of Shekhar's men. Mrs Laura is still so ignorant of Malaysian ways and Mariel could see that she was shocked to the core – confused and uncertain as to whether she should be using Shekhar's Gardening Services.

Shekhar, a Malaysian Indian, was born and bred in a *kampong* village not far from Kuala Lumpur but he has many connections in India – connections that he's cleverly exploiting for the benefit of his business. He has a genuinely beautiful face, a kind and helpful manner, and extraordinary eyes that dance in the Malaysian sunlight. Mariel knows that Mrs Laura had been taken in by him. How could she not be? He's mastered the skill of working the expat wives – flirting with them and persuading them that he provides the best-priced, most reliable gardening service in the Bukit Tunku and Bangsar suburbs. Of course, he doesn't tell them that his men are not paid, that they're only given basic sustenance and locked in warehouse dormitories at night with nothing but a roll mat to sleep on. And he tells himself that he has saved these men from starving in their rural Indian villages, where conditions are so desperate that many are indeed grateful to have found employment that merely feeds and houses them.

Mariel had only revealed all this to Mrs Laura because of her ulterior motive – to persuade her to hire Vijay as a live-in gardener and caretaker. She's sure that today is the right day to make her proposal and yet she's nervous. The possibility that she could live with Vijay before they've waited the full ten years for her divorce and that they could stay working and living together in KL before moving back to the Philippines seems so close that she can almost touch it.

She and Vijay have been lovers for twelve years now – during which time she's always worked as a full-time live-in maid. And of course, to some of the families she's worked for, full-time means twenty-four hours a day, six days a week – sharing a room with the baby and seeing to it during the night. At least with this family she has plenty of time to herself – but she longs to be with Vijay every day, to have some privacy to make love and, when the family are out, to have some quiet moments when they can sit on the veranda and talk, or maybe not talk – just be together with time to spare. Besides, Vijay needs a better job – his work in the factory is badly paid with irregular hours. Not good. If he can work for this family, the salary will be *mat salleh* price, enough for some left over once he's sent back what's needed to his parents and siblings in India.

Vijay is a kind man – he doesn't beat her like her husband, Vincente, did back in the Philippines – and he's always smiling. She loves him with every fibre of her body. Indeed, she loves him so much she's been willing to sacrifice seeing her children for ten years in order to be able to get a divorce, marry him and grow old with him. For, if they don't get married, they'll have to move back to their respective countries once they stop working – they're only permitted to stay in Malaysia on immigrant work visas. Retirement here is not an option. And having found Vijay's love, she couldn't bear to grow old without it.

He would do a good job looking after Mrs Laura's garden, and he can fix things round the house. And he can service the pool. For the last few weeks Mariel has been talking with the man who comes to the house from the pool-servicing company and carefully watching what he does – how much of the chemicals he puts in, how he works the pump. She and Vijay have agreed that, if Mrs Laura asks, they'll say he knows how to service the pool and then later Mariel will show him what to do.

The smell of the spices infusing the kitchen interrupts her thoughts and she briskly stirs the chicken into the curry paste. Normally she only gives the gardeners Nescafe 3 in 1 with biscuits, so they'll be very surprised to be served a proper meal of chicken curry. It may well be the first meat they've ever tasted.

*

Later, when their work is finished, the three men squat on their haunches on the paving outside the back door and cram the curry and rice into their mouths – speedily, in case the madam changes her mind and takes it away. Not even a drop of gravy is left – all carefully wiped up by the rice skilfully squashed together with their fingers. The young one, with the shy smile, already enthralled by the Western woman, is now smitten.

The men's bellies, not used to such rich quantities, hardly have time to digest before Shekhar arrives to collect them in his dusty red truck.

"Thank you, madam, very nice to see you, madam. You're looking lovely today, madam – always lovely. Very good of you to give men curry, madam," he says, giving his usual film-star smile. But, as Mrs Laura pays him, she avoids his gaze while she counts out the ringgit notes.

"Thank you, Shekhar. See you next week," she replies,

without flipping back her hair like she normally does and in a much less friendly tone than usual.

Mariel goes back to the kitchen and sits on the high stool to gather her courage. Through the doorway she can see Mrs Laura in the sitting room returning her purse to her bag. She knows that in a moment she'll come into the kitchen for a glass of water. Mariel takes a deep breath and holds the edge of the worktop to steady her shaking hands.

"Mariel, do you think there are any other reliable gardening companies working in this neighbourhood?"

"Don't know, mam." She hesitates. "Maybe Vijay, my husband, can do work for you, mam? He can do gardening and pool and clean storm drains and fix roof where water coming in girls' playroom, mam." Looking down at her lap and rubbing her knees with her hands, she holds her breath as she waits for Mrs Laura to answer.

*

The following Sunday Mariel waits for her taxi in the shade of one of the three frangipani trees by the high white wall that guards the bungalow. She twizzles one of the flowers between her forefinger and thumb, drinking in its sweet scent and admiring the delicacy of its custard-yellow centre spreading out to firm white petals. With her left hand she swats the mosquitoes congregating on her calves.

She'd called for the taxi half an hour ago, knowing that it would be slow to come up to Bukit Tunku. A prickly sweat gathers around her hairline and meanders downs her face, streaking her makeup. She dabs at it carefully with a tissue. Previously, she'd envied maids with jobs near bus stops who don't have to spend money on taxis, but now she wouldn't swap her position with any of them. The extraordinary feeling of happiness that's been coursing through her veins since Friday starts to swell again. She checks it, fearing it – hers is not a life for happiness. But the joy is unstoppable – she can't wait to tell Vijay, to see the look on his face, to show him the house, the room where they'll live as husband and wife, finally, even before they're properly married.

She'd been floored by Mrs Laura's response. "What a brilliant suggestion," she'd said. "I had no idea your husband was living here in KL, I'd assumed he was back in the Philippines with your family. I can see you must want to be together and, if he's happy to work for us as a gardener and handyman, then that would be perfect."

Of course, Mrs Laura is right, Mariel's husband *is* back in the Philippines – Vijay is not her husband. Her heart had stopped for several beats but then she'd decided she must continue with the lie, trusting that Mrs Laura won't care, that she has modern views on adultery. When the moment is right, she'll explain to her that they hope to be married in a year, after Mariel's got her divorce. There is a risk – if Mariel's misjudged Mrs Laura and she feels they've deceived her, they could end up both losing their jobs and be deported immediately, but Mariel's confident that that's highly unlikely.

She hears the taxi trundling up the hill towards her – from its coughs and splutters she can tell it's one of the old red and white ones, running off a gas tank in the trunk and with a belly so rusty that the road whizzing by is visible through various holes. The smell of cigarette smoke and food permeates the interior, but the toothless Chinese driver is friendly and chats about the lottery, traffic congestion and the smoky haze that floats over from Indonesia.

Vijay is waiting for her at their favourite banana leaf curry place. Restoran Bestari stands in the middle of a row of dilapidated shop houses, nestled between a hardware store and a pirate DVD shop. It buzzes with noisy people and wafts its aromas, both the delicious and the stale, along the entire row. Waiters with green aprons and caps and tired, humourless faces bustle around the customers – one sets down the banana leaves, another rice, another curry, another dhal and another a variety of chilli sauces in little metal bowls.

Vijay is with a small group of men he knows from the factory. Perched on three-legged stools, they huddle around one of the scratched white plastic tables drinking fresh watermelon juice, half of which is sugar syrup.

He looks up and sees Mariel winding her way through the crowded tables. Her eyes give away her news.

"Can be caretaker?" he asks.

"Can, can, *boleh*," she replies, and his face breaks open into a delighted, beaming smile, his arms beckoning her closer, to sit down and tell all.

*

Later, bellies full of curry and hearts full of joy, they return to the bungalow. Despite her descriptions, he's surprised by the dated look of the house and daunted by the unusually large garden. He's seen big properties before but generally they're very modern with balconies and verandas and paved courtyards instead of gardens – to reflect the owners' sophisticated and developed taste and show how far they've come from the jungle of their forefathers.

Mariel had never dared to bring him back to her room on previous Sundays, although now she knows Mrs Laura better, she thinks she probably would have allowed it. Certainly, none of her previous bosses would have permitted any visitors at all. She leads Vijay down the steps at the side of the main house to the separate, much smaller bungalow that overlooks the swimming pool and shares the shade of the jacaranda tree. Her home, their home.

"Can go in," she says, opening the door and gently nudging him forward. He stands in the small hallway, inspecting the clean, simple bathroom to the left and then delights in repeatedly opening and closing the sliding doors of the built-in cupboards on the right. She follows him through to the bedroom, where he sits on the double bed, bouncing slightly and laughing. She laughs too when he lies back, spreads out his arms and floats amongst the red hibiscus flowers of the batik bedspread.

After they've made love quietly and tentatively, neither used to nor entirely confident of their newly won privacy, they lie on the bed, Mariel's beloved bolster cushion comfortably wedged between them, half-watching a Malay soap opera that's flickering on the TV. The thin yellow curtains do little to keep out the strong afternoon light.

"Like married now," he says, gently stroking the back of her hand.

"Yes," she replies, "like married. One year more then I can get divorce and can be proper married." *And I can see my children*, she thinks, *after ten long years of not even visiting once a year. And I can meet my new granddaughter.*

She looks across to the photos on the bedside table – the little baby smiling in her frilly pink dress, the small gold stud earrings that Mariel had sent, shining in the child's newly pierced ears.

And once again she checks the rising tide of happiness within her.

PART 2

November 2006

The Indian husband and the van man

"Peter, wake up! There's someone outside in the garden!"

Laura jumps out of bed and opens the curtains a crack. It's still dark. She can't see much – only the faintest streak of dawn winking through the jungle trees at the bottom of the garden.

Peter rolls over and attempts to open his eyes and focus. "Sounds like someone's sweeping leaves – strange thing for a burglar to do."

"Don't joke! I'm frightened. It could be a drug addict – I've heard they take refuge in the jungle."

She draws the curtains back a little more. There's a stillness in the garden at this time of morning – she's noticed it before when the call to prayer has woken her. But right now the sound of rhythmic sweeping can clearly be heard. She scans the dimly lit garden and there, sweeping up leaves around the swimming pool, is a short, slightly pot-bellied, dark-skinned man. Feeling foolish she realises that it must be Mariel's husband, Vijay, who'd moved in yesterday and who's going to help with the gardening and the house maintenance.

She'd seen him and Mariel arrive in a taxi yesterday, but they'd gone straight to the staff bungalow, and she hadn't felt it was the right thing to disturb their Sunday to say hello. He must be trying to make a good impression by starting work so early in the morning – that and avoiding the heat of the day. Laura is impressed. She decides that rather than staying in her pyjamas as usual, she'd better get dressed before going downstairs.

As she pulls a light cotton dress over her head, she recalls how pleased she'd been when Mariel had suggested that her husband could come and work for them. She'd been so horrified when Mariel had told her about Shekhar's men's working conditions. And had felt sick to the stomach and disgusted with herself for fantasising about him seducing her. How could she have been so naïve, not realising what he was up to? After all, his workers looked as though they'd barely eaten for weeks. And having worked in the fashion industry, she knows well enough about unsavoury labour practices – sweatshops in Asia where textile factory workers are made to work in terrible conditions for not much more than basic subsistence. But there'd always been significant pressure to brush over this dark side of what was otherwise such a glamourous and glittering industry. Perhaps she'd succeeded in white-washing her brain so effectively that she'd failed to spot similar labour abuse when it was staring her squarely in the face?

So, Laura had been more than delighted when Mariel had suggested her own husband as an alternative to Shekhar's men. Although, she'd been surprised as she hadn't realised that he was in KL but had assumed that he was still living in the Philippines. The plan makes perfect sense for everybody – it means that Mariel and Vijay can live together, although Laura and Peter would've been perfectly happy for him to move in even if he hadn't been working for them, especially as the staff bungalow is so separate. Plus, they really do need help with the house maintenance, particularly as Peter is working such long hours.

She'd said yes straight away, and it was only afterwards that she'd worried she should have interviewed him first. But life has improved so much since Mariel arrived and Laura just wants to do everything she can to keep her happy and make sure she stays. And, although she's only known her for a short time, Laura trusts that Mariel wouldn't have suggested Vijay for the job if she wasn't confident that he'd do it well. After all, she wouldn't want to put her own job at risk. They've agreed that Vijay should do a month's trial, although it would clearly be very awkward not to keep him on. Laura's confident that all will be well.

Suddenly feeling a little shy about meeting him, she waits for Peter to finish his shower so that they can go down together. But when they get downstairs Vijay's nowhere to be seen. The children are both sitting on the stools at the kitchen table having their cereal. Tilly looks up from her bowl and her face lights up. "Mummy, Daddy

– Mariel's husband is here! He's come to live with us. He's called Vijay, he's from India and he's got a moustache."

Laura's a bit taken aback by this titbit of information. She'd assumed he was Filipino. She can see Mariel looking at her nervously. Peter gives both the girls a kiss on the top of their heads and says, "How exciting! Where have you hidden him? Can we meet him?"

Aggie giggles. "We haven't hidden him, silly. He's in their house."

"He jus' washing, sir, after gardening. He come soon." Mariel's nervousness fills the room. Beads of sweat appear on her forehead.

Peter skilfully eases the tension by suggesting that he and Laura start breakfast on the veranda and that Vijay should come through to say hello when he's ready. Tactfully, he adds that he doesn't have to be at work until a little later than usual today.

They've only been sitting at the table for a few minutes when Mariel comes out of the kitchen swing door carrying a platter of fresh fruit, followed by Vijay. Laura's surprised by how small he is – smaller even than Mariel. He's very neatly dressed in a well-pressed polo shirt and a tidy pair of cargo shorts.

Laura and Peter immediately stand up, shake his hand and say hello slightly over-enthusiastically. He's clearly embarrassed by this and extremely nervous. To them both, separately, he says, "My name Vijay, sir," nodding his head slightly.

Laura has encountered this before in Malaysia – being called 'sir'. At first, she couldn't understand it at all because with her mane of blonde hair she's not at all manly looking, but she'd later discovered it's just a general term of respect.

Small talk is clearly not an option and so Peter artfully takes Vijay off to show him the notorious water pump. Laura, deciding it's best to leave them to it, tucks into the papaya and mango. But moments later they return and stand in the doorway of the playroom. Peter is talking about the hole in the roof. Vijay is just nodding. Sensing the level of awkwardness rising, Laura gets up and walks over to join them.

"Oh, goodness, look at the time – I must go." Peter looks at Laura apologetically.

She wants to show Vijay the broken panel on the front gate which, for security reasons, she feels is a priority for him to fix. She's endlessly hearing about burglaries, although normally they're in the gated communities favoured by expats. Presumably the robbers know there are rich pickings to be had there – they regularly manage to hit more than one house at a time. She explains to Vijay that she'd like to show him the broken gate and so together they follow Peter out of the front door.

Prakash, the driver, is leaning against the car reading *The Star* newspaper.

"Morning, Prakash," says Peter. "This is Mariel's husband, Vijay. He's come to live with us and is going to take care of the house and garden."

Prakash looks completely confused, as if Peter has made a mistake and got his facts wrong. He turns to Vijay and speaks to him in Malay. His tone is questioning and a little confrontational. Laura catches the word 'Filipino' and is pretty certain that Prakash can tell immediately that Vijay's not from the Philippines and is asking him about this. Vijay mumbles a response, shifts from foot to foot and suddenly Laura feels irritated with Prakash for interrogating him – it's no business of his. Indicating that Vijay should follow her, she walks up the driveway towards the big white wall and its wooden front gate and points to where one of the panels is coming away. Vijay inspects it silently, his nervousness still palpable.

Getting in the car, Peter lowers the window. "Bye, darling, have a good day."

Hearing the electric motor of the front gate whirring, she and Vijay stand back as it starts to swing open. She waves at Peter as she heads back into the house, Vijay behind her, and there in the hall is Mariel helping the girls to put on their shoes and socks for school. Laura smiles at her encouragingly and watches a look of relief spread across her face.

"Come on, you two. We'd better get going or you'll be late." She ushers the girls out of the house and into her car.

"Bye bye, Vijay," pipes up Tilly shyly, mimicked almost immediately by her little sister, who gives him a huge cheeky grin which he returns with a wonderful white flashing smile. Laura's touched that he's so obviously delighted by his new young friends.

In the car on the way to school the girls are chatting away, but Laura keeps missing what they're saying because she's so engrossed in her thoughts about Mariel and Vijay's relationship. How would Mariel, who's from a small village in the Philippines, a very Catholic country, have met and married a man from rural India, who's presumably Hindu? Perhaps they'd met in KL and got married here.

Or maybe they're not married at all, just pretending to be, which Laura can understand now that she knows Malaysia to be such a conservative country. That would explain why they'd both been so nervous. Well, it's Mariel's private life and, Laura decides, no business of hers. She wouldn't dream of saying anything.

This morning it's Laura's turn to help out on the reading table in Aggie's class. The teacher had sent out a request for help to all the parents and her tone had been so firm that Laura hadn't felt she could refuse. And besides, now that Mariel's running the house so well, she's beginning to have too much time on her hands. Although she's constantly surprised by how the slow pace of life in the tropics makes it easy to do very little during the day. But Presbyterian guilt is creeping in, and her self-respect is telling her that she really should do more; after all, in London she'd worked flat out five days a week and loved it. She'd asked the few mums at school she knows best what options there are around for work. But they'd all looked at her blankly. Little Mia's mum said, "I'm getting stuck in to being a lady who lunches. For me it's payment for this hardship posting. I know it's not one officially, but it practically is."

When Laura arrives home later, her patience entirely used up after spending an hour with a class full of four-year-olds, she finds both Mariel and Vijay hovering in the living room, like naughty schoolchildren waiting for the headmistress.

Mariel hands her Vijay's passport. "He got visa for working at furniture factory. Old boss say OK him work here – till arrange papers."

Laura looks at the passport, which confirms that he's from India, not the Philippines. He doesn't share the same last name as Mariel – that doesn't necessarily mean they're not married, but she's pretty convinced that they're not.

"So, do we need to arrange for his visa to be transferred to Peter's passport like we did with yours?"

"Yes, mam. Mrs Faridah can do."

Vijay looks sweaty and uncomfortable and is pulling at the sides of his moustache. Laura senses that he doesn't mind Mariel speaking on his behalf. She's beginning to think that perhaps he doesn't speak very good English.

"Isn't his boss at the furniture factory annoyed with him for leaving so suddenly? Doesn't he want compensation?"

"No, mam, Vijay arrange for his cousin to take job, so boss happy. He talk to him this morning."

Laura suspects that money has already changed hands but decides not to interfere. She and Peter will have to pay the fees for Vijay's immigrant work visa in any case – she understands now that this is part of the package when you employ foreign staff. It's become apparent to her that there are hardly any Malaysian maids or gardeners. All the lowly menial jobs seem to be done by immigrant workers from rural villages in the Philippines, India, Bangladesh, Indonesia – anywhere where the line between life and death can be so narrow that you must flee, whatever the cost, for your survival – often leaving behind a family, or indeed an entire village, that will then depend on you.

Laura looks up from the passport – the two of them still look terribly anxious. This constant nervousness is beginning to irritate her.

"Well, it looks like there's nothing to worry about then. Welcome to the household, Vijay – would you like me to ask Mr Peter to drop off your passport at Mrs Faridah's office tomorrow?"

To her relief she senses their tension dissipate and is rewarded by one of Vijay's beaming smiles.

"Can, mam, *boleh*. Thank you, mam," he replies, nodding his head again – a mannerism she now recognises.

Mariel is smiling too. "Thank you, mam. Vijay hard worker – can look after house no problem."

She turns to him and says in a slightly matriarchal manner, "Can go fix playroom roof now."

He seems delighted by this instruction and walks off with a purposeful air, still grinning from ear to ear.

*

Later that morning Mariel sets about preparing a tuna salad for Mrs Laura's lunch. She and Vijay will just have rice and left-over curry. Mariel likes to eat rice for breakfast, lunch and dinner; she was brought up that way – without rice a meal just doesn't seem complete. She nibbles at a bit of the crisp yellowy green lettuce that Mrs Laura buys from the *mat salleh* supermarket. *So tasteless, lah! Why does she like to eat it all the time?*

Vijay is up on the roof fixing the broken tiles. Mrs Laura is at her desk in the living room, on her computer. Mariel's relieved and grateful that she hadn't asked lots of questions about whether she and Vijay are married. It seems that she does have the modern Western attitudes. Mariel has heard that Western people, *mat salleh*, often don't get married – just live together 'like married'. And she knows it's quite common in the West for people to marry someone from another country, which is probably why Mrs Laura didn't say anything about Vijay being from India. After all, Monsieur Duras's wife, who died, was Malaysian. A shiver creeps across her spine at the thought of Monsieur Duras. Not having to provide him with extra services anymore has eased a tension between her and Vijay – it's only the release of that tension that makes her realise how taut it had been.

A horn is honking outside the front gate. It'll be the van man. He's a wily old Chinese Malaysian who runs a mobile market stall. Every day at crack of dawn he goes to the wet market to stock up with fresh meat, fish and vegetables. His van is an open-backed truck with a frame built over it. The frame has a solid roof, but the sides are bamboo-slatted blinds that can be pulled up into a big roll – displaying the produce to the customers. The bamboo blinds are a dusky pink colour – originally painted red, now faded by the sun and the repetition of being endlessly trundled up and down. But the colour looks perfect, framing the piles of lush green vegetables and brightly coloured fruits. He keeps the meat and fish in insulated cooler boxes, and to present them to the customers he lays them on a huge pile of ice which melts gradually throughout the day, flowing into a clever gulley and drain system.

Every day the van man drives around the wealthy neighbourhoods of KL selling his produce, particularly to the *mat salleh* who don't seem to want to haggle in the wet markets. Mariel knows him because he used to come to Monsieur Duras's condo. He has a weather-beaten face and eyes that disappear into a mass of friendly wrinkles when he smiles. And he has a deferential manner. She likes him and admires the fact that he's wise enough to always be kind and polite to the maids. When he came to the condo, which had eighty apartments, there'd be quite a queue, and he was always cheery and respectful to every maid, especially the down-trodden ones from Indonesia.

A couple of days after she'd started working for the family Mrs Laura had come back from the wet market in an irritable mood with some fish and chicken which Mariel could tell weren't fresh that day. Mrs Laura hadn't seemed to notice. But Mariel knew that the stall holder had sold day-old produce to a *mat salleh* who didn't know she was being cheated. When Mariel suggested using the van man Mrs Laura really liked the idea. She explained how relieved she'd be not to have to go to the wet market again and Mariel smiled to herself, thinking what a clever man he was. She immediately sent him an SMS telling him that her new boss would be another very good customer. Now he comes to the house every Monday and Thursday.

Mariel goes upstairs to the front door, presses the button to open the electric gate and stands there watching him drive in, a steady drip of fishy water coming from the small pipe sticking out of the back of his truck. Little puffs of steam rise up from the hot tarmac.

"Hello, Uncle." She always uses the polite Asian term to address him – she has no idea what his real name is.

"Hello, Mariel. OK, lah?"

It was only when Tilly had mentioned how nice it was that Mariel could see her uncle twice a week, now that he was delivering to the house, that she'd realised Tilly thought he was her relation. Mrs Laura had explained that in England you only call a family member or a very close friend of your parents' 'uncle'. But when Mariel had enquired what the polite way to address someone like the van man was, Mrs Laura had seemed a bit perplexed and had said, "That's a very good question, we don't really have an equivalent term for 'uncle' in England. Do you use the term 'auntie' in the same way?"

"Yes, mam."

This morning Mariel and the van man chat amiably as she admires the beauty of his produce. She loves the sight of the deep purple brinjal leaning against luscious piles of water spinach and skinny stalks of green choy sum with a few timid yellow flowers sprouting from their tops. It's the vibrancy of the colours that cheer her soul – the buxom watermelons so proud and strong – even the meat and fish look gorgeous, the pink scales of the red snapper glistening against the ice.

For a moment her sense of peace is so complete she considers introducing him to Vijay, who she can still hear hammering on the roof. But she decides against it – that can wait for another day and perhaps it will be better not to draw attention to the fact that they're a couple. 'Uncle' is bound to be conservative, like the rest of them, and she'd miss their friendly talks if he decided to be disapproving.

Suddenly Mrs Laura appears at the front door and turns to the van man. "Hello, *Uncle*, how nice to see you again."

His smile and the mass of wrinkles flash in and out of view as he bows his head repeatedly in greeting.

"I just wanted to say how grateful I am that you're able

to deliver to our house. It's made such a difference to me not having to go to the wet market."

"No problem, mam. Very pleased can help, mam." He looks across to Mariel and his eyes twinkle.

*

After Mariel has cleared away the lunch Mrs Laura lies down on one of the loungers on the veranda – this seems to be the spot where she likes to have her siesta. Mariel and Vijay retreat to their room. It's that hour of the day when it's too hot for anything other than rest.

Vijay is scowling as he lies down on the bed and leans back against the pillows.

"Got problem with Mr Peter driver, Prakash."

His words immediately wash away Mariel's sense of peace.

"What you mean, problem? What he say?"

"Boss tell him that I your husband. Prakash look at me like I cheat boss. He speak Malay and he say, 'You not Filipino. When you marry Filipina girl? You think boss stupid? He gonna find out.'"

Mariel's tension eases. "Is OK. Mrs Laura see your passport this morning. She see you Indian – she don't ask how we married. I think she understand we just 'like married'. She don't mind these things." She strokes the side of his face and watches her words soothe him. "When I get quiet time with Mrs Laura I going to tell her I getting divorce and that we get married next year. Maybe Mrs Laura and Mr Peter and the girls like come to our wedding?"

At that suggestion his eyes light up. She knows that

nothing would make him prouder than to have his bosses attend his marriage. She makes them both a cup of 3 in 1 coffee and asks how things went up on the roof. He tells her that he thinks he's fixed it but won't know for sure until the afternoon's rainstorm. Then he mentions that that morning, when he'd been sweeping up the leaves around the pool, he'd seen a large black cobra slither into the undergrowth.

Mariel shivers instinctively. "Always get snakes in this neighbourhood but I don't think Mrs Laura understand that. We must be so so careful 'cos those little girls always playing in pool and in garden. They only babies really – snake bite will kill them quickly."

Vijay's face blanches – she can see him realising that it's his job to shield them from these dangers. Yet she also knows that part of him will adore being their protector – he's naturally paternal and she can tell that although he hardly knows the children yet, he'll go out of his way to keep them safe.

He turns to her, his eyes serious with responsibility, and says, "I get sulphur powder. Put outside of house – snake don't like smell, keep away."

"Can, can – you a kind and good man, Vijay."

She sets the alarm clock just to be sure she wakes up in time for the girls' return from school and then curls up in the crook of his arm and doses off.

Sammy

A week later Laura presses the remote control for the front gate, waits for it to open and pulls into the driveway. She's collected the girls from school and they're desperate to get home and down to a game of cards with Vijay – this is their latest passion. In the car on the way back they'd been trying to explain the game to her – as far as she can tell it's an Indian version of Old Maid.

"You have to keep a totally straight face, Mummy. You mustn't let anyone know if you've got the black Jack."

"Tilly says I mustn't giggle." Aggie immediately starts giggling.

As soon as Laura unlocks the front door the girls kick off their shoes in the hallway, throw down their school bags and scamper down the stairs to find Vijay. She's aware that Mariel's only been working for them for six weeks and already the children have grown used to someone picking up after them without complaint. Their nanny Tracy had always been very strict about this kind of thing. Laura has

131

asked Mariel a couple of times to tell the girls they must tidy up after themselves, but she's noticed that she doesn't and she's beginning to realise that she won't, however many times she's asked. Laura believes that Mariel has an underlying fear of getting into trouble if ever she were properly strict with Tilly and Aggie. With a slight sigh she picks up their bags and hangs them on the pegs, and places both pairs of shoes neatly on the hallway shoe rack.

As she walks into the kitchen the girls are disappearing into the utility room. Mariel follows them with a plate of sliced watermelon and some banana muffins. Vijay is already in there, settled at the table, shuffling the cards. Fixing herself a glass of juice, Laura calls to the others that she's going to her desk to write some emails. She wants to reply to Louise, her old PA, who'd emailed to tell her that Anna Wintour, editor of US *Vogue*, is rumoured to be coming to this year's London Fashion Week, which would be a huge deal as, for the last few years, she's snubbed the event. *Typical*, Laura growls to herself, *the one year I won't be going.*

Just at that moment Mariel comes back into the kitchen and asks if they could have a 'quick talk'. Laura is distinctly taken aback – it's out of character for Mariel to ask to talk. Perhaps something's wrong. She hopes she isn't unhappy with the job. She couldn't bear for her to leave now.

Together they walk into the living room. But Laura's not quite sure where they should sit down. After hesitating for a moment, she sits on the sofa and suggests that Mariel sit next to her. Mariel does so but seems extremely awkward, keeping her hands on her knees and looking down into her lap.

"Mam, I got something I must tell you."

"Oh, OK..."

"Vijay not my husband."

"Yes, I'd guessed that," replies Laura, trying to hide her relief. She leans back against her favourite cashmere throw which is draped over the back of the sofa and sips her juice.

"Very sorry, mam. I didn't mean not tell you whole truth."

There are beads of sweat on Mariel's top lip and her hands are trembling. In the short period of time that Laura has known her she's seemed strong and determined sometimes, and yet at other times, like now, she's apparently plagued by fears and conservative morals.

"My husband in Philippines. He not a good man. I going to divorce him and marry Vijay. But cannot get divorce till I've been separate from my husband, not gone back to Philippines, for ten years. Lawyer in KL tell me this. He expensive but worth it to know that I can get divorce."

"But doesn't that mean you also won't be able to see your children for ten years?" Laura is appalled. She crosses her arms protectively and wonders how such a cruel law can exist. She knows the Philippines is a very strict Catholic country but to be separated from your children for such a long time would be awful.

"Yes, but nearly over. Is already nine years."

"Oh my goodness, that's so sad – you must have missed them so much! You have two girls and a boy, right?" Having recently started to truly enjoy spending time with her own children Laura is profoundly affected by this news. "What about your husband? Does he have to agree to a divorce?"

"He cannot stop it after ten years separate – lawyer say that." There's now a resolute tone to Mariel's voice. "Long time we have nothing to do with each other. I give money to my children and my mother. I don't give money to my husband."

"Do your children live with him?"

"Before I come KL, we all live in small house with my parents. So, when I get first job here, they all stay together in that house. My mother take care of children." She's visibly relaxing as she unravels her tale – her hands now lying comfortably in her lap, her fingers gently curled. She looks directly at Laura, something she rarely does, and in her eyes Laura detects a glimmer of pride. "My job in KL pay for everything. My husband sometimes get work in paddy field but not much. Farmer say he not reliable." Laura is both amazed and delighted that Mariel is finally opening up. "After first nine years working in Malaysia, I make enough money to buy plot of land and build proper concrete house for my mother and children – best and biggest one in village. My father already pass away."

For a moment Laura's tripped up by the term 'concrete house' until she realises that the previous one must have been bamboo.

"I tell my husband he can keep old house. He happy 'cos now he can have naughty girls come round."

"You must have been so pleased to be able to build a new house. But the long separation from your kids must have been terribly hard."

"Yes, mam, very hard." She looks down at her lap again and for a while is silent. Then, as she continues, there are tears in her eyes. "I call them every week and we send SMS too. And we mail photos to each other."

"Will you and Vijay get married in the Philippines?"

"No, mam. We plan get married in KL. Maybe you and Mr Peter and the girls like come to wedding?"

"Oh yes! We'd love that." Laura finds herself increasingly caught up in the romance of it all. "What about the future? Will you stay in Malaysia or go back to the Philippines, or India?"

"Can only stay in Malaysia if got work visa, mam, but there are not many jobs like this one for married couple. So, if OK with you and Mr Peter, we stay working here till you go back to live in England? Then we go to live in Philippines."

"Yes, of course you can stay till we go back."

"And, please, mam…"

"Yes?"

"You remember I take leave in August? That's when I will go to Philippines to visit my family and get divorce."

"Oh… yes, of course. I'd forgotten. Now I understand what a special trip it will be. We'll probably also go on holiday in August so that'll fit in well."

"Thank you, mam." She lowers her eyes. "Sorry again, that I not tell you before we not married. I mus' go back to kitchen now." She stands up and walks back to the kitchen, leaving Laura lost in her thoughts.

Finishing her juice, Laura reflects on the hard life that Mariel has had – not only did she have to leave her own country to find well-paid work, but she hasn't even been able to visit her family for nearly a decade. Laura thinks she couldn't bear to be separated from Tilly and Aggie for that long. Just the thought of it makes her stomach lurch. Not for the first time she feels guilty that Mariel doesn't live with her own children in order to take care of Tilly and Aggie. And the fact that Laura doesn't even have a job or any real purpose to her day makes her ashamed. At least Mariel has found happiness with Vijay – a happiness that looks like it will soon be completed when they get married. *But*, Laura wonders, *how will they be received by her family when they return to the Philippines? Might there not be some stigma to her being divorced? Surely their marriage won't be recognised by the Catholic Church. Will Vijay be accepted into the community?*

She stands up, having forgotten all about Anna Wintour and replying to Louise's email, walks through the kitchen, where Mariel is now cutting up more watermelon, and into the utility room to see how the card sharks are getting along.

The utility room is a bright and airy, welcoming room. Like the kitchen and the bedrooms, on one side it has wide metal-framed windows which give a cinematic view of the garden. The wall opposite the windows has two rectangular ceramic sinks side by side. The other two facing walls have full-height cupboards painted a gentle duck egg blue which makes a stark contrast to the ugly brown of the wooden cupboards in the neighbouring kitchen. The back door leads out to the pool and the staff bungalow. Unusually it's shut. Normally all the downstairs doors and windows are left open to encourage a flow of air through the house.

In the centre of the room there's an old-fashioned

rectangular table with a white Formica top and wooden legs painted the same duck egg blue. One of its short ends is pushed up under the narrow window ledge and Aggie is sitting cross-legged on the top of this table, her back against the window. She has a fierce look of concentration on her face. Tilly and Vijay are sitting at the table on chairs, their faces equally serious. The game appears to be reaching its climax, so Laura doesn't interrupt. Aggie slams a Joker down on the table.

"S'not fair!"

Vijay and Tilly take no notice of this outburst. Aggie then wriggles her little body backwards off the table – first dangling her feet and then gradually lowering herself to the floor. Her face is scrunched up in a furious frown.

"Shall we play snap now?" Tilly asks Vijay, continuing to ignore her little sister's strop. He nods his assent, and the game starts.

As Aggie stomps towards the back door, Laura watches her, slightly transfixed. Reaching up and placing her small hand on the handle, Aggie opens it a little but then closes it suddenly.

"There's a snake."

"What?!"

"It's black."

The game of snap stops abruptly and Vijay stands up with a jerk. Tilly looks terrified. She brings her knees up towards her on the chair and clutches her arms around her legs. Aggie, on the other hand, seems relatively unperturbed. Mariel is standing in the doorway between the kitchen and the utility room, looking with horror towards the back door.

Without really considering what she's doing Laura rushes towards the back door and opens it a crack.

"No! Mam!" Vijay croaks.

A squeak emanates from Tilly.

There, on the small back porch, is a black cobra – its body an immaculate coil, its hooded head raised, its jet-black eyes staring directly at Laura. She slams the door shut immediately.

"Oh my God! Aggie's right, there's a black cobra there. Quick, Vijay, do something!"

There's a moment's hesitation and then, as though courage is surging up from his toes and coursing through his body, Vijay opens his arms wide as if to herd the girls and says to them, "Upstairs! *Go, go, go*, with Mariel."

"Yes, go upstairs with Mariel right now. And stay there till we tell you."

Mariel grabs the children by their hands – slightly roughly but they seem happy to let her – and the three of them rush through the kitchen towards the stairs.

Laura and Vijay wait until they've gone up and then turn their attention to the closed door. Vijay, grabbing a broom, approaches it. Laura steps back instinctively. As he raises the broom, she can see the muscles tense across the back of his shoulders. Tentatively he opens the door an inch but then immediately drops his arm and opens it completely. Sensing the danger has passed, Laura comes closer. Together the two of them watch the large black snake slither across the last stretch of paving between the swimming pool and the staff bungalow and into the undergrowth.

Laura's initial sense of relief is immediately swept away by the realisation that even though it's now in the perimeter of the garden, it might come back to the house at any time. She rushes into the kitchen, grabs two saucepan lids and then without even registering Vijay's astonished expression, runs towards the stretch of jungle on the far side of the pool, bashing the lids together as hard as she can, hoping that that will be enough to scare the creature away.

*

When Peter gets home from work that evening, he's hardly through the front door before the girls start to regale him with the day's drama.

"Ah, Sammy the snake – I thought he might like to live in a beautiful garden like ours." He's sitting on the chair in the hall, having taken off his shoes. The children have just had their bath and smell deliciously of Johnson's Baby Shampoo. Lovingly he pulls them towards him but looks at them sternly.

"Girls, you must remember that Sammy the snake is *not* friendly. You must *never* go near him. And you must *never* go near any of the bushes or big trees in the garden where he might be hiding. Do you promise me?"

Tilly nods her head vigorously, but Aggie is distracted by the little bow of ribbon on her nightie and Laura worries that she's not paying attention.

"Aggie, are you listening to Daddy?"

She looks up from the ribbon and says, "And Mummy ran around banging saucepan lids to scare the snake!" Aggie's clearly too caught up in telling the story to concentrate on her father's warning. Laura sighs inwardly, the knot of anxiety in her stomach tightening.

"Well, I'm sure Mummy did manage to scare it away. But it wouldn't have been the sound of the saucepan lids that did it but the reverberation of her running up and down. You see, snakes don't have ears. But they know where you are by feeling your movements through the ground."

Hearing this Laura feels a fool. How does Peter always know these things? He and Tilly are so similar – brains like sponges, always soaking up information. She feels even more foolish at the thought that Vijay and Mariel probably know this about snakes but were too embarrassed to tell her.

After Tilly and Aggie have gone to bed, Laura and Peter sit down at the table on the veranda to have their dinner.

"My God, that was a close call for you all. Just imagine, Aggie could've wandered out there to say hello to it – doesn't bear thinking about. We must try and find a snake catcher – if such a thing exists." He pours them both a glass of wine then stares at his thoughtfully before taking a swig.

Laura is still irritated with him for being such a know-all about snakes being deaf. It's alright for him – swanning in at the end of the day from his interesting job – but it's her that has to be in the house all the time dealing with its difficulties. Even though she now has Vijay and Mariel to help, there are clearly still challenges, and today's had been a terrifying one. She looks up and says tersely, "Yes, I was talking to Mariel earlier about snake catchers. She said there's a phone number you can call – some local municipality office. I can't remember the name."

Just at that moment, Mariel appears carrying a steaming dish of asparagus risotto.

"Thank you, Mariel, that looks delicious. Peter and I were just talking about getting rid of the snake. What was the name of the agency you mentioned?"

"Can call Dewan Bandaraya, mam, DBKL. But can only call if know exactly where snake is, mam, so they can catch it."

"So, they won't come if the snake's in the garden then?" Peter helps himself to a large dollop of risotto while Mariel holds the dish for him.

"No, sir, must trap snake someplace."

"Oh. Well, it looks like we'll have to pray that it stays in the jungle, away from the house, then."

"This evening Vijay already put sulphur powder round house, sir. Snake don't like smell. But problem is rain always wash powder away."

"Well, please thank Vijay and tell him to continue putting the sulphur powder out."

"Yes, sir."

Mariel returns to the kitchen, and Peter and Laura fall silent for a while as they eat their dinner and ponder Mariel's information. Laura suddenly remembers her earlier conversation with Mariel about the divorce – the drama over the snake had completely swept it from her mind. She tells Peter about Mariel's very nervous confession that she and Vijay are not actually married. And that she hasn't seen her children for nearly ten years and how heartbroken she is clearly.

"Can you imagine leaving Tilly and Aggie, and not

seeing them for that long?"

Peter's face, normally so calm and composed, takes on a harrowed expression at this suggestion. "My God, that's some sacrifice to make. She must really want the divorce." He takes another large swig of his wine. "I thought there was no divorce in the Philippines. You don't think she's been misinformed, do you?"

"No, it's some kind of loophole which means that because she's been living abroad, she can take advantage of this ten-year law."

"Do you think we should check? Say something to her?"

"What are we going to say? 'By the way, Mariel, we're concerned that you might have spent the last decade away from your children all for nothing.' If we did that, she'd have a complete breakdown. No, I'm sure it's all fine. She saw a proper lawyer here in KL and paid a full fee and everything."

*

Later that night when Peter goes to bed Laura decides to stay up a little longer. Sitting on the veranda she stares out into the garden. The moon is high and nearly full, and she can see it floating serenely above the treetops – their dark outlines contrasted against the silvery light of the sky. She wonders where the snake is now and instinctively brings her feet up and wraps her arms around her knees just like Tilly had earlier that day. She reflects that although she's recently started to appreciate her own private jungle, the appearance of the snake has once again made her apprehensive and resentful. How will they ever be able to relax in this house knowing that there's a snake in the garden? Why does everything always have to be so difficult? She's trying to be happy in her new life, to embrace all the different things that she can learn and experience, and to enjoy being with her children. But how can she when she has this list of dangers to contend with? Snakes, poisonous centipedes, rabid monkeys, monitor lizards, dengue fever and even bolts of lightning?

Just at that moment her attention is caught by a group of fireflies weaving their fairy magic in and around the leaves of the rambutan tree on the far side of the pond, their sparkling reflections twinkling in the water. Yet again she marvels at the constant contrast of beauty and danger. *Perhaps*, she thinks, *it is this that makes this place so beguiling, and I must learn to live with both the shadow and the light.*

A gilded cage

"I thought instead of coffee we should have one of KL's best treats – a spa pedicure and manicure. Do you know the hairdressers Careful Cuts in Bangsar Shopping Centre? I've booked us in there for 11am. Hope that's OK?" Evi's voice has a gentle Dutch lilt to it.

Laura loves the idea, tells Evi so and hangs up the phone. She does indeed know Careful Cuts, having had her hair cut there a few weeks previously and been delighted by how well they'd blow-dried it. Laura's very proud of her long blonde mane and she was flattered when the hairdresser spent ages smoothing it out and treating it with veneration, almost as if it were real gold.

After they'd met at the ikebana lecture Evi had texted suggesting, initially, that they meet for coffee, but a mani/pedi sounds much more fun. Laura really appreciates that Evi's coming over to her side of town – she knows she lives in Ampang on the east side of the city, popular with expats whose kids are at the American school.

Evi is waiting for her by the reception desk. It's a large and noisy salon. Most of the customers, even the male ones, are having manicures and pedicures at the same time as getting their hair done. The design of the salon places it firmly in the First World – huge mirrors, black and chrome chairs, bright lights, and giant-sized photos of stunning models with extraordinarily luscious hair. The number of staff, especially those kneeling on the floor massaging feet, subservient expressions on their faces, tells a different story – one that's closer to the Third World. It occurs to Laura that Malaysia is between the two – in the Second World.

"Laura, hi! It's good to see you again." Evi greets her with three kisses and Laura is immediately charmed by this. Her grandfather was Dutch and always did the same.

The tall, sharply dressed Chinese receptionist, who has the air of a New Yorker, shows them to their seats. Almost immediately a woman settles down at Laura's feet and places them in a bowl of warm water which has flower petals floating in it. Another woman takes one of her hands and gently puts it into a manicure bowl. Evi is sitting next to her – their chairs obviously positioned for conversation, as if this is a typical way to socialise in KL. She also has one woman working on her feet and another on her hands.

"Wow, this redefines being pampered!"

"Just wait till you see what they do to your feet."

"Thanks for organising this, Evi. It's really sweet of you."

"My pleasure. Friday is my day off, so I try to do something nice."

The pedicurist covers Laura's left foot in a delicious-smelling salt scrub and massages with a strength that belies her delicate appearance. The manicurist carefully trims her cuticles.

"So, you work four days a week at the Burmese refugee school? Do you teach as well as do the organising?"

"Yes. To be honest, I do a bit of everything: teaching – I have a TEFL diploma – also organising, shopping for food and books, managing the property. We rent a house – the rooms double up as classrooms during the day and accommodation for some of the refugees at night."

Now the right foot – salt scrub and massage.

"And you don't need a work visa to do that?"

"No, you're allowed to do charity work without a visa. Officially I'm a volunteer with the UNHCR, who oversee the school. The whole refugee thing is a bit of a grey area – the Malaysian government never really clarifies whether they're allowed in the country or not. Most of the time it turns a blind eye as long as the refugees don't work or go to school."

Now Laura's feet and lower legs are firmly wrapped in hot, damp towels which are wonderfully warming in the cold of the intense air-con. She'd remembered from her haircut visit how cold the salon was and had brought a cardigan. It's the first time she's worn one for three months and it's strangely comforting.

"Of course, many of the refugees do work illegally and occasionally there'll be a big crackdown by the authorities. A couple of times the school has been raided and everyone taken to a detention centre. But luckily, so far, no one has been sent back to Myanmar. And most of them were released after twenty-four hours."

"God, that must be really stressful." Laura tries to remember the little she knows about Myanmar – 'The Lady', Aung San Suu Kyi, who's under house arrest, campaigning for democracy against the ruling military junta. She knows it's the harshness of the dictatorship that leads to so many people fleeing the country.

"Well, it's OK for us volunteers because we have the official protection of the UNHCR, so the authorities don't detain us. But it's very stressful for the refugees – never knowing when the next raid will be. It's the older children who get anxious – the ones that have some understanding of what's going on. Anyway, the UNHCR work as hard as they can to get them repatriated to other countries, and although it can take up to two or three years, it's generally a successful programme." Evi's feet, also wrapped in hot towels, are now, like Laura's, being slowly unwound. "The majority go to live in the US – many of the Christian churches there are keen to sponsor refugees – and we've recently had quite a few go to the Czech Republic. Obviously, that's quite a challenge for them as there's yet another language to overcome. Only this week, we had a letter from one of our former refugee teachers who'd moved there with two of the children. She said she loves it except for the fact that she can't buy decent dried chillies so could we please send some! She's got herself a job as a classroom assistant in an English-speaking school."

Suddenly, Laura flinches at the sight of the pedicurist holding what appears to be a potato peeler. She's horrified when she starts to peel her heels with it. But more horrified at the sight of the peelings. She can't quite see if

Evi's peelings are as disgusting as hers, but Evi seems to be completely at ease, so Laura resolves to be the same.

"I really envy your sense of purpose."

"Do you have any plans for what you want to do while you're here? You're a fashion journalist, right?"

"Yes, I used to have my own column at *The Sunday Times Style Magazine*," she replies, with pride. "I didn't plan what I was going to do once we got here but I hadn't realised that legally I wouldn't be allowed to work. I miss my job so much. I think I'm driving my old PA mad because I keep emailing her for an update on what's going on. And I never thought I'd say this, but I miss the deadlines – the adrenalin rush. The only deadline I have now is getting the kids to school on time." Laura looks thoughtfully at the freshly manicured fingernails of her free hand. "Don't get me wrong, I'm loving the luxury of having staff and being able to swan around like a princess, but it's beginning to feel like a gilded cage. I need to do something more than play tennis and go to lectures on flower-arranging, fascinating though they might be!" They both laugh. "My husband is totally into his job. He's so obsessed about making a success of the company he's developing, he can't think about anything else. I don't think he realises how frustrated I'm getting. To be honest, it's really beginning to get me down."

"Oh… I'm sorry to hear that," Evi says kindly. "You could always come and volunteer at the refugee school. We're always in need of helpers, especially ones who have English as their first language."

"Oh, I couldn't do that," replies Laura, feeling very uncomfortable. "I'd be a terrible teacher. I don't have the patience, let alone the training. I'm not great with kids. It's only since we came here that I've started to spend proper time with my own children. And I never know what to do with them. I'm hopeless at creative games and arts and crafts and all that."

"Well, the offer holds if you change your mind. You wouldn't have to teach, just help out – you can always just come along and read a story or sing a song in English. To be honest, anything is better than nothing. We don't have enough trained teachers, Burmese- or English-speaking, so half the time the children just have to study their workbooks by themselves."

Laura's distracted by the fact that her feet and legs are now being covered in copious amounts of lotion and wrapped up in cling film. "This is so weird – I've never experienced anything like it. And I've had quite a few pedicures in my time!"

"This'll be the best you've ever had. By the end of it your feet will feel like a baby's bottom – I'm not joking you!"

They're both laughing as they're each brought a cup of jasmine tea with a lid on it, which Evi explains is to stop any stray bits of cut hair falling in. Laura's manicurist suggests she drinks it now before she starts to paint her nails.

"So, how's your house?" asks Evi. "Last time we met you were complaining about it being a bit run-down."

"Well, one day I like it but then the next day I hate it. It's beautiful and romantic, especially the garden. And I love the light – the way it twists and bends. I like to sit on our veranda and watch the sunlight weave its way around the passionflower – it feels almost heavenly."

Evi explains that it's because of the humidity – the sunlight refracts through the water vapour in the air so there's light where there should be shadow. There's a moment of silence as Laura takes this in and then she says, "But there's always something dangerous in the house or garden that frightens me." She surprises herself – being so honest with Evi and by the sudden welling of tears in her eyes. "A couple of days ago my four-year-old daughter found a black cobra on the back porch. It could have killed her. Luckily it slithered away, but I'm terrified it'll come back. Our garden is so big it'd be impossible to find, let alone catch."

Evi looks at her sympathetically. "I'm afraid snakes are a fact of life out here – you even get them in modern houses. The only way to avoid them is to be in a high-rise apartment. Apparently, you can also avoid dengue if you live above the fourteenth floor because supposedly mosquitoes can't survive that high up. Although I'm not sure that's been scientifically proven!" An infectious chuckle ripples through her, and Laura, grateful for being encouraged to laugh when she'd felt she might cry, thinks how much she likes her. She feels there's every possibility that they'll be true friends. Evi continues, "We had a snake in our bedroom once. I shut it in there and went to call the snake team. But by the time they arrived it had gone. They said it could've been anywhere. Seemingly, they can slide into gaps between the floorboards and the skirting boards. The snake catchers refused to look for it – they just left. I couldn't sleep for at least a week after that, but it never came back."

"Oh God, now I'm going to be picturing the cobra under our floorboards. Already, if I wake up at night for a wee, I have to turn on the light and hang over the bed to check if there's anything under there! It's driving Peter crazy." She forces a laugh as she says this, knowing with dread that now she'll find it even harder to sleep.

The two of them choose the same red nail polish and, while congratulating each other on their good taste, agree that they should get together to do this at least once a month.

The great protector

Mariel is at the kitchen sink, looking out of the window while washing up. She's made her speciality chocolate-chip cookies for the girls – carefully timed so that they'll be ready and still a little warm when they get back from school. She can see Vijay scooping leaves out of the swimming pool. This is one of his daily tasks, for the jacaranda tree provides beautiful shade but, like so many trees in Malaysia, it constantly sheds its leaves.

It's been two weeks since Vijay moved in and the two of them are gradually becoming accustomed to living together. Now it's clear that Mrs Laura and Mr Peter don't mind that they're not married, they're more relaxed and many of their days are joyous – eating their meals together at the table in the utility room, far enough away from the family out on the veranda to have a private conversation, chatting about everything and anything, and sometimes just sitting in comfortable silence.

Even though it means more work, Mariel's enjoying

cooking separate meals for her and Vijay – spicy food to feed his chilli addiction. Before he'd moved in, she'd generally eaten whatever the family were having, often a Western dish, and added a bit of rice, of course. She doesn't mind Western food, but she knows that for Vijay it's disgusting. She'll be forty this year, but she feels like a young bride in a romance novel, smitten with her new husband, wanting to spoil him and make their new and unexpected home together as comfortable and happy as possible.

She still can't get used to the amount of privacy they now have – able to make love every night if they want. And most afternoons there's time to rest and relax in their little bungalow. Earlier this week the family had all been out; Mariel had been ironing in the utility room when Vijay had come in from the garden through the back door. He'd walked over and kissed her on the back of her neck – a gentle, lingering kiss. She could sense him breathing in her scent. Never in her life had she experienced such a surprisingly romantic moment – she finally understood what it meant to go weak at the knees. She'd seen this kind of thing on *Marimar*, the Filipino TV drama that she loved to watch, but she'd always thought that the swooning romance was completely unrealistic. She'd never once dreamed that her life could be like that.

Of course, there'd been romantic moments over the twelve years that she and Vijay had known each other, particularly in the early days, but the lack of privacy, especially in his crowded apartment, hadn't allowed for much intimacy. When they'd initially met, she'd still been working for her first family, a Chinese Malaysian family with two children called Jade and Zhin. The family had gone on holiday and, unusually, had left Mariel behind. She'd had plenty of spring cleaning to do, but the driver, Rajen, who she got on well with, had nothing much to do other than occasionally drive her to buy groceries. So, he'd spent most of his time sitting in the back kitchen, the 'wet kitchen', reading the newspaper and smoking cigarettes. One day, in the early evening, a friend of his had come over to play cards.

The two men were clearly enjoying themselves – sitting at the table, laughing and cheering, or groaning, depending on who was winning. Mariel went through to say hello and the moment she set eyes on Vijay she was struck by his beautiful, generous smile. For the next four evenings he returned to play cards with Rajen, always making sure to talk to Mariel and to compliment her on something – her silky hair, her lovely brown eyes, how well she kept the house. On the fourth evening, the Friday evening, Mariel treated the two men to her homemade cookies, and before he left Vijay asked her if she would meet him on Sunday at Megamall, suggesting that they went to the food court together.

Within a few weeks she felt completely transformed, not only by her love for him but by the sensation of being deeply loved for the first time in her life. Her husband, Vincente, had never loved her. He'd just wanted a pretty young wife to cook and clean for him and to have sex with. Her parents had never shown her any affection. She loved her grandmother, her *lola*, and the feeling was returned, but her relationship with Vijay was something completely different. It enveloped her completely, made her feel brave and brought her a joy she'd not known existed. Before long a steely determination grew in her to do whatever was needed to protect this love and it was that that led her, two years later, to seek advice from a lawyer regarding getting a divorce from Vincente.

She got the idea from her employers who were themselves getting divorced. She'd overheard various snippets of conversation – 'my lawyer said this, my lawyer said that' – and, realising that *she* would need to consult a lawyer, wondered firstly how she would find one and secondly how much it would cost. Then, one day, she was taking Jade to a dance class in a newly developed part of town when she noticed that the building next door was a small law office with a discreet sign on its door. So, while Jade was learning to do her arabesques and pliés, Mariel nervously knocked on the law firm's door, hoping that Rajen, the driver, wouldn't spot her from behind his newspaper as he sat waiting in the car which was parked further down the street.

The receptionist seemed surprised by her request for an appointment. "OK, I can revert to his schedule, but he is busy man and very expensive – minimum fee RM70 for one hour." Mariel tried to hide her shock at this sum – that was nearly her daily wage – but she knew if she wanted to get divorced, she needed to seek legal advice.

Taking a deep breath, she arranged an appointment for the same time the following week, when Jade would be at the dance class again. She hoped that the lawyer would be able to tell her all she needed to know during one appointment.

She didn't confide in Vijay or anyone else about this meeting, and when the lawyer told her about the ten-year separation rule, she thought about it for several months. The idea of not going home for her annual visit to see her children for such a long time was dreadful. Just thinking about it brought tears to her eyes. She loved them so dearly. Her marriage was a burden, but her children were a gift. But if she didn't get divorced and marry Vijay they would have to separate when they stopped working in Malaysia. They were only allowed to live in Malaysia on immigrant workers' visas and they wouldn't be able to live in each other's respective countries unless they were married. She couldn't bear the idea of losing Vijay. So, after much difficult deliberation, she decided that not going home for ten years was a sacrifice she'd have to make. When she told Vijay her plan, he was surprised by her decision but also overjoyed and they agreed that they would be married the moment the divorce was finalised.

Now, as Vijay bends over the edge of the pool scooping out leaves with a net on the end of a long pole, she can see the back of his neck. She loves the warm, dark skin there – for her it's always a pillow of comfort for her cheek when he lies in bed with his back to her, and she wraps herself around him.

Suddenly her attention is caught by a terrible shrieking and screaming from the bottom of the garden. The noise is coming from the family of macaque monkeys who have made their usual stop-over. Their picnic on the grass, of bananas and papayas, has been disturbed by a large eagle that is circling menacingly, its beady eyes on a new and fragile baby monkey that's clinging pathetically to its terrified mother. She and the rest of the troop rush frantically to the increased safety of the trees, their squeals of hysteria flowing in their wake. The alpha male, however, remains. He bares his teeth and shrieks with extraordinary ferocity at the attacker, his chest puffed up and his shoulders rolled forward, his full body strength on show. Mariel is awestruck by this extraordinary display of protectiveness. The eagle rapidly assesses that its prey is too well defended and circles back in retreat, high up into the sky.

Standing by the pool, Vijay has also been watching the scene but, when the eagle has given up and the monkeys have fled, both he and Mariel return to their work. As Mariel pushes the large mixing bowl, encrusted with cookie dough, into the water, down below the Fairy Liquid bubbles, she can't stop thinking about the monkey and its powerful instinct to protect its troop. She smiles to herself – Vijay may not be made of muscle to quite the same degree, but he does have a very protective nature, always keeping her close whenever they're out on a Sunday, especially in the busy shopping malls. And he's already being protective of Tilly and Aggie – trying to keep them safe from the dangers in the garden, especially that devil of a snake. But her smile fades as she thinks of her husband, Vincente, back in the Philippines, how he'd always been too drunk to protect her or her babies.

The night before her wedding Mariel's father, also a violent bully, had locked her in the house to ensure she didn't run away. He'd chosen her husband for her – she was sixteen and Vincente was thirty. The two men were drinking buddies, frequenting the same small bar, so even before they were married, she'd had some idea of what to expect. Her father would invite Vincente over to their house to 'court' Mariel. He would tell her to fetch them beers and then the two friends would sit down together on a couple of old plastic chairs in the dusty space that was their front yard, under the shade of the coconut tree, some hens pecking at the dirt. They would completely ignore Mariel, laughing loudly at their own jokes while she hovered awkwardly, longing to retreat inside but knowing that she was expected to stay. Then, when Vincente got up to leave, he would leer over her as he said goodbye, stroking her hair and stinking of drink.

She'd begged her father not to make her marry him, but he'd insisted – determined to honour the agreement he'd made with his drinking partner. She'd cried all night curled up on her roll mat, wondering why her mother and especially her grandmother, who seemed so strong and wise, were not trying to stop the marriage. But deep down she'd known that they'd both always been under the yokes of their husbands – it was just the way things were. So, on the morning of her wedding day her grandmother had bathed her red and swollen eyes and helped her into the lacy satin wedding dress that had already been used by her cousin while her mother put her hair up into an elaborate bun. Her father, meanwhile, stood leaning against the doorframe, keeping a close eye on them all.

Looking down at her hands Mariel realises she's still washing the same mixing bowl even though all traces of cookie dough have long gone. She rinses it off and places it carefully on the drying rack, thinking with a good deal of satisfaction how far she's come since her wedding day. She's now entirely financially independent. In fact, she's a wealthy woman back home and it's her family that's financially dependent on her. For many years she's been earning a top maid's salary, and every month, as well as sending money home, she's added to her savings. These savings have enabled her to build a proper modern house for her family, to put Mila through nursing college, for Vito to start vet school, and last year to buy the village bakery and give employment to Rosa and Luis, her son-in-law. Her father had died of a heart attack a few years after she'd left for Kuala Lumpur, so the only yoke remaining is her husband, and in less than a year she'll be free of him too.

She starts at the sound of the timer – the cookies are ready. Their delicious aroma, already seeping out of the oven, completely fills the room as she takes them out and lays them on the rack to cool. She smiles contentedly.

December 2006

Church

It's Sunday, late afternoon, and Mariel is sitting in the back of a taxi going to church. She's feeling guilty because it's the first time in ages that she's been, certainly the first time since Vijay moved in. Her Filipina friends, Jenny and Faye, will be there. She's hasn't told them yet about Vijay moving in and, after the reaction of her daughter, Rosa, last night on the telephone, she's feeling nervous. She and Rosa had, of course, spoken Ilocano, their local dialect, together.

"But I thought he was just a boyfriend you went out with on Sundays – nothing serious. You can't live with a man unless you're married to him – it's shameful."

Mariel thought of the many maids in KL sleeping with men they're not married to – some enjoying themselves, others less so, but she said nothing.

"If your boss finds out you're living in sin with a man you'll be fired. Your friends will reject you. And even if you weren't already married, you couldn't marry Vijay because he's a Hindu."

Without thinking Mariel replied, "But in a civil marriage it doesn't matter what religion you are."

"Oh my God! Are you planning to marry Vijay? Is that why you've got this crazy idea to divorce Dad?"

Choosing her words more carefully this time, Mariel said, "As I've told you many times before, I'm divorcing your father because he's a drunken bully and I don't want him in my life." She brought the conversation to a close by saying she had to go, that they could talk again soon, and hung up. Rosa rang back immediately but Mariel didn't answer.

Since she'd woken this morning, she'd been expecting another call from Rosa or to hear from either of her other children, Mila and Vito, but nothing yet.

The taxi, its brakes complaining, pulls up in front of St John's Church. A large group of people are milling around its grand entrance – most of them Filipino. She can see Jenny and Faye chatting to each other as they walk into the church. She knows that they'll save her a seat. She pays the cab driver. "*Terima kasih.*" Thanking him she jumps out and walks briskly into the church, pretending she can't hear her name being called by a maid she knows from Monsieur Duras's condo. She doesn't like her and knows that she's exactly the type that would spread nasty gossip about her and Vijay living together.

The church is long and wide, its beautiful arched windows, running the length of each side, filling it with light. Rows and rows of traditional wooden pews face the altar which sits in an alcove adorned with three stained-glass windows whose detailed designs have on many occasions caused Mariel to lose concentration during sermons. Jenny and Faye have indeed saved her a place – she can see them on the end of one of the middle rows. Thank goodness she won't have to push past people to sit down. Today she really wants to be as invisible as possible.

She greets her friends with a brief hug and a hushed exchange of pleasantries, and then settles into the pew. The mass is long, and the hard benches succeed in their task of being uncomfortable enough to keep the congregation awake. As always, the priest encourages them to pray for forgiveness and Mariel worries whether God will forgive her for sleeping with Vijay and for divorcing Vincente. This brings her thoughts back to her conversation with Rosa. She'd known she'd have a strong reaction to him moving in – she's never been positive about Vijay because she doesn't like foreigners, which is why Mariel had delayed telling her. Rosa has spent her whole life in the village and married her high-school sweetheart (a privilege that she doesn't seem to appreciate). So, she's more narrow-minded than Mila and Vito, who are both now living in Manila – Mila working there as a nurse and Vito studying there at vet school. But Mariel's worried that even Mila and Vito won't find it easy to welcome a Hindu into the family. And she can't even begin to think about how her mother will react. It's becoming more and more apparent to her how hard it's going to be to persuade her family to accept her plan to marry Vijay and even harder to get them to accept him into the community when they move back to the Philippines.

After the service Mariel, Faye and Jenny leave the church and make the twenty-minute walk to Jalan Alor, one of KL's best spots for hawker stalls selling street food. The three women have known each other for seventeen years – they'd met a couple of years after Mariel arrived in KL. They were all working in the same apartment block. Mariel was with the first family she worked for, where she'd ended up staying for ten years, the Chinese Malaysian family that had treated her well but who had sadly moved to Australia. Faye and Jenny were working together in the apartment across the hall, for the family of a well-known Chinese Malaysian politician for whom they still work but now in a fancier apartment.

As they stroll along, Faye updates Mariel on *her* family news – she's very excited because her daughter, also a nurse, has got a job in Canada and is moving there in less than a month. Not wanting to hijack the conversation, Mariel decides to wait until they're eating to tell them about Vijay moving in.

By the time they reach Jalan Alor it's already a hive of activity with an array of stallholders selling a variety of Malaysian culinary specialities. Most of the stalls have colourful signs and bright lights – some have Chinese lanterns swinging from them. The three women push through the crowds of people wandering about, many of them tourists, spoilt for choice as to what to eat, although some are unnecessarily searching for the 'cleanest'-looking food – the least likely to give them diarrhoea. Amongst the noise of the customers chattering and the hawkers shouting can be heard the sizzling and spitting of the food cooking. And, of course, so many smells waft their way down the street and into every nearby alley – the smell of curries, coriander, satay, fried noodles, pineapples, boiled eggs, *pisang goreng* and coconut rice all mixed up with the whiff of stale cooking oil and cigarette smoke.

The friends know exactly what they want to eat – Mariel and Jenny always have *char kway teow*, deliciously greasy noodles topped with prawns and bean sprouts, and Faye has *laksa*, a sour and spicy fish soup. All three of them have sweet *teh tarik* to drink. They carry their food to a metal table under a makeshift awning of blue plastic and sit down on small red stools. And, because they don't share the same dialect, they talk in Tagalog, the national Filipino language.

"Girls, I've got some news to tell you," says Mariel hesitantly, poking at her noodles with her chopsticks. The other two stop eating and look up at her curiously.

"Vijay has started working at the bungalow as caretaker. He's moved in – sharing the maid's room with me." She feels suddenly hot and flushed, and starts fanning herself with her left hand.

"*Aiiiiiyaaaaa*" – long and almost whispered from Faye. A silent, dumbfounded expression from Jenny. Mariel looks from one to the other, wondering if she should say more.

But then Faye asks, "What about your boss? She'll find out you're not married."

"She knows. I told her. She doesn't mind."

"Phew – lucky."

Jenny finds her voice again. "What about your kids? What have they said?"

"I called Rosa last night. She was very shocked. My mother has trained her well to be full of morals. I made a mistake pretending all this time I wasn't serious about Vijay. So, she wasn't prepared for the news."

"And Mila and Vito?"

"Haven't spoken to them yet."

The three women sit in silence for a while, eating their food – Faye and Jenny digesting Mariel's news and Mariel hoping that they'll understand. Her guarded nature has meant she's never let her friendship with them become too close, but she values it nonetheless and would hate for it to be damaged by her change in circumstances.

Then, looking up, Faye says, "Well… sounds like a good situation to me. And it's only a short time until you can get married, after all, even though it'll only be a civil wedding." Mariel lets out a sigh of relief. "And it's good you've got Vijay to keep you company in that crazy jungle house. I've always felt so lucky being able to work with Jenny, not having to be in a job by myself, even though we must share that stupid small bedroom." Faye and Jenny look at each other and grimace. "You were lonely working for your old boss when there were plenty of other Filipina in the condo. Just imagine how lonely you'd get stuck by yourself in Bukit Tunku."

Mariel, conscious that Jenny seems less approving, nevertheless smiles at them both, grateful that Faye, at least, seems happy for her and is not judging her.

Then Jenny says thoughtfully, "But I still don't understand how you can get divorced. I've never heard of anybody back home getting divorced."

"Amy Perez, that TV host, the one that always wears those big earrings – she's applied for a divorce. And I've told you, it's different if you live abroad for a long time."

The street is even busier than before as the tourists are now out in force. Having finished their meal, they're glad to be leaving. Again, they push their way through the crowd and, once past the worst of it, link arms like teenagers and head off down the adjacent street to the bus stop. The bus will take Faye and Jenny home, but it doesn't go to Bukit Tunku so Mariel needs a taxi. Luckily in this busy part of town she's able to flag one down easily. It shrieks to a halt, brakes complaining, like its predecessor. Mariel hugs the others warmly, jumps in and waves goodbye – she's so relieved that her friends seem to have accepted her actions but increasingly worried that her children won't.

A tea party and a dinner party

Battling with her mascara, Laura is getting ready to go out to what she hopes will be a very elegant dinner party given by Arpana, the grand Indian lady she'd met at the ikebana lecture, and her husband Shiv. It's the first time in weeks that Laura's been positive about anything. More and more these days she feels adrift in a sea of uselessness. The active, successful woman that she once was has slipped away.

Arpana is well known for giving good parties. Shiv's job comes with a grand house – one of the few original colonial houses in KL that hasn't been demolished as part of the drive to build a modern Malaysia and wipe out references to its subjugated past. Apparently, the house has beautiful reception rooms and gardens which Arpana fills with an eclectic mix of interesting people. And she has a cook from northern India whose food is renowned to be some of the best in KL. Laura's looking forward to the evening but she's nervous. If she's going to meet the interesting people of KL, she wants to make a good impression and as a result has spent a lot of time choosing what to wear – finally deciding upon a strappy silk Nicole Farhi evening dress that's cut on the bias. It's one of the samples she'd been sent, back at work in London, for her 'Must-Haves' column.

The sound of Peter singing in the shower floats through as Laura wipes away the third black smudge she's made with the mascara wand. She's just making a fourth attempt when Aggie wanders in from the girls' bedroom.

"Mummy, Sammy's under my bed."

"Is he? Is he having a tea party with Ted Ted and Blue Bear?" Mascara successfully applied at last, she carefully reapplies her under-eye concealer.

"No, he's curled up looking at me wiv a cross face."

"Well, perhaps he's cross because he *wants* to have a tea party."

"Do snakes like tea parties?"

"Of course they do. Everyone likes your tea parties." Making a strange O shape with her mouth Laura applies lip liner, remembering how well made-up Arpana always is.

"OK, he can have my *best* pink plate. Do we have any mice? Vijay says snakes think mice are yummy."

"Sorry, sweetheart, what did you say?"

Comprehension dawning slowly, like a gradual Suffolk morning rather than the sudden turning up of the lights that is the tropics awakening, Laura sets down the lip liner, turns towards her younger daughter and asks in as calm a voice as she can muster, "Aggie, is there a snake under your bed?"

"Yes, that's wot I said. Sammy, the black one we saw the other day. I'm going to ask Vijay for some mice for him. I fink he's cross 'cos he's hungry."

Using a tone that she knows Aggie will recognise as 'do exactly as I say or else', Laura tells her that she's changed her mind and she doesn't think that snakes like tea parties. Aggie is to go downstairs and find Tilly, and they're both to *stay* down there with Mariel and Vijay.

Clearly disappointed that the tea party is off and alarmed by her mother's sudden change of mood, Aggie runs downstairs as fast as her little legs will carry her, at which point Laura gives in to a rising sense of hysteria. She walks into the bathroom, opens the shower door, grabs Peter by the arm with a vice-like grip and pulls him dripping, naked and with little meringue blobs of shampoo in his hair, through into the girls' bedroom. She doesn't even give him time to grab a towel. She crouches down in the far corner of the room and looks across at Aggie's bed. He follows her lead and there under the bed is a beautiful black cobra, its magnificent hood giving it a Darth Vader-like appearance, rising above its neatly coiled body.

The moment of awe is broken by a whispered command from Laura: "Stay there. *Don't* take your eyes off it. If it moves, for God's sake make sure you see where it goes. I'm going to call the DBKL snake catchers. I know for a fact that they don't come unless you can assure them you know exactly where the snake is." She takes a deep breath, attempting to slow the rush of adrenalin. "If it slithers away and we don't know where it's hiding, the snake team will refuse to do anything. I couldn't bear that – we'd have to move out of the house."

169

Leaving Peter looking unnerved, she darts back into their bedroom and grabs the cordless phone and her address book from the bedside table. Riffling through the pages, she tries to remember whether she wrote the number under D for DBKL or S for snake. Her fingers are shaking, and her eyes seem to be too – she can't focus on any of the entries in the little book. Finally, she finds it. It's under S for snake. Dialling the number, she takes the phone back with her into the children's room and, seeing Peter, registers, as if for the first time, that he's crouching stark naked on the floor, has little rivulets of soapy water running down his face, and that his arms, crossed in front of him, are doing their best to protect his modesty. But that can't be helped – this is a serious emergency. The number rings and rings.

"I don't think you should look the snake in the eyes in case it hypnotises you," she whispers.

"I think that's pythons, not cobras. And it's probably a myth but, just to be safe, I'll focus on its tail rather than its eyes. No answer from the snake team then?" Nervously he flicks shampoo out of his eyes.

"No. What are we going to do?" Her panic is rising so fast she feels she might pass out at any moment.

"Try again – maybe they were having their dinner break."

At that moment Vijay comes in through the door off the landing. He takes one confused and horrified look at Peter, retreats, shuts the door swiftly and says through it, "Sorry, boss, sir, very sorry, boss. Mariel tell me come upstairs. She call DBKL – they come soon." Despite his embarrassment it's clear from his tone that he's wondering what in the name of Shiva his employer is doing.

"Oh, Vijay, that's such a relief," says Laura. "I was trying to call them myself but there was no answer."

Peter, who's clearly as disconcerted as Vijay to be found watching over a snake stark-bollock naked, stands up abruptly and flees through the other door, the one to the master bedroom, leaving Laura to keep guard. His sudden movement causes the cobra to hiss and snap, and Laura jumps back in shock.

"I… er… oh… Vijay… please could you come in here and watch the snake until the DBKL arrive?"

"Er, yes, mam, but, er… what about sir, mam?"

"It's OK, Mr Peter's gone through to our bedroom."

"Thank you, mam." He opens the door carefully, clearly conscious of not wanting to scare the snake away.

She looks at him with relief and gratitude. "Thank you, Vijay."

Quietly, Laura joins Peter in their bedroom and the two of them nervously continue to get changed – trying to distract themselves as they wait for the snake team to arrive. It feels like a long wait.

In fact, the snake catchers arrive in about fifteen minutes. There are two of them – big, strong, burly Malays wearing singlets and cargo pants and tall thick rubber boots. One of them, the team leader, has a baseball cap on backwards and is carrying a long metal rod with a hook on the end. The other has a large hessian sack. Anxiously Laura wonders where the rest of their equipment is. Surely they need more than just a stick and a bag. She shows them into the girls' bedroom and Vijay greets them with a look of relief. He steps back, leaning against the window, as they approach Aggie's bed. Laura and Peter hover in the doorway, wanting to watch but not wanting to get in the way. Taking comfort in his nearness, Laura clasps Peter's hand.

The man in the baseball cap crouches down to get a better look at the cobra.

"OK, lah. Can catch no problem."

Laura's alarmed by his nonchalance. *How can he be so sure?*

"Is very good, sir, that you watch the snake" – he appears to be addressing them in general – "'cos these ones will hide and then very difficult to find."

Laura feels pleased with herself that she'd known to do this – she must remember to thank Evi for telling her. But her thoughts are quickly interrupted – using the hook the snake catcher suddenly pulls the cobra out from under the bed. It thrashes about in the middle of the bedroom floor, biting and snapping angrily at the two men's boots, its fury further inflamed when it finds thick rubber rather than flesh. But to Laura's surprise it calms down quickly and raises its head back up to take stock of the situation, swaying slightly from side to side like a boxer in the ring, recovering from a hard blow, readying himself to fight again.

Using slow but deliberate movements, the snake catcher takes off his baseball cap and places it on the end of the metal rod, covering the hook. Holding the rod in his left hand he slowly positions the baseball cap to one side of the cobra, not more than a foot away from its head, and moves it from side to side, mirroring the snake's own swaying motion. Of course, the cobra immediately focuses all of its attention on this new and nearby threat.

Laura holds her breath and squeezes Peter's hand as she watches the snake catcher take advantage of the reptile's momentary distraction to grab it around its neck from behind its hood. At the moment of capture the snake snaps its jaws wide open in angry shock and a little croak of alarm escapes from Vijay's throat.

As if it's the most normal of everyday events, which of course for him it is, the snake catcher then puts down the metal rod, picks up the cobra's tail with his free hand and bundles the serpent into his colleague's bag. Tying up the neck of the sack, he turns to Laura and Peter. "Thank you, sir, we go now." And the two men walk out of the house with their captive, leaving the others lost for words.

While Vijay goes downstairs to tell Mariel and the children that the snake's been caught, Laura and Peter return to their bedroom, where, her nerves frayed, she announces dramatically, "Well, we can't go out to dinner now."

"Why on earth not? It's fine – the snake's been caught."

"But what if there's another one hiding under the floorboards? That's the children's bedroom – we can't just leave them to sleep in there."

"Laura, I know it was frightening, but I think you're over-reacting. The snake catcher would have told us to look out for another if he thought it was likely that there'd be one. And Mariel and Vijay will be here to watch over the children. I'm sure Mariel will sit with the girls in their room for a bit while they're sleeping if you ask her nicely. She did that before when Tilly was frightened of having that bad dream again."

Laura walks towards the door to the staircase landing, fidgeting nervously with her wedding ring. "Well, I'm going downstairs to tell Mariel to keep a very careful lookout and if she's at all concerned to call me immediately."

*

By the time Laura and Peter get to the dinner party they're nearly an hour late. Taking their shoes off in the front hall, Laura immediately clocks the various brands of designer shoes and sandals left by the other guests and is relieved that Peter has finally conceded to having pedicures, like most Malaysian men, so that his bare feet, toenails, in particular, are acceptable to look at.

The guests, about twenty of them, are all happily mingling on the candlelit terrace drinking cocktails. There's a wonderful smell of jasmine. Laura looks around trying to spot where it's growing, then sees hundreds of fat jasmine flowers, like the ones that are threaded into necklaces and sold outside Indian temples, sprinkled across a long dining-room table that's been laid up on the veranda. The delicate white flowers tinged with pink soften the grandeur of the starched white linen tablecloth and napkins, the shining silver cutlery and the tall, stemmed wine glasses that have been so well polished the table settings reflect in them.

They are given Bellini cocktails by a waiter and Laura's just sensing the alcohol calm her nerves and wash away the image of the snake when Arpana, wearing a shimmering red silk sari, sails towards them and gushes, "Welcome, my dears! I'm so glad you were able to make it – thank you for calling to say you'd be late. What an ordeal you've been through. You must tell us all about it

– we're just about to sit down to dinner." And she ushers them towards the table.

"I really am sorry we're so late. I do hope we haven't held up the evening."

"Not at all, not at all." The rest of the guests are slowly making their way towards the table and finding their places. "Now, Laura, you're sitting there, between Krish and Augustus." Above the place setting is a small card with 'Laura' written in beautiful calligraphy. "And Peter, you're over there next to Linwen and myself."

Laura's immediately conscious of what a compliment it is that Peter's been put next to Arpana and is relieved that they'd managed to make it to the party. She looks across at him and thinks how handsome he looks in his cream linen trousers, his piercing blue eyes picking up the colour of his shirt. He was right not to wear a tie; none of the other men are. In fact, many are wearing brightly coloured patterned shirts. The women, she notices, are extremely well dressed and generally seem to have a confidence about them that makes Laura strangely alert.

She's feeling the heat even though her arms and shoulders are bare and is grateful for the ceiling fans ticking away above them.

"Hi, you must be Laura. I'm Krish. Let me get your chair for you." A good-looking Indian man in his late thirties with a pukka English accent gallantly pushes her chair in under her. "And this wicked Chinese bloke on your other side is Augustus," he says, laughing.

Augustus is elegantly dressed and serious-looking despite his mischievous smile.

"I should warn you that we're both lawyers so likely

to bore you rigid." He also has a perfect English accent. "I gather you've already had to fight off a cobra tonight."

"Yes, to be honest, it was terrifying. I was not brought up to cope with snakes. But fortunately, the DBKL snake team came and took it away."

"You were lucky then – more often than not they make some excuse about why they can't come."

A wide variety of dishes are brought in by an army of waiters and placed on the table. The smell is delicious. Laura spies one with cauliflower in a tomato sauce; another of sliced French beans with potatoes, onions, tomatoes and lots of green chillies; also, various dishes with chickpeas; and a chicken curry with coriander leaves sprinkled prettily on the top.

"May I help you?"

"Oh yes, please do."

Krish starts to give her a small amount of every dish within his reach.

"These are specialities from northern India, which is where Arpana is from. Her family cook has been with them for years and moves with them wherever they go. So… did you see the DBKL men catch the cobra?"

She tells the tale of the snake's dramatic capture. Both Krish and Augustus are gripped by her story, and she enjoys having such an attentive audience.

"You should have seen the snake's face when he grabbed it round the neck – it was furious."

"Wow! How skilful. But rather him than me!" Augustus laughs. With the snake safely caught, he politely turns his attention to his neighbour on the other side, leaving Laura and Krish to continue their conversation.

"So, Krish, tell me about yourself. Are you from KL?"

"Yes. I am, as we like to say, Chindian – my mother is Chinese Malaysian and my father Indian Malaysian." He looks across the table at the woman sitting next to Peter. "And that's my wife, Linwen. She's an interior designer and an art consultant."

Laura feels herself tensing. Across the table is possibly the most stunning and sophisticated-looking woman she's seen since she's been in Malaysia. She's wearing a lovely, figure-hugging, black dress and having an extremely animated conversation with Peter. Gazing at this beautiful career woman, Laura senses envy slithering up her spine.

"Peter will be thrilled to be talking to her. He loves art. In fact, we bought a painting at the WWF exhibition at Rimbun Dahan a few weeks ago."

"Ah yes, that was a great show."

Laura's suddenly overwhelmed by the need to defend her unemployed status. "Of course, I'm not allowed to work here – your government are very strict about these things. I'm a fashion journalist – back in London I had my own column in *The Sunday Times Style Magazine*."

"Linwen will definitely want to hear all about that – she loves fashion. We go quite often to London to shop. It must be hard for you giving up a job like that to become an expat wife here in sleepy KL." His sympathy lowers her defences an inch.

"Yes, actually, it's *very* hard. I'd taken some comfort in the assumption that it was the norm for Malaysian women not to work, when they can afford not to. But clearly that's not the case."

"I'm afraid not, Malaysian women tend to be rather

career-minded. I think most of those that are here tonight have quite good jobs. Augustus's wife, Casey, works for Citibank."

This information starts a fire within her which, fuelled by the adrenalin left over from the snake incident, burns throughout the rest of the evening. She's relieved when Peter signals that he's ready to go home.

*

Prakash drives them. This luxury is a perk of Peter's job that they're rapidly taking for granted. And now they both tend to drink too much when going out. Peter chatters away about what an excellent evening it was. Laura murmurs in agreement, but the fire of frustration is still smouldering, and she has to focus on keeping it under control. Later, when they're home – he's putting toothpaste on his toothbrush:

"I also had a good chat with that woman called Sarina." He starts brushing his teeth and continues, mumbling through the foam, "She owns that groovy furniture shop in Bangsar Shopping Centre – the one that we said was KL's answer to the Conran Shop. Apparently, it's a really good little business with more and more Malaysians wanting contemporary furniture. She says she loves it, especially as she gets to travel quite a bit."

Another successful career woman – it's too much for Laura and suddenly the smouldering fire inside her explodes.

"Right, that's it! I can't fucking take anymore! I've had enough!"

Peter looks utterly bewildered. His toothbrush, halted unexpectedly, leaves a frothy river running down his chin. Laura bursts into angry tears, collapses onto the closed loo seat and starts sobbing into her hands.

"What the hell am I going to do in this bloody place?" Furiously she pulls at the loo roll and unravels much more than she needs. She blows her nose loudly. "It was one thing when I thought all Malaysian women were good little housewives, but now it turns out that there's a whole load of them with glamorous jobs, not to mention their own businesses. Whereas I'm stuck in the house fighting off bloody cobras. And Linwen flies to London to buy her clothes!"

Peter, traces of white still coursing down his face, kneels beside her. "Darling, I'm sorry. It was unfair on you having to give up your job. But it's not as bad as all that, is it?" He puts his hand on her shoulder.

She shrugs it off and gives another heartfelt sob. "I don't feel like *me* without my journalism," she sniffs, "and there's no sense of achievement to my day. Without it I feel incomplete – like there's nothing to me except my children, like I've let the side down for the modern feminist movement. You know, I was actually grateful to that snake tonight because it gave me an interesting topic of conversation."

"Look, if things keep going as well as they are, Spears Anderson should be able to sell Sweet Stevia by next September and then we can go home. And until then, why not enjoy the expat life – being waited on hand and foot, not even having to stack the dishwasher? Many women would give their eye teeth not to have to work."

She looks at him in disbelief, stands up and pushes past, storming out of the room.

*

The guest room is hot and smells musty. She turns on the air-con. Why can't he understand better how she feels? Now he's made her feel like a spoilt brat. Of course, she's enjoying having Mariel and Vijay working for them – it's absolute luxury. But her self-respect demands that she do more with her life and Peter should understand that. They've both been brought up to be ambitious and hard-working, Laura especially. She's always believed that she owes it to her mother's generation, who'd still been held back by society, to go out there and prove that a woman can have it all – marriage, career and a family. She realises that at the core of her soul she thinks that to be a housewife with a houseful of staff and therefore nothing to do is shameful. It flies in the face of everything her generation of women have fought for. She knows she's losing her self-respect and can feel dark clouds of gloom gathering around her.

What *is* she going to do? The suggestion of helping at Evi's refugee school is a complete non-starter. She hasn't done a Teaching English as a Foreign Language course – she'd have no idea what to do and the thought of trying to keep a class of thirty Burmese kids under control fills her with horror. She'd probably do more damage than good.

She curls up on the bed. The air-con is kicking in but it's still too hot to get under the sheet. She flinches – on the wall there's a *chik chak*, a gecko, with a cockroach in its mouth. The gecko is not much bigger than the cockroach but has its jaws firmly around its head. The cockroach is still alive – moving its antennae and legs in a feeble attempt to free itself. The gecko has spotted Laura. It is stock-still, eyeing her warily, determinedly keeping hold of its prey.

Part 3

April 2007

Saga seeds

"Mam? Mam? I've brought you a cup of green tea." Mariel touches her shoulder gently.

Mrs Laura rolls over and looks at her blearily.

"Hmm? What time is it? Oh... Mariel, it's you – I must've fallen asleep."

"It's six o'clock, mam. Tilly and Aggie have had supper and are ready for bath. Aggie is asking if you're doing bath, mam?" Mrs Laura pushes herself up and leans back against the pillows. She looks tired and worn. Mariel hands her the cup of tea.

"Yes, I'll do bath time. Of course. I hadn't realised it was so late. Thank you – for the tea, and for waking me up. I'll be down in a minute."

Mariel leaves her and heads back down to the living room to check on the children, who are watching *Dora the Explorer*. She's worried about Mrs Laura. She's been worse in the last few weeks – sleeping almost every afternoon, spending less and less time with the children.

This had all started in December, before Christmas – suddenly her mood got bad and stayed like that every day. And she's become more and more like a regular boss – demanding and impatient, always leaving everything for Mariel to clear up. She'd seemed a bit better around Chinese New Year – more cheerful. She'd said she loved the fireworks and the lion dances. There'd been a lion dance performance at school and Mrs Laura had invited Mariel to go with them. Mariel was surprised that the family had never seen one before – she'd assumed there must be Chinese New Year festivities in England. Mrs Laura said she thought it was fantastic – the men dressed as the lion, dancing their dangerous acrobatics on the vertical poles. Tilly had worried that they'd fall off. Aggie hadn't liked the noise of the Chinese drums and cymbals, and had hidden behind Mariel's legs. They'd all decorated the house with Chinese lanterns and bowls of mandarins, and Mrs Laura had laughed so much when the kids had tried to teach her how to say '*Gong Xi Fa Cai*'. But after the holiday she'd again been sad or cross every day and had complained of being tired. That was when all the sleeping in the afternoons had begun. Mariel knows Mr Peter's worried about her too. She'd heard him talking to Mrs Laura – encouraging her to stop skipping her tennis lessons and keep active.

One evening he'd come home from work, and she'd still been napping. Mariel had already given the children their bath and was getting them ready for bed.

"Mariel, you must make sure Laura doesn't sleep this late in the afternoon. It's not good for her. Just knock on her bedroom door and tell her it's time for the girls' bath or whatever. This really can't go on," he'd said, and she could hear the angst in his voice. Then he'd gone in to wake her himself and Mariel had overheard their conversation about the tennis lessons.

When Mrs Laura had finally got up, she came in to say goodnight to the children and Mariel went back downstairs. Mr Peter was sitting on the sofa, his head in his hands, staring at the floor. Mariel felt embarrassed finding him like this and stood there frozen for a moment before walking as quietly as she could back into the kitchen.

This evening the children are engrossed by Dora the Explorer's latest adventure. Mariel goes into the kitchen and starts washing up the dishes from their supper. After a short while she hears Mrs Laura come down and take Tilly and Aggie back upstairs for their bath, and so decides to go and phone Rosa, while she's not needed – she doesn't want to leave it till Sunday. They've been arguing for months about whether she should marry Vijay and now they've started arguing about who will run the bakery when they move back.

Entering their little bungalow, she can hear Vijay in the bathroom showering.

"Vijay!" she shouts through the door. "I ring Rosa now – think it better we talk and solve problem." The noise of the water stops, and Vijay comes out of the bathroom with a towel tightly wrapped around his generous waist.

"What you tell her? Tell her I going to work in bakery?"

"Yes, I'm going to tell her we definitely get married. And when, in future, we move home, we will *all* work in bakery. *I* bought bakery for them so *I'm* the boss – she

187

cannot argue with me." She rummages in the drawer of her bedside table for her little Nokia handphone and her international phone card. "But I also tell her that if all four of us work there, we can make more – cookies and cakes as well, not just bread and rolls. Then we will sell more and plenty of work for everyone."

She sits down on the hibiscus-patterned bedspread, swings her legs up on to it and starts punching the numbers into the phone. Vijay gets dressed slowly. She can tell he's hovering in order to overhear the conversation.

"Hello? Rosa? Hi, it's Mom."

"Hang on a moment – let me give the baby to Luis so we can talk properly." Mariel can hear her granddaughter babbling away and Luis welcoming her into his arms. "Look, Mom, this idea to marry Vijay is crazy. I've talked it over with the rest of the family. We all agree, it's not right." Mariel starts pulling angrily at the edge of the bedspread. "We understand that you want to divorce Dad, but you'll be the first divorced woman in the village. And remarried to a Hindu? People won't like it – it's wrong. And, besides, a civil marriage is not a real marriage."

Vijay is still hovering in the doorway. He doesn't speak Ilocano so can't understand anything they're saying, but Mariel doesn't want him listening, just in case. She looks at him fiercely and shoos him out. Reluctantly he leaves the bungalow.

"Rosa, I'll be proud to be the first divorced woman in the village. I bet there are others who want to get divorced – if I'm the first then I might do some good. Anyway, I'll also be the richest woman, living in the biggest and best house, especially after Vijay builds on another room – that will bring respect."

"Yes, that's another thing, Mom, this Vijay guy is just after your money."

Mariel is truly angry now – she clenches her jaw. "I won't have you speak about him like that! I've been with Vijay for twelve years now – if I want to give him my money then that's my business. The three of you have had plenty of it already. Not to mention the bakery I bought for you!"

The argument continues with Rosa making her claim that she and Luis will be out of a job if Mariel and Vijay both work at the bakery – Mariel counters with her plans for expansion.

"I'm going now – the little *mat salleh* will want their hot chocolate. We'll talk again on Sunday. Please, Rosa, try to understand how important this is to me." She hangs up before Rosa has time to say anything else.

Vijay is sitting at the table in the utility room scratching at a lotto card – leaving a little spray of silver dust on the white Formica top. He'd said he was confident of a prize this week because he'd chosen his number combination from the number plate of a car in a big crash he'd seen – looked like at least two dead. He was using the local Chinese strategy – believing that the number on the car plate had just had so much bad luck it was now due some good.

"Ah-ha!" He raises his lotto card into the air in triumph. "Twenty-ringgit prize – not so bad, good profit. I tell you, Chinese way is good. What Rosa say? You tell her?"

"Yes, I told her. No more argument." His face lights up with his beautiful smile and he stands up and gives her a kiss. "Vijay!" She giggles as she pushes him away. "Stop now, boss might see!"

"You are my woman! I buy you present with my winnings. What you want? New blouse? New lipstick?"

She blushes and smiles at him. "Hush now, I'm busy."

She goes through to the kitchen and starts heating up some milk in a pan on the stove. Tilly and Aggie come in, in their nighties, and clamber up onto the two bar stools that are on either side of the small high table that Mariel uses for chopping. Tilly looks serious.

"Mariel, can we give Mummy the saga seeds we collected this afternoon? She seems really sad today and I know they'll cheer her up."

That afternoon there'd been yet another power cut. The rainstorm and the lightning had come at lunchtime and the power had been off for nearly four hours afterwards. There seem to be more power cuts up on Bukit Tunku than in the areas where she's worked before – probably because the hill attracts the lightning. After Mrs Laura had brought Tilly and Aggie back from school, she'd said she was going to her room to read (sleep more like it). With the fans and air-con not working the children had soon become tetchy from the heat so Mariel had taken them for a swim in the pool.

They always have so much fun in that pool – Mariel loves to watch them. This afternoon they'd started by playing on the little slide – shooting down as fast as they could go. Sometimes they went together, Aggie sitting in front of Tilly. Then they devised a game where one of them held the inflatable crocodile at the bottom of the slide while the other had to zoom down and land on it.

After that, they spent ages practising 'big girl' strokes, with Tilly confidently showing Aggie how to do freestyle, and Aggie determinedly swimming width after width trying to get it right until Mariel, worried that she was getting dangerously tired, suggested it was time to get out.

Slipping hooded towelling dresses over their heads, Mariel had asked them if they'd like to collect saga seeds from the base of the saga tree round the back of the staff bungalow. The tree stands outside Mariel's bedroom window, and she'd been very happy when she'd first spotted it there. She'd explained to the children that in Asia the dark red saga seeds – in the shape of squashed spheres the size of small peas – are a symbol of deep love. This is because they're so hard they're almost impossible to crush and their colour *never* fades. Even at four and six the girls have had enough romantic stories dripped into them to be delighted by this.

"Let's collect loads of them up and put them in a bowl for Mummy. Then she can look at them every day and remember how much we love her."

"Can, *lah*. Mummy will like that. But listen now," she'd taken them both by the hand and looked at them sternly, "you mus' not eat. Understand? Will make you sick if eat. So cannot, OK?"

"Do you mean they're poisonous?"

"Yes."

"OK, we'll remember, won't we, Aggie?"

Aggie had nodded her head seriously, looking like she'd gone off the whole project a bit. But once they'd started to collect the seeds she was soon distracted by the richness of their colour and their beauty.

191

Now, the two of them finish their hot chocolate, get down from the bar stools and put their mugs in the sink.

"Thank you, Mariel, night night," they chorus. Mariel says goodnight and pats them both on the head at the same time, one with each hand. She feels a surge of affection which she knows from bitter experience she should try to suppress when Aggie kisses her on the side of her thigh, the nearest part of her body that's available, and then dashes after her sister to find the bowl of red seeds.

Through the kitchen doorway she watches them as they give their mother the little bowl of love. She can see Mrs Laura, tearful and overwhelmed, hugging both of her children close to her. *Why does that woman not realise how lucky she is? She's got her family and this big house, her health and enough money to pay a doctor when she needs one. She must stop feeling sorry for herself. Life is hard but she's got it easy.*

Mini Mars Bars

There's a terrible scrunching sound as the back wheel arch and the bumper scrape against the concrete column in the entrance of the car park.

"Shit, shit, shit." Laura reverses but the corner of the bumper has got caught on the column so is wrenched off further. "Oh God. This is ridiculous. I can't even drive the car properly!" She rests her forehead on the steering wheel and bursts into tears. Aggie joins in, wailing.

Tilly is craning her neck, trying to see the side of the car out of the window. "Mummy, what's wrong? What's happened? What was that noise?"

Laura pulls herself together. "Sorry, darlings, it's nothing serious. I don't know why I got so upset. I've just scratched the side of the car on that pillar. It's these stupid shopping mall car parks – the entrances are so narrow."

Aggie stops wailing, but her next few breaths are a shudder. A couple of the cars in the queue behind start honking their horns.

"Alright! Alright!"

Laura gets out of the car to inspect the damage. The heat envelops her, and her anxious sweat is joined by a humid one. She feels like she can't breathe. The bumper is hanging off – trailing on the ground. "Oh, fuck, I can't drive the car like that." She yanks at the bumper and the rest of it comes away. So, she opens the boot and throws it in.

They're at the car park of the new mall, Bangsar Village II. Having picked up the girls from school she's taking them to buy some new sandals. The widths of the parking bays in the car park are also absurdly narrow and she nearly takes out the other side of the car pulling in to one.

The day hadn't started well either. She'd had a call that morning from Barbara Johnson, the editor of *The Expatriate Magazine*, saying they were sorry but 'they couldn't accommodate any more contributors at the moment'. Laura had been speechless with disappointment. She realises now that she'd been rather arrogant and naïve to assume that they'd snap her up because of her experience at *The Sunday Times*. Barbara had quickly disillusioned her of that idea: "I'm afraid we don't tend to run articles on fashion – the magazine is more about exploring Malaysia and its culture." *Patronising cow*.

It seems that there are numerous expat spouses who want to write pro bono for the magazine, but the current team is a small circle of close friends. Laura hadn't even realised that *The Expatriate Magazine* existed until her friend Evi had told her about it recently. Not for the first time she'd ended up crying while having lunch with her.

Evi had recommended that she needed something to focus on and had suggested pitching to the magazine. She'd been so excited at the thought of doing some journalistic writing again. She should have known better than to get her hopes up.

And now she's gone and bashed up the car. Peter will pretend not to be cross even though it will be expensive to repair. Imported cars and their parts are extortionately expensive in Malaysia because of the protectionist duties. Malaysian cars, Protons, are renowned for being tin cans on wheels, which is why they'd bought a Japanese car.

Peter is making such an effort to be nice to her at the moment, but it isn't helping. In fact, it's making her paranoid that he's having an affair. Often, he comes home late saying that he hadn't been able to get away from work. And then there was that weekend when he went off to the Cameron Highlands with his work colleagues for a bonding weekend. He was in such a good mood when he came home. Laura couldn't help but worry that something had gone on. Actually, she feels anxious about everything. Indeed, these last few months she's felt like she's wading through mud – tired all the time, everything an effort. Every time she tries to do something it invariably goes wrong. And having once been enchanted by the light, she now thinks of it as the enemy. It's the glare – it gives her a headache. She can't seem to get away from it.

Luckily the sandal shopping is successful, and morale is further improved when they find a bag of mini Mars Bars in the mall's supermarket. They haven't had Mars Bars since they've been in Malaysia, let alone mini ones – somehow their cuteness makes them even more special.

Quite a few are consumed in the car on the way home. They taste a little different from the ones in England but none of them are surprised by this – they'd noticed the same with the KitKats that can be readily bought in the supermarket, and Peter had told them it's because the recipe is altered to stop the chocolate melting in the heat. Anyway, the Mars Bars are delicious, and the sugar does a good job of restoring their depleted energy levels.

When they get home the girls announce they're going to do their Disney Princesses jigsaw puzzle, so Laura decides she'll sit down and help them before ringing Peter at the office to tell him about the car. She's trying to make more of an effort to be cheerful around the children – they were so endearing when they gave her those beautiful saga seeds. And she doesn't want them worrying about her. She just feels so worn out – all the time.

Dumping her handbag and the bag of mini Mars Bars on the veranda table, Laura settles herself on the living-room floor, her back to the veranda. She stretches out her legs, enjoying the coolness of the marble on her bare skin. Tilly goes to the playroom to fetch the jigsaw while Aggie clambers onto Laura's lap. Her little body is hot and sweaty, but Laura doesn't have the heart to move her. She's still a bit unsettled after the incident in the car park.

Just then Mariel appears bringing them each a glass of her delicious ice-cold homemade lime juice which she makes from *calamansi*, the Philippine lime. It tastes like a mixture of orange and lime and Laura particularly loves its smell.

"Oh, Mariel, thank you so much. We've had a bit of a dramatic afternoon—"

"Mummy *crwaashed* the car!" Aggie gives another of her dramatic, shuddering sighs.

"I just scratched it while driving into the mall car park."

"She *says* it's not serious," Tilly is busily laying out the jigsaw pieces, "but the whole back bit has come off. We had to drive home with it in the boot."

"Oh my goodness, mam, sound serious."

"No, no, it's just the bumper. Mr Peter can ask Prakash to take it to the mechanic tomorrow."

Mariel returns to the kitchen. Laura can tell that she's not on great form either; recently she's been looking a little tired and harassed herself. Laura often thinks of the emotional toll that leaving her children for such a long time must have taken on Mariel, and she feels guilty for feeling so utterly miserable when by comparison she's really got nothing to complain about.

The children start to work on the puzzle, but Laura finds it hard to concentrate. Again, she's thinking about her conversation with the woman at *The Expatriate*. Why did she have to be so snooty about having a piece on fashion? Surely a lot of their readership would be interested. More and more malls are opening – the new one they went to this afternoon has a shop that sells lovely Asian clothes that are more modern, often with a Western twist. Laura's already bought three pairs of floaty trousers there and several very pretty blouses. And she's heard, via an old work friend in London, that both Hermès and GAP are planning to open in KLCC, the big mall below the Twin Towers. But bloody Barbara Johnson didn't even give her a chance to make her case.

Laura had *so* hoped that the magazine would be the solution to her problems – help her to keep the black dog at bay. It's been sniffing at her heels since she'd been depressed after Aggie was born. She'd had it under control – securely tied up in its kennel – but now she fears it's got the better of her again.

"Mummy! Mummy! The Mars Bars!" Tilly's face is horror-struck.

Turning round Laura catches sight of a monkey bounding away. Sliding Aggie off her lap she gets up and hurls after it with an explosion of aggression, surprising herself almost as much as the monkey.

"Give those back, you brute!"

The villain picks up speed, not knowing that its swag of loot is hanging open. As it runs down the terraces towards the wilder part of the garden it leaves a trail of little black and red rectangles, and escapes with nothing but an empty bag.

"Serves you right, you bloody thief!"

Laura is panting, sweat running down her face and into her eyes. The girls are watching from the veranda – a look of awe shining from both their faces.

"Oh, Mummy, that was brilliant. You scared him so much he dropped them all."

Laura starts walking slowly back up the garden, picking up the scattered Mars Bars as she goes. "There was no way I was going to let him have them – they're our treat and we need them to cheer us up."

But she doesn't feel cheered. In fact, the sudden adrenalin rush and the hundred-metre sprint in 35°C have left her feeling utterly depleted, and the familiar sense of weariness creeps back over her. She puts the Mars Bars in the fridge, tells the girls they can watch TV and goes upstairs to bed.

A trip to the cinema

It's been a long week for Mariel. Unusually, for the last four days, there's been no rain, so the heat has become intense. Mariel can take heat, but working in the kitchen this week has been hard. She certainly doesn't miss working for Monsieur Duras, but when it's as hot as this she misses the air-con in his kitchen. And Mrs Laura is still napping every afternoon, leaving her to mind the kids, although Vijay often does this. In fact, he loves looking after the kids – as well as playing card games with them he also spends hours pushing them on the swing at the far end of the veranda. He's such a kind and patient man. It makes her happy that his relationship with Tilly and Aggie is some compensation for not having had kids of his own. Occasionally she reminds him not to allow himself to get too close, but she knows that she herself is falling into the same trap.

Unfortunately, despite her efforts, the argument with Rosa has still not been fully resolved. This week she's sent Mariel a string of SMSs claiming that they'll all be shunned by the village community if Mariel gets a divorce, that Rosa won't be able to hold her head up high in church, where she's an active member of the congregation, and she's still going on about Vijay being after Mariel's money. The language barrier generally shields Vijay from these remarks, but he's picking up on the gist of the argument and it's clearly beginning to make him uncomfortable. He's always known that it won't be easy for the village to accept him – they'd talked about that problem ages ago when they'd first decided to get married. But she knows that he's shaken by how hostile her children, especially Rosa, are being towards him.

So, this Sunday, after such a difficult week, she's treating herself to a trip to the cinema with her friends Faye and Jenny. They're going to the 7pm showing of the new James Bond movie, *Casino Royale*. They're all keen to see what this new actor, Daniel Craig, will be like as James Bond. Mariel's not convinced he'll be as good as the handsome Pierce Brosnan.

She's waiting for her friends outside the Megamall cinema. It's crowded, but it always is on a Sunday, especially if it's hot – everyone enjoying the cool of the mall's air-con on their day off. Faye and Jenny are a bit late, but they generally are, so Mariel's bought the tickets and some popcorn – they'll pay her back later.

"Oh my goodness, Mariel, the bus was so slow – thought we'd never make it on time." Faye is running towards her from the direction of the escalators with Jenny not far behind.

*

They enjoy the movie – all three agree that although he's not as attractive as Pierce Brosnan, Daniel Craig is good. But it's a long film so it's after 9.30pm by the time it's finished and they all want to get home, ready for another hard week's work. Mariel walks with her friends to the bus stop – she'll get a taxi from there. But when they get to the bus stop there's a huge queue – everyone is leaving the mall at the same time. So, despite the heat, they decide to walk fifteen minutes to another bus stop, on a different route, which they figure will be less crowded. Mariel says she'll go with them but, if she sees a taxi on the way, will grab it.

They talk as they stroll – Mariel tells them all about her long-running argument with Rosa.

"She just goes on and on about how shameful it will be for her, how shocked her friends will be – she only thinks of herself these days."

"I can see her comments are hurtful, Mariel, but you can't deny that it'll be a big deal returning to the village divorced and living with a Hindu man. After all, have you ever heard of anyone back home who's divorced?"

"I've told you before, Jenny, that TV host, Amy Perez, is getting a divorce. Anyway, it's a price I'm willing to pay and, after all I've done for them, I expect my family to be more supportive."

They're so engrossed in their conversation they don't notice the police van drawing up quietly behind them. Mariel hears car doors opening and shutting but thinks nothing of it until she realises that there are two policemen standing one on either side of them. Neither are big men, but they're mean-looking and both are resting a hand on their gun holsters.

"*Selamat petang.* Show us your papers, *boleh*?"

Mariel's whole body starts shaking instantly and she sees the colour drain from Faye and Jenny's faces. Of course, they have copies of their papers with them – they would never go out without them. All three of them rummage nervously in their purses and then hand their papers to the taller of the two men, the one that had spoken. He glances at the documents.

"Papers not in order. Get in van."

Faye looks outraged. "But papers good, sir!"

He ignores her. "Get in van."

There are two other Filipina maids already in the van. They are both young and very pretty. Mariel is too shaken to speak – she's worried she might just burst into tears. But Faye asks the young girls, in Tagalog, "Do you know which police station they're taking us to? Where did they pick you up?"

The girl nearest the van doors replies, "They picked us up on the same street as you. We'd only just got in the van when they stopped again for you. We think they're taking us to Mid Valley *Pondok Polis* as it's the closest."

This is the first time this has happened to Mariel, but she's often heard of it. She'd thought that now that she was older, she'd be less of a target, which is why she'd become braver about going out without Vijay. But clearly these policemen are not fussy and don't just want young and pretty girls.

Jenny has now started to cry. Faye takes her hand.

"Jenny, Jenny – no need to cry. I'm ringing the boss now. He will call the police station. He's the MP for this constituency – as soon as the police hear he's our boss they'll let us go." She looks over at Mariel. "Mariel – you must call Mr Peter now."

By the time Mariel has got her handphone out of her purse and shakily punched in Mrs Laura's number, because she doesn't have Mr Peter's, Faye has already spoken to her boss. Mariel wishes that she was working for an important Malaysian MP and not a Western expat. Maybe the police won't respect *mat salleh*? The phone is ringing and ringing with no answer. Maybe Mrs Laura's already gone to bed and left her phone downstairs?

"Mariel? Is that you? What's wrong?"

"Oh, Mrs Laura, mam," she starts sobbing as she speaks, "I need Mr Peter come quick to Mid Valley *Pondok Polis*. Please, mam, tell him come quick, please, mam." Her hands are shaking so much she must hold the phone with both of them.

"OK, Mariel – I need you to talk more slowly and explain what's happened. Where are you? Is Vijay with you? Peter is here with me – he's listening too."

"No, mam, Vijay at home. I don't want ring him 'cos he go crazy. Please tell him mus' stay home." She takes a deep breath and tries to slow down. "I at *Pondok Polis*, mam, near Mid Valley Megamall. *Polis* say papers no good, mam. I know they will say mus' have sex if want to be released."

She feels her scalp reddening and hears Mrs Laura's sharp intake of breath.

"Mariel, this is Peter talking. Do you have your papers on you?"

"Yes, sir, of course. I show them but they say are no good."

"Right… I see. Well, my copy of your papers is in the office so we will have to go there first to collect them. But you must tell the police that we're coming."

She wonders if he hasn't understood the seriousness of the situation. "But sir, mus' come quickly. There's not much time, *please*, sir?"

"You need to stall them, Mariel. We will come as quickly as we can but it's vital we do the right thing. We need to be careful. Remember, you were supposed to go back to the Philippines for three months before your visa was transferred to us? Maybe this is why they're saying your papers are not in order. We need to be careful because they could use it as a reason to revoke my visa as well. We'll be there soon, I promise." And he hangs up.

Mariel is speechless. What is Mr Peter talking about? Does he not understand that these policemen don't care at all how she got her visa, whether a bung was paid or not? They're just saying the papers are no good as an excuse to take the maids to the police station and lock them up so no one can see what they do to them. *Why are Mr Peter and Mrs Laura so blind?* Fury surges through her.

Just at that moment the van pulls to a stop and then the back doors open, and they're told to get out. Jenny is still crying – Faye has her arm around her. She takes Mariel by the hand, and they huddle together as they're all ushered through the reception of the police station, past a man behind the desk who doesn't even bother to look up from his phone, and into a dingy waiting room. A few grey plastic chairs are scattered about. It smells stale

– stale sweat, stale food, stale cigarette smoke. The two policemen follow them into the room and lock the door behind them. *How am I supposed to stall them?* She can't decide if it's fear or anger that's making her shake – both, perhaps. Immediately the policemen grab one of the two young girls, the one that had spoken to Faye in the van and, taking an arm each, they pull her into an adjoining room. She starts screaming and struggling, and before the door closes Mariel sees one of the policemen clamp his hand over her mouth, muffling the noise.

*

"Quickly, Laura – go and talk to Vijay. Be very calm with him and don't let him know how freaked out Mariel was." Peter is moving fast, putting on a clean work shirt and a tie – clearly intending to look business-like and authoritative. "I'm going to have a quick look at the map to see where Mid Valley Police Station is. Then, as soon as you've finished talking to Vijay, we'll go to the office and get the documents. We *must* hurry."

Laura dashes downstairs and runs through the house and out of the backdoor. Taking a deep breath to calm herself, she knocks firmly on the door of the staff bungalow. She can hear the TV.

"Vijay, it's Laura. Can I have a quick word?" She feels awkward and knows he'll be confused by this intrusion as she never normally goes to the staff bungalow. In fact, she hasn't been in it since the day Mariel arrived.

"Coming, mam." The TV goes quiet, and he opens the door. "Yes, mam?"

"Vijay, Peter and I are going to Mid Valley Police Station to collect Mariel – there's been some confusion over her papers. You're not to worry – Peter will sort it out and we'll be back very soon." He looks startled but her firm and calm demeanour seem to do the trick and he remains reasonably composed. "Please could you come and watch the TV in our living room, just in case one of the girls wakes up?"

"But, mam, I mus' go *Pondok Polis* with you – help Mariel."

"I think it would be better if you stayed here – just in case the police argue that your papers are not in order as well." A deepening of the crease between his dark eyebrows displays his longing to argue against this. But logic wins him over and his eyes soften in agreement. Laura smiles at him encouragingly. "We'll be back soon." And she runs up the steps to the drive, where Peter is waiting in the car.

"OK, let's go. I've worked out where the police station is – it's literally just behind Megamall," he pulls the car out of the front gate, "but can you keep the map on your lap just in case I get in a muddle?"

Peter drives fast and in less than fifteen minutes they've reached the office. He dashes in, leaving the car idling on the side of the road and Laura waiting in it. She can't bear the wait – he seems to take so long – the office is on the fifteenth floor and the lifts aren't particularly speedy.

What the hell is going on? Surely the police don't just randomly rape Filipina maids. Maybe Mariel's over-panicking, catastrophising. But what if they declare her visa illegal and force her to go back to the Philippines?

There must be some reason behind their claim that her papers are out of order.

Peter, out of breath, jumps back into the car and chucks a document folder onto her lap before driving off at speed. In another fifteen minutes they're at the police station. Before they get out of the car Peter takes a big breath and rolls back his shoulders, puffing out his chest. "Come on then, let's do this." They jump out and march into the reception area.

The policeman behind the desk is slumped in his chair smoking a cigarette. On seeing Peter and Laura he stands up abruptly, his eyes wide with surprise. Peter's Malay is poor but better than Laura's.

"My maid, Mariel Ramos, here. I want see her, please."

The policeman looks both taken aback and surly. He replies in English, "Wait here. I get station manager." His tone implies that it's verging on insulting that Peter and Laura have come to the police station – as though as foreigners they should mind their own business.

"Please tell the station manager that I have her official papers with me which show that her visa is all in order." The man looks at Peter uncomprehendingly then turns and leaves them.

Laura's so nervous she has to hold her sweaty hands together to stop them from shaking. She looks around. The reception area is basic – just a large counter with a chair and pigeonholes behind it, and doors leading off to the left and the right. The tiled floor is slightly chipped and grubby. On the wall above the desk she spots the obligatory pictures of the current *Agong*, the king, and the prime minister.

The sound of a door opening startles her. The policeman from the front desk walks in with Mariel and two other young and pretty Filipina girls – but no station manager. Mariel's hair is mussed up and her mascara is streaked across her cheeks. She looks coldly at Peter and Laura, and then her head drops forward and her shoulders start to convulse with sobs. The two other girls have both clearly been crying – their makeup also smudged, and their eyes swollen. The policeman's expression is now positively aggressive.

"Can go now, *boleh*!"

Laura is horrified. Why are they not asking to see the visa papers? Thoughts of what might have happened race through her mind. She steps towards Mariel and goes to put her arm around her, but when Mariel flinches she withdraws it self-consciously. Mariel takes a huge intake of breath, as though to draw in strength, and stops crying.

Peter's expression has clouded with anger and comprehension. "Right then, let's go." His voice is strong and commanding. He steps towards the entrance but then hesitates. Turning towards the two young girls, he asks gently, "Would you like us to drop you somewhere?"

One of them replies, "Jalan Gallagher, please, sir."

Laura and Peter both know this road. It's near to where they live and boasts a string of expensive houses owned by wealthy Malaysians.

It only takes them about ten minutes to get to Jalan Gallagher, but the heavy silence in the car makes it seem like an eternity. The young women are both quietly effusive in their thanks as they drop them off at the guardhouse in front of the property.

"No problem at all," replies Peter, obviously embarrassed.

Once the Filipina girls are out of the car Laura turns round to look at Mariel in the back seat.

"Mariel, are you OK? I mean… did anything happen?" Once again Mariel's shoulders slump forward. She starts to weep but says nothing. "Oh, Mariel, oh no… Oh God, I'm *so* sorry. We should have got there quicker." Laura wants to touch her, to comfort her, but she's wary after her last attempt and, as she processes the reality of what has clearly happened, a terrible feeling of nausea rises in her.

Mariel still says nothing – her body rigid, her head bowed, tears splashing into her lap. Laura, panicking that she's going to vomit, instinctively opens the car window, but then, remembering where they are, shuts it as the blanket of humid air slides in and starts to smother her. She puts her hand to her mouth, partly to stop the vomit from coming and partly to catch it if it does. As she mumbles through her fingers, "I'm *so so* sorry, Mariel," she starts to cry silently – her tears splashing on the back of her hand.

"Were those two other women your friends?" Peter asks.

Mariel's head snaps up and she stares with a fierceness Laura's never seen in her before. "No, my friends' boss come straight away when they call him, before bad thing happen. He Malaysian politician. He know *polis* want bad thing, that they jus' use visa papers as excuse."

Laura starts to sob and even Peter's voice has a shakiness to it. "Mariel, I really *am* very sorry. We didn't understand. We genuinely thought that it would be best if we could show them the proper documents. I will make a formal complaint to the police authorities."

"No, sir! Mus' not do that. This my business, sir. I do not want speak to authorities. And please don't tell Vijay. He mus' not know otherwise he try kill *polis*. I tell him they jus' want money."

They're pulling into the driveway as she says this, and as soon as Peter stops the car, Mariel opens her door, gets out and, without turning back, heads down the steps to the staff bungalow.

*

Walking down the steps Mariel takes a Kleenex from her purse and wipes away the mascara smudges from under her eyes. She smooths down her hair before opening the door to the little bungalow.

Vijay's anger is visceral. "What they do, those bastard *polis*? They hurt you? I kill them!" He raises his fist as he spits out the words.

"No, is OK. They jus' want money. Two hundred ringgit. Mr Peter pay them. Is all OK now."

"You been crying, I see you been crying. Why you been crying if they not hurt you?"

"I got frighten. Mr Peter and Mrs Laura very slow coming. But is OK now." She's trying to keep her voice calm and soothing. She needs him to believe her and for his anger to subside. Her own anger is almost overwhelming – she can't cope with his as well.

"Why they slow coming? They leave soon as you call – Mrs Laura come down here and tell me."

Mariel, still smoothing down her hair, is hovering by

the bathroom door. She can feel the stinging sensation of vomit rising in the back of her throat. "They go first to Mr Peter office to get visa papers. They so stupid, they think *polis* truthful when they say they want see my papers even though I tell Mr Peter come straight away... that it urgent... that *polis* jus' just use papers as excuse... that they jus' want... money." The tears threaten to come again, and she must use all her willpower to stop them.

Vijay is calmer now. He sits back down on the bed. "Sometimes I sick of these *mat salleh*. Why they always think they know best? If *polis* had hurt you – I kill them and I kill Mr Peter and Mrs Laura."

"Hush now, Vijay. Is all OK. I mus' have shower. Is late and we got work tomorrow." She backs into the bathroom and locks the door. Turning the shower on to full power, she prays that the sound of it covers that of her retching into the toilet bowl.

I will not let that bastard polis ruin my plan.

Taking off her dress, she screws it into a tight ball and hurls it into the corner of the bathroom, swearing that she'll never wear it again. She checks her reflection in the mirror – looking for any bruises that she'll have to hide from Vijay.

I'm going to marry Vijay and we're going to have a good life back in the Philippines.

There's a red mark on her collarbone where his hand, especially his thumb, had dug into her. But, she hopes, it doesn't show too much. She had held still.

She scrubs at her skin until it looks as angry as she feels. She knows perfectly well that only her willpower can wash away the night – hot water, soap and the loofah will do nothing. Resolutely she pictures herself playing with her little granddaughter, Gloria, in the front yard of her house in the Philippines, and chatting with her daughter, Rosa, Vijay happily weeding the vegetable patch at the back of the house.

When they last spoke, Rosa mentioned that the paddy field adjacent to the house is up for sale – the local farmer has run into some debt. Feeling her steadfast soul reasserting itself, Mariel thinks that perhaps she'll buy the field – she knows she can haggle the farmer down on the price, and then she'll rent it back to him. Land is security.

She's washed her whole body now but somehow she can still smell the policeman, still feel his foulness on her skin. She starts all over again, first her hair and her face, then her private parts – scrubbing and scrubbing, wishing that she had an electric razor like Mrs Laura's to shave off her hair down there. Perhaps she will borrow it quickly tomorrow when she's taking the girls to school. But how will she explain her sudden baldness to Vijay?

Finally, she turns off the shower and leans against the tiles. Their coolness soothes her. She hates lying to Vijay, but she must. Otherwise, the plan will unravel – he will not be able to stop his anger and any trouble at all with the police, even just shouting at them, would lead to his arrest and deportation. She won't allow that to happen, not after everything she's sacrificed.

We will grow old together – as man and wife.

She creeps out of the bathroom and approaches the bed. Vijay's already asleep – still frowning. She curls up next to him and prays for sleep to steal her away from her own company.

May 2007

From the streets of KL

Laura's tennis is rusty after not playing for more than three months. She's also terribly unfit. This morning Rama has her and Guilia running all over the court. She's exhausted and stops for some water and a rest, leaving Guilia to keep going on her own.

"Laura, don't worry, your fitness levels will return quickly, no problem. Have a break and then join back in when you're ready." Both Rama and Guilia have been gently sympathetic towards her all morning and she's grateful. She hasn't explained her long absence from the lessons, but they seem to have guessed that the last few months have been a struggle for her.

She takes a big swig of water and then downs a can of 100Plus energy drink. It's the last few weeks that have been truly awful. She and Peter are both racked with guilt about what happened to Mariel, not to mention feeling utterly stupid for misunderstanding the reality of the situation. Also, furious that such a discriminatory and criminal practice is apparently not uncommon. Peter spoke to Jim in the office, who told him he'd heard of this before and that he guessed Mariel didn't want to make a complaint because she knew it probably wouldn't achieve anything other than her getting a black mark against her name at the immigration department.

Laura and Peter had tried so hard to do the right thing, by going to collect the visa papers, but in doing so had done the worst thing possible. Mariel had been raped – and it was their fault. How would she ever forgive them? She'd probably hate them forever. If only Laura could find a way to make it up to her, but how could anything make up for that? And what if Vijay ever found out what had actually happened? Surely he would blame Laura and Peter. What if he became violent? Vijay seems like such a gentle person, but the reality is, they know nothing about him. They didn't even get a reference for him – just blindly trusted Mariel's word. Anxiety crawls all over Laura's skin.

"I just can't get over how evil the whole thing is," Peter had said in the privacy of their bedroom, to be sure that he wouldn't be overheard. "How can Mariel bear to live in a country that treats her so badly?"

"Presumably because she doesn't have much choice, and I don't suppose she was treated much better in her home country."

Mariel's not hiding her anger towards them. Her shy smile seems to be a distant memory and has been replaced by a blank mask. She never speaks unless spoken to, although luckily her manner with the children is as

215

warm as ever. But Laura knows that Mariel would never punish the girls for their parents' idiocy. Every day Laura's overcome with relief when Vijay remains his usual smiley self and she wonders what Mariel has told him to explain her fury towards them.

So, the atmosphere in the house has been very tense. Laura's realised that there's no point in continually apologising – it's devaluing the power of the words. Mariel's fortitude and determination seem extraordinary. Despite her anger, she appears to want to move on and put the whole thing behind her, as if it was simply one of life's dreadful curveballs that must be dealt with. Ideally, of course, she should talk to a therapist, but from conversations with Evi Laura knows that mental health issues in Malaysia remain very much taboo – apparently children with learning difficulties are still kept out of sight. So, it's unlikely that they'd be able to find a therapist even if Mariel agreed to it. When Laura had asked her if she'd like to talk about it, she'd replied pointedly, "No good talking, mam. Nothing can be done *now*. Is past – I jus' want think about future when I marry Vijay." And when Laura had suggested she take some time off work, she'd said she'd rather keep busy, a response Laura well understood herself.

Laura feels shamed by Mariel's strength, shamed that she's allowed herself to get depressed just because she's had to give up her job, to get depressed when she's living a life of luxury in a beautiful house with a husband who is good and kind, and with her adorable children.

So, she'd determined to pull herself together, to be more positive. Last week she'd been to another of the Enjoy Malaysian Culture lectures organised by Susan – on the history of the *kampong* house. And on Friday, after their monthly mani/pedi, she'd taken Evi out to a Vietnamese restaurant to thank her for always listening so patiently to her grumbles. These outings had made her feel better. But she can't shift the feeling of guilt – guilt that Mariel has been dealt such a crappy set of cards and that by their idiocy Laura and Peter have added to them.

She's endeavouring not to nap every afternoon, although there are still some mornings, like today, when she has to drag herself out of bed. But thinking of Mariel instils in her a resolve that wasn't there before, so this morning she'd successfully forced herself to get up and go to the tennis lesson.

"Right then," she says running to the back of the court, "I'm fully recharged. You can put me through my paces."

*

Later that evening, at dinner, Mariel is once again taciturn as she puts the food on the table and retreats to the kitchen, leaving Laura and Peter feeling admonished. There's something about Mariel's anger that's almost a little frightening. Laura's just wishing she could think of a way to repair things when Peter surprises her by asking, "Do you think it might be a nice idea to get a puppy?"

Back in England the girls had regularly asked for a dog, but she'd always said no, believing that it would be too much for Tracy, the nanny. But now, she thinks, she's not working, and they have Mariel and Vijay to help, so why not? She knows that Mariel loves dogs, as she'd once asked if they were planning to get one, and had often mentioned the beautiful Alsatian that one of her previous employers had had. Perhaps a puppy would cheer Mariel up. As for Laura, she's secretly always longed for a dog. She'd never had one as a child. Her father had died when she was only ten. Childhood after that had been difficult for her and her brother as they'd negotiated the miasma of grief that had engulfed their home. When a family friend had suggested a puppy, her mother had said she couldn't cope with a dog as well as everything else. As a compromise Laura was given a guinea pig called Missy who she'd adored and who'd lived for years mainly because Laura had lovingly nursed her back to health when she'd suffered a terrible attack of mange mites.

"Yes, a puppy, how lovely! What a great idea. But I think we should get a small breed so it's manageable. Should we just buy one from a pet shop or try to get one directly from a breeder?"

Peter looks a touch uncomfortable and shifts in his chair. "Well, erm… I've sort of got a specific puppy in mind. I may have already, err… slightly committed us to having it."

"What? What do you mean?"

Peter explains that Jo-Anne, one of the admin staff in his office, had come in this morning asking if anyone would be interested in adopting a sweet and very friendly stray puppy. Apparently, it had befriended her own golden retriever which she leaves out in her yard every day when she's at work. Jo-Anne had foolishly made the mistake of feeding the puppy one time and now it won't leave. It's just a stray street mutt – offspring of one of the many feral dogs that roam the streets of KL. Jo-Anne's husband had even tried driving it a couple of miles away to Sungai Buloh, where there are masses of strays, hoping that it would find its pack. But the next evening, when they'd returned from work, the puppy was back at their front gate wagging its tail and giving them a beseeching look with its large, endearing eyes. So, Jo-Anne had set herself the task of finding it a good home. Rather sheepishly, Peter confesses that on hearing this tale he'd found himself agreeing to re-home the puppy before really thinking it through.

But Laura is also charmed by the story, by the idea of rescuing this little orphan who needs their help. She's suddenly filled with a glowing sense of optimism, that this dog will bring joy and happiness to them all, that it will be the symbol of her new and positive life in Malaysia. She smiles. "Well, it looks as though we're going to have a new addition to the family. The children will be beside themselves with excitement. When can we go and collect it?"

Clearly relieved and rather amazed by her upbeat response, Peter suggests that they shouldn't tell the children quite yet and that tomorrow Laura should go to see the puppy just to check that she likes it.

*

Jo-Anne's house is in a respectable middle-class suburb on the outskirts of KL. Laura had arranged to meet her there at 5.30pm, once Jo-Anne was back from work. She'd been concerned that it would still be raining but luckily on the way there the rain stops and according to the car dashboard the temperature has dropped to a cool 27°C.

The houses in the street, all in the same monotonous modern design and painted the same colour of beige, are built-in rows, and are detached, but only just, with a very narrow alley between each one. The streets are laid out in a grid and numbered rather than named, as though the city planner didn't have the time, energy or creativity to think of names. In front of each house is a covered porch and a yard neatly enclosed by a tidy fence.

Jo-Anne is waiting for Laura in her front yard accompanied by a huge and very fluffy golden retriever, which looks ready to keel over in the heat, and an extremely skinny mongrel puppy.

Laura walks towards the small front gate and, on seeing the puppy, worries that she's made a mistake. The little thing is emaciated. It has golden copper-coloured fur, huge ears and eyes, both of which appear totally out of proportion to its body, and a long tail that curls upwards which it starts to wag frantically when Laura opens the front gate.

"Laura, hello, please come in. Good to see you again."

Laura has met Jo-Anne a few times at Peter's office. She's a slim, plainly dressed Chinese woman with a warm but slightly deferential manner.

As Laura enters the yard, the puppy bounds towards her, making little welcoming yelps – the kind of greeting she'd always dreamed of from a dog. She kneels down to say hello and it clambers onto her lap, tries to lick her face and pees on her skirt – its tail wagging so fast she wonders how it doesn't fall over. Thank goodness she'd had the foresight to wear her oldest, scruffiest summer skirt.

"Oh no! I'm sorry. Puppy's done pee-pee on you. I'm afraid it's just excited. It's actually quite well trained."

"Don't worry, it's not a problem," she replies, laughing, surprised herself that she genuinely doesn't mind. "It was only a little bit. The puppy's adorable and so friendly."

Laura and the little mutt are still embracing. She strokes its head, marvelling at the softness of its ears. It can't stay still and tries to nuzzle its nose into every part of her. There are tears in her eyes. At the age of thirty-five she's finally found her longed-for puppy and the scruffy little canine knows this too – eventually rolling onto its back and succumbing to a tummy tickle but still unable to control its excitable wriggling. *Maybe*, she thinks, *helping this little one will help me to help myself.*

The puppy is a female – another little girl. Poor Peter – he'll be even more outnumbered. Laura arranges with Jo-Anne that the whole family will come back tomorrow, Saturday, to collect her.

*

For the past few weeks, since the night the policeman forced himself on her, Mariel has tried to control the rage searing through her, but it's been hard. She's done her best to put the incident behind her and only think of the future, but the effort is exhausting. When she's least expecting it, the image of his filthy, leering face jumps out at her and almost floors her.

She'd had to wait quite a few days before she'd had the house to herself – Mrs Laura had taken the kids to school and Vijay had gone on his scooter to buy sulphur powder. Then Mariel had lain on her bed and howled – trying to rid herself of the grief and the anger and the self-disgust.

She'd cried and cried until her breathing was ragged and at moments had even allowed her arms to flail about as though conducting her symphony of anguish. Afterwards, the improvement she felt was only physical. The tension in her head and neck had eased a little, but the pain and fury in her heart hadn't shifted.

This morning, however, as she approaches the back door of the main bungalow at 6.15am and notices that the lights in the kitchen and utility room are already on, a small smile steals across her face. Ever since the puppy arrived, Aggie has been coming downstairs as soon as she wakes up and curling up in its bed. Mariel looks down at her with tenderness. She's wrapped round the little dog as it sleeps in the space under the utility-room worktop, next to the washing machine.

But the respite from the battle against dark thoughts is only fleeting. There are chips on the tiled floor next to where the child is sleeping and suddenly Mariel's mind is back at the police station.

She'd known better than to resist him – best to get it over with. But she'd wanted to fight: to scratch at his eyes, to kick him in his private parts, to bite him wherever she could. It had been like that with Vincente, who'd always been rough and taken her without any gentleness or attempts to woo her, his own wife, and certainly no interest in her own possible pleasure. And the policeman had smelt like Vincente – breath foul with alcohol and cigarettes, dirty, sweaty clothes. And just like Vincente he'd simultaneously made her ashamed and utterly furious – wanting to scream at the universe for being so cruel and unfair. And now she feels drained by it all – she only wants to forget, to plan for her trip home, her divorce, and her and Vijay's wedding day.

She is, of course, also incredibly angry with Mrs Laura and Mr Peter. How can they still be so naïve? Understand so little about Malaysia? Why did they not do what she'd asked? She knows that *mat salleh* are famously ignorant of Malaysian ways, especially when they first arrive, but she'd tried to educate them, to make them wise to the wicked things that go on. They understand *now*, that's for sure. The two of them look so ashamed when she gives them her cross face that she almost feels sorry for them.

Aggie stirs and the puppy nuzzles its nose further into the crook of her arm. Mariel likes dogs very much, but she can't understand why Mrs Laura got this wild street dog when she could easily have afforded a beautiful pedigree one from a pet shop. Although, this puppy does have a very friendly nature, which is unusual for a street dog. Normally they won't come anywhere near you unless you tempt them with food, and even then, they're usually cautious. Vijay likes the dog too – he's already enjoying taking it for a short walk every evening, just after sundown, along the road to the condo further up the hill. He likes to chat with the security guards at the gatehouse there.

They have similar street dogs back in her village in the Philippines, scavenging around waste dumps and hawkers' stalls – looking out for scraps but always wary of an angry kick. Mariel had been shocked by the state of the puppy when they'd first brought it home. You could see its skeleton and a lot of its skin was scratched raw. But the family seemed determined to care for it – Mariel had never seen the kids so excited, and Mrs Laura seemed properly happy for the first time in ages. This was a relief because Mariel wasn't sure she could take much more of her being sad. *That woman has no idea how blessed she is.* After the rape, she finds it harder and harder to be patient with her.

Tilly and Aggie had played with the puppy for the whole weekend – chasing it round the little lawn at the top of the garden, playing tug of war with its towel, teaching it to fetch a ball – only stopping to feed it and cuddle it while it slept.

"Aggie, Aggie, wake up now. Is time to get up." Mariel crouches down to shake her little shoulder, for the child is right underneath the worktop. Aggie opens her eyes, looks at Mariel, smiles and stretches as best she can in the cramped space. The puppy also wakes, lifts its head with a yawn and then drops it again onto its paws – utterly content. Mariel knows that Tilly is jealous of this new morning routine of Aggie's. The elder sister longs to join the younger one but she's a sleeper in the mornings, never managing to wake early.

The puppy is called Mutty – the girls had been allowed to choose the name. Apparently in England they call a street dog a 'mutt'. Both Mariel and Vijay had been dismayed by this choice of name because Mutty sounds like *mati*, the Malay word for death. If they call it that, the dog will surely bring ill fortune. She and Vijay had talked about whether they should say something to Mrs Laura and Mr Peter but had decided they'd better not in case they were insulted. And Mariel's determined not to do anything that might jeopardise her plans for the future.

Since the night at the police station, she's been more and more concerned with bad omens. And she's been struggling to sleep at night. Sometimes she wakes with a start – again convinced that she can smell him, that he's hovering somewhere close to her. Not being able to share her distress with Vijay has made things even harder. Thank God he'd believed her story about the police just wanting money. She'd been right not to tell him the truth. If he'd gone to Mid Valley Police Station in a blind rage and been locked in jail or deported back to India, she would have collapsed – she couldn't have borne it. He'd asked her a few times why she was still so angry with the bosses, and she'd just told him that she was fed up with idiotic *mat salleh*. And Vijay had told her to be careful – she couldn't afford to annoy them and risk being fired. But she's struggling to think of an excuse as to why she doesn't want to make love. 'I'm too tired, it's been a long day' had worked at first, but now Vijay is beginning to look perplexed and hurt. She hates the thought of him thinking that it's his fault in any way – she would never want to wound his male pride. But of course, she can't tell him that she feels dirty and that her body is no longer what it was – a gift that she loved to give him. She knows that if she wants to protect his pride and her secret she'll have to give in soon. Right now, however, it's too much.

She'd also lied to Faye and Jenny – told them that Mr Peter and Mrs Laura had arrived in time, minutes after they'd left with their boss. She couldn't bear the shame of her two dear friends knowing what had really happened. But when Faye had said, "Thank goodness you've got a sensible boss who understands how to deal with these situations," Mariel had had to turn away and pretend to be coughing to stop herself from shouting out in anger that her *mat salleh* boss had certainly *not* understood the situation. So, without Vijay, Faye or Jenny to help her, she's bearing the burden of her pain alone.

She helps Aggie up onto the stool at the little high table in the kitchen, to wait loyally for her sister before giving Mutty her breakfast – to do that would cause a terrible row. Mariel ushers the puppy out of the back door and into the garden to do its business – she's keen to avoid having to clear up any puddles or messes in the house. There have been a few, but generally the puppy is good and knows to go outside. Of course, Mrs Laura didn't think to ask Mariel and Vijay before bringing home a dog even though they'll be the ones that must look after it most of the time. The children are very keen now, but they'll soon tire of the mundane jobs, and Mariel and Vijay will have to do them.

Before long Tilly comes downstairs – still in her nightgown – and the two sisters carefully measure out the puppy's food and refill its water bowl with cold, fresh water. *That puppy*, thinks Mariel, *must be the luckiest dog in the whole world – maybe it'll bring good luck and not bad after all.*

After dropping the children at school Mrs Laura comes home again to pick up the dog and take it to the vet. She treats it like it's her third child – always hugging and kissing it and talking to it as though it can understand. This is the third visit to the vet and Mariel knows that it's costing a fortune. Who in their right mind spends that kind of money on a street dog? They'd collected it on Saturday and Mrs Laura had rung the veterinary surgery straight away, but they wouldn't give her an appointment until Monday. She'd got angry and was quite rude to the receptionist, who'd obviously remained firm and said she'd have to wait until Monday and that they didn't normally treat strays at all.

After that first appointment Mrs Laura had come home in a total fluster because the vet had told her it would be better to euthanise the puppy. In the privacy of their room, Mariel and Vijay had laughed – they could have told her that for a cheaper price. Mariel thinks the vet must have started seeing dollar signs the moment Mrs Laura walked in. After she refused to have the puppy put down, he told her it needed a series of expensive transfusions because it was probably carrying the parvovirus, plus it needed a course of antibiotics for its skin infection and some fancy shampoo and skin cream, which Mariel knows cost more than any beauty products she's ever used on herself. Just thinking of all the money spent on the animal infuriates her, but what really makes her fume is that Mrs Laura is still being so foolish, that she doesn't appear to realise that the vet is cheating her.

She and Vijay have an early lunch in the utility room while Mrs Laura is still at the vet's – she throws together a quick egg-fried rice, adding a tin of tuna and some frozen peas.

"That vet mus' think Mrs Laura completely stupid! When she gonna learn you mus' sit on these people's head or they jus' cheat you?"

Vijay strokes his moustache. "She *mat salleh* – she never gonna understand. Maybe nobody cheat in England?"

*

Later that afternoon Tilly and Aggie are sitting on the sofa watching *Angelina Ballerina* on the TV. The puppy is cuddled up between them – three happy little monkeys. And, as so often at this time of day, the TV volume is turned up to max to drown out the noise of the afternoon rainstorm which is pounding the house. Huge droplets are bouncing off the swimming pool.

Suddenly there's an almighty bang and a sizzling sound from the TV as lightning strikes. The howls of terror from the puppy are hard to distinguish from those of the children, and the three of them bolt into the utility room and hide under the worktop – curled up like frightened pangolins squashed into Mutty's sleeping quarters.

Within minutes Vijay is assessing the burnt-out television and checking that it's not going to cause a fire – carrying out his duties as guardian of the house. Despite the aftershocks of fear still thumping in her ribcage, rattling her shattered nerves, Mariel can't help but smile with tenderness at the sight of her brave lover at one end of the house and the slightly less brave but endearing children in her care at the other.

Stones in the salad

Laura is disappointed. The girls are thrilled with the puppy and even Peter is pretty smitten, but Mariel doesn't seem pleased at all. If anything, she'd been irritated by its arrival, muttering under her breath, "I hope it knows to do its business outside. I already got plenty work to do."

The puppy is such a sweet little thing – Laura had really hoped it would cheer up Mariel. It had certainly helped Laura to feel better, although today she's feeling anxious about the dinner party they're giving this evening. Laura's still not really in the mood for being sociable, but Peter had insisted they needed to return Arpana and Shiv's hospitality before it looked rude. Laura knew he was right but her heart had sank when he also invited Susan and Jim. She really didn't feel strong enough for Susan's bossy suggestions on how to do things the 'right way'. And then he'd also gone and asked Krish and Linwen, which had really bothered her. Peter's so fired up about his work at the moment – he's all buzzy and flirty and she knows he's going to flirt with Linwen, which just feeds her paranoia. He says he wants to invite them because he wants to get to know Krish better as he's thinking of using his law firm for the sale of Sweet Stevia. But Laura worries that's just a convenient excuse.

As well as being sexy and beautiful Linwen is also a vegetarian. Laura's mind had gone completely blank trying to think of a good vegetarian recipe they could serve. She'd decided that the food should be Western – Mariel is so good at cooking Western food and that way they wouldn't be trying to compete with Arpana's dinner. But what on earth could they serve? Peter is very much a meat and two veg man, so she hardly has any knowledge of vegetarian recipes. Then she remembered the delicious asparagus risotto that Mariel makes so well and realised that it could easily be made with vegetable rather than chicken stock. So, she'd asked Mariel to serve roasted red peppers as a starter (or capsicum, as Mariel calls them), followed by the risotto with a nice green salad. For pudding she'd decided to cheat regarding the Western theme and serve dragonfruit with pineapple, which was her new favourite. She'd given Mariel very specific instructions regarding the salad because the previous week Mariel had served one which had obviously been sitting waiting for a while and the avocado had started to turn brown.

"Mariel, if you make the salad in advance, which I can see you'll probably want to do, could you please leave the stone in the salad when you add the avocado. That helps stop the avocado from turning brown."

On hearing this Mariel's eyebrows had visibly risen, clearly questioning the truth of this practice. And Laura had wondered for a moment whether it was in fact complete nonsense but then, she thought, she'd been doing it for years and the avocado never did seem to turn brown.

*

The evening had started off well. So as to have some guests she genuinely wanted, Laura had also invited Evi and her husband, Rudy. Over drinks everyone seemed to be getting on well and Peter did indeed talk mostly to Krish. Laura had done the place settings – she put Peter next to Susan (his punishment for inviting her) and Evi, who knew all about Laura's worries that he might be 'playing away'. Next to herself, Laura had placed Rudy, who seemed as passionate as Evi about helping the needy, and Shiv, who was very easy to talk to – he was so full of himself all you had to do was press 'play' and then just sit back and listen.

Now they're all sitting at the table, having just finished the starter. Vijay is helping with the serving. He's laying out the main course plates when Mariel comes out of the kitchen, proudly carrying Laura's best Sophie Conran serving dish filled to the brim with steaming risotto.

"Ah, risotto, how delicious, my favourite," says Krish politely.

"Yes, how charming," purrs Arpana. "I love *rustic* Italian food."

Laura, unsure whether this is a compliment or not, replies, "It's asparagus risotto. I'm not sure how many Italian peasants treat themselves to asparagus." And then she laughs, trying to cover up the tone of defensiveness.

Mariel carefully goes round the table and is just serving Susan when Vijay returns from the kitchen carrying a big wooden salad bowl. As he sets it down on the table, Laura sees to her horror that there are four large grey pebbles lying on the top of the salad, nestled amongst slices of slightly browning avocado. She recognises the stones as having come from the pot that the passionflower on the veranda sits in. Unfortunately, Krish has also spotted them – he raises his eyebrows and smirks at her.

Desperately trying to ensure that no one else sees them, she leans over to pick up the salad bowl and deftly whips away the stones with one hand, shielding her action from the rest of the guests with her floaty sleeve. She knows that Krish is watching her and hears him sniggering and, despite her embarrassment, can't help laughing herself.

"What's so funny?" asks Peter.

"Nothing, nothing," she replies, stifling her giggles when she catches a glimpse of Susan's disapproving expression.

Settling back down in her seat she watches Mariel and Vijay return to the kitchen and tries to remember what exactly she'd said to Mariel about leaving the avocado stone in the salad bowl and wonders how she could have misunderstood her so completely. Had she done it on purpose to embarrass her because she's so angry? Could she be that calculating? Once again Laura feels paranoia creeping through her veins and the episode no longer feels funny at all.

Everyone starts eating the main course and before Laura has even taken a bite there's an embarrassed hush around the table. Thinking that perhaps they had all noticed the stones she wonders whether she should say something – make a joke of it. But then she eats a mouthful of the risotto and realises that the silence has nothing to do with the stones in the salad. The risotto tastes of nothing – just boiled rice with asparagus in it – no flavour whatsoever.

Flushing red with mortification she says, "Oh my goodness, I'm so sorry, this risotto is completely tasteless. In fact, it's disgusting. I don't know what went wrong – Mariel normally makes it so well."

Coming to her rescue, Peter adds, "Yes, this is very unusual. She's generally such a good cook. I'll pop into the kitchen and get some parmesan – that should perk it up a bit."

"Oh, Laura, I've told you before, it takes ages to train up these maids. Perhaps she's just not as good as you think she is." Susan gives one of her smug smiles and Laura wants to slap her. "Also, I notice she hasn't laid the table properly." Pointedly, Susan moves her pudding spoon and fork which have been laid horizontally above the place setting and positions them vertically on either side of her plate. "You really *must* tell them again and again how you want things done. It requires patience but it's worth it in the end."

Laura can't quite believe what she's hearing and is profoundly grateful that neither Mariel nor Vijay is in the room. Her hackles rising, she replies, "Mariel's an exceptionally experienced maid, she certainly doesn't require any further training. I'm sure there's a perfectly good explanation as to why the risotto has turned out like this. And I really don't care how she lays the table – I think there are more important things in life to worry about!"

Everyone looks from Laura to Susan, who takes a sharp intake of breath. Arpana then glances at her fingernails, apparently admiring her manicure.

"Right, I'll get that parmesan." Peter, clearly flustered, gets up and heads into the kitchen.

"Well, we Dutch like our food plain, so personally I think this risotto is delicious. Please don't worry about it, Laura." Laura smiles at Evi with gratitude – she's such a good friend.

Peter returns with the parmesan, a purposefully cheery expression carefully pasted across his face. "Now, Susan, what's all this I hear about you organising a Scottish ball at the Selangor Club? I love a bit of Scottish dancing, especially the Gay Gordans!" Susan's face lights up as she starts to tell everyone about her plans for a Highland fling and to Laura's relief the convivial atmosphere is restored.

But, despite Evi's encouraging words about the risotto, Laura *is* worried, not so much about her dinner party being awkward but more about whether Mariel is trying to ruin it on purpose. Why on earth had she made such a disgusting risotto? She's made this recipe a thousand times before and it's always been delicious. Although normally she does use chicken stock but surely using vegetable stock wouldn't change it that dramatically. Maybe she'd wanted to purposefully embarrass Laura, to get back at her. Maybe she was more calculating than Laura had ever imagined. As these dark thoughts start to envelop her, she wonders whether the couple that she's invited to live in her house are in fact not the people that she thought they were.

The great escape

It's Saturday afternoon and Mariel is catching up with a large pile of ironing. She's taken it into her bedroom so she can watch the TV while doing it. Vijay is up on the roof of the main house fixing a small leak that has recently sprung in Tilly and Aggie's bedroom. The family are out – they've gone to Petrosains, the science discovery centre in KLCC, which has great attractions for small kids. With them all out she's comfortable ironing in her bedroom rather than in the utility room, but she worries about using the air-con in her room during the day. She and Vijay have been sleeping with the air-con on since the start, luxuriating in the pleasure of a night's sleep with no oppressive humidity, no fighting with a sweat-drenched sheet kept only to protect from the mosquitoes. Mrs Laura has never commented on this, and Mariel can't decide whether it's because she hasn't noticed or is too naïve to realise that staff aren't normally allowed to use the air-con. She and Vijay had argued about this. He'd insisted that they should be careful not to cheat the boss – that it wasn't worth it just for a bit of rich man luxury. But Mariel had overruled, confident that Mrs Laura wouldn't mind, so the air-con has been humming its bliss every night.

But after the disastrous dinner party she's more nervous of annoying Mrs Laura so she leaves the air-con firmly off. She'd never seen her boss so bothered.

"Mariel, what on earth happened to the risotto? It was totally tasteless."

"Really, mam? Oh no, I sorry. I don't know what happen. I never taste food when I cook. I follow recipe same as usual, but I use vegetable stock, like you ask, mam."

"Did you use vegetable stock cubes, or did you make it yourself?"

"Oh, mam, I don't know vegetable stock cubes. I just boil water with carrots and onions. Oh, mam, I sorry, I think I make a mistake."

"Right, well that explains it. No wonder it tasted of nothing. My fault, I should have told you you'd need to use a stock cube. Sometimes I forget that Western food is foreign to you." And Mariel had thought irritably, *Yes, you should have explained exactly what you wanted.*

Mr Peter, who was standing behind Mrs Laura, started laughing. "It was funny watching Arpana eating it all up politely. She was literally wrinkling up her nose with each bite. Shiv, on the other hand, was so busy banging on about how successful he is, he hardly seemed to notice what he was eating and just gobbled it up."

Mariel was relieved she'd been in the kitchen while the guests were eating. She loves to cook and she's proud of her skill. Hearing that it hadn't tasted good made her feel so embarrassed. Her ears burned red just at the thought of what the guests must have said, and her annoyance with Mrs Laura for not giving clear instructions grew stronger.

"And I meant put the avocado stone in the salad," Mrs Laura had continued, "not stones from the garden! Luckily, I managed to extract them from the salad bowl before any of the guests served themselves."

"Avocado stone, mam? Sorry, I don't understand."

"The stone in the middle, the pit."

"The pit? You mean the seed, mam?"

"Yes, the seed, we call it the stone in English."

At this Mariel hadn't been able to stop herself from giggling. Covering her mouth with her hand she'd said, "Oh, mam, I understand now. I thought was very strange when you say put stones in salad. But then I thought maybe that's what you do in England, maybe like tradition or something."

"That's brilliant!" said Peter with a real belly laugh. "I didn't even notice. Thank goodness Susan didn't get one on her plate. Can you imagine the fuss she would have made?" And Mariel had been relieved when Mrs Laura had started laughing too.

Now, smiling at the memory of how much Tilly and Aggie had laughed when she'd told them about the stones in the salad, she starts the ironing with Mr Peter's shirts, always her favourite thing to iron. Whilst working she makes a mental list of presents that she wants to buy her children. It's only three months now until she'll make her first visit home to see them in ten years and enjoy a whole month with them. She knows they'll be expecting her to arrive laden with gifts, which of course she'll do, and planning what to get is thankfully keeping her mind busy. A flat-screen TV for definite and an electric rice cooker. Also, she wants to buy lots of pretty little clothes for the baby.

Having finished five shirts, she decides to take them upstairs and then fix Vijay a drink. She worries about him working outdoors in the heat of the day. As she walks through the house and upstairs into the master bedroom, she has the sensation that something's not quite right. But it's not until she's back in the kitchen mixing up some orange barley water that she realises what it is. She rushes out into the garden, onto the small lawn, and calls up to Vijay on the roof, "Vijay, where's the puppy?"

He's dripping with sweat and looks confused. "Puppy? Huh? Don't know. In utility?"

"She's not here. Oh my God, she's gone! Vijay, come down, quickly, help me find puppy!"

She runs down the terraces towards the thicker parts of jungle at the bottom of the garden and shouts the dog's name again and again, frantically. But it's a hateful process for her to be calling out, "*Mati! Mati! Mati! Death! Death! Death!*" as though summoning it to her. Within moments Vijay joins her. He's carrying his gardening machete and cuts away at the tangled jungle plants. He whistles for the dog, refusing to say the name. But Mutty is nowhere to be seen. They search the whole garden, including the patch behind the staff bungalow, where the saga tree grows, and there they spot a little tunnel through the undergrowth clearly made by animals. After ten hard minutes of cutting back, slashing away again and again, Vijay reveals a narrow pathway all the way to the wire fence that borders the road. There, in the fence, is a hole just big enough for a skinny puppy.

"Oh my God, Vijay, what have you done? Mrs Laura will blame *us*. She will fire us…" Mariel collapses onto her haunches and puts her head in her hands.

Vijay stands there looking at the dog's escape route, his face contorted with angst. "I never check fence. I think no way can get out – jungle too thick." The machete blade is dangling by his side, glinting in the sunlight.

"We mus' find dog before they get back home. Check all streets in area, ask all security guards. I go this way," she points left down the hill, "you check that way. I think we got one hour maximum."

*

With every step she takes along the hot tarmacked road the pain of anxiety intensifies in her chest. What will happen to them? Mrs Laura loves that puppy like her child. She will be heartbroken; the children will be heartbroken. Vijay should have made sure the garden was secure – he's ruined everything.

Carefully she scans the road – there's no pavement; it's bordered either by jungle growth or fences. Further down she can see a troop of monkeys tightrope-walking across the telephone wire that traverses the road. They take little notice of her.

If she and Vijay are fired, their visas will be invalid. Vijay will be sent back to India. She'll be sent back to the Philippines and the ten-year separation will be ruined. The lawyer had been very clear that she must not return to the Philippines at all, to prove that there had been a complete separation from her husband. The ten years is nearly finished. If she's sent back now, it'll all be wasted – not seeing her children for so long will have been for nothing. Even if she manages to persuade Mrs Laura to let her stay until she finds another job, the Immigration Department will never allow a visa transfer again so soon after the last one. On that terrible night Mr Peter was wrong to think that the police cared that'd she'd transferred her visa without returning to the Philippines, but the Immigration Department care about these things. Even they will only allow a certain number of 'visa transfer penalty payments'.

Tears start to stream down her face. Through the blur she sees something moving in the undergrowth just up ahead on the right. She runs forward, calling the dreadful name again, but on reaching the spot catches sight of the back of a monitor lizard as it waddles its way deeper into the jungle. If she and Vijay are not able to get married, they'll have to separate. He can't go back to the Philippines with her unless they're married, and they can't stay in Malaysia without work permits. The idea of living life without him is intolerable.

The hour ticks by and she passes four enormous residences, all hidden behind huge fences and gates, with security men idling in small guardhouses. She asks each one if they've seen the dog, but they all look at her with bemusement because there are always street dogs scavenging around in the area, all with the same copper-coloured fur and slight curl to their tail.

She knows she can't blame Vijay entirely – she should have done the ironing in the utility room and kept an eye on the cursed puppy or at least shut it in there while she was in her room. How could Vijay have ever known if the fence was secure all around the garden? In most places it's completely inaccessible – buried beneath thick, twisted vines and vegetation. She must say sorry; she's surely worsened his pain by blaming him. She looks at her watch – it's nearly four o'clock – and calls Vijay's handphone. He can't have found the dog, otherwise he would have messaged.

"Vijay, go back now. We will have to tell them she's gone."

As she walks back up the hill, swatting at the mosquitoes feasting on her arms and legs, she berates herself for ever believing that her plan could work. She feels once again in her heart of hearts that hers is not a life for happiness. Why did she ever convince herself that it could be? She hears a car drawing up behind her and turns to see Mr Peter driving, Mrs Laura in the passenger seat, the children in the back and the car slowing to a halt beside her.

"Mariel, hi! What are you doing out on the road? Do you want a lift back?"

Mariel looks at Mrs Laura through the open car window then down at her feet in her flipflops on the hot, steamy tarmac. "Oh, mam…" Her voice falters. "Very sorry, mam, Mutty run away."

"What…? What do you mean?"

"She find path through jungle and hole in fence, mam… onto road, mam." Mariel keeps her eyes cast down – she can't bear to look at the children.

"You mean there was a hole in the fence, and she found a way to get to it?"

"Yes, mam."

"But how can there have been a hole? Surely Vijay checked that the fence was secure?"

"Yes, mam, but difficult to see when jungle is thick."

"Oh God, oh no… my little puppy! Where's she gone? What will happen to her?"

Aggie starts crying and wails, "Mutty! I want Mutty!"

"Mummy, Daddy, quickly, we must find her." Mariel can see Tilly struggling to hold back her tears.

"Right then, Mariel," says Mr Peter firmly, "jump in and we'll drive round the whole neighbourhood and look for her. Where's Vijay?"

"He walk up hill looking for her, sir, but I think he gone home now."

"OK, can you SMS him and tell him to stay at home in case she comes back of her own accord?"

Mariel clambers up into the back seat of the car, sits between the two girls and types out a message to Vijay: *Stay home. I go boss car look for dog.* Then she takes each girl by the hand and gives a gentle squeeze.

"Is OK, she a clever dog, she be OK." But Mariel doesn't believe her own advice.

They drive slowly up and down every street of Bukit Tunku – the windows down, calling out the dog's name. Mrs Laura's voice is shrill and almost hysterical. The cloying heat invades the car and wraps around them, and Mariel's head clamours with the sound of *mati*, again and again, in four different voices – *death, death, death, death.* She feels increasingly desperate, almost claustrophobic with tension. What if they don't find the dog? Surely she and Vijay will be blamed.

After they've been searching for nearly an hour Mr Peter stops the car and turns round to look at them.

"I think we'd better go home now. It's getting late." At this sign of defeat Mrs Laura bursts into tears, which sets off the children again. "Now come on, all of you, be brave. Mutty's probably gone into another house, which is why she can't hear us calling. Knowing her, she'll have made friends with somebody who's giving her a delicious dinner right at this very moment."

"But what if they keep her and we never see her again?" Tilly's eyes are all red and puffy.

"She's got our name and Mummy's phone number on her collar, so I'm sure they'll call us."

"But why haven't they called already?"

"They probably haven't spotted it yet. Now come on, let's get you home. It's time for your tea."

Mrs Laura and the children look encouraged by Mr Peter's explanation, but Mariel wonders why he'd told this story. Nobody would take in a street dog except maybe *mat salleh*, and there aren't that many of them in this neighbourhood. But perhaps he doesn't know that. Maybe in England people are always taking in street dogs.

*

The evening drags on as the family apparently wait for someone to call. It's agonising. The four of them sit quietly together at the veranda table while Mariel brings the children their tea. Neither Mrs Laura nor

243

Mr Peter say anything angry either to her or to Vijay. In fact, they don't really say anything at all. When Mrs Laura takes the girls up for their bath Mr Peter goes off to have a shower, leaving Mariel and Vijay in a vacuum of silence.

Vijay hovers anxiously beside Mariel's shoulder while she's doing the washing-up. She sympathises, but it's irritating and his anxiety is infectious, that is, if it's possible for her to catch any more.

"Here now," she hands him the tea towel, "dry dishes."

He takes the large wooden salad bowl and slowly wipes the towel round and round it. "Why they say nothing? I don't understand. They know is my fault. My job is to keep garden and guard house. My job to find path in jungle and fix hole in fence."

She places her hand, wet with Fairy Liquid bubbles, onto his shoulder. "My fault too. I know you were busy on roof. I should have kept puppy near me when doing the ironing. I also don't understand Mrs Laura and Mr Peter. I think maybe they hope for real that someone find her and call them. Maybe they get angry when they know for sure she's gone."

Later, when Mr Peter and Mrs Laura put the children to bed Mariel can hear, through the bedroom door, Mr Peter reassuring Tilly and Aggie that the puppy's safe in someone else's house. After they've said goodnight to the children, Mrs Laura asks Mariel to come downstairs and talk to her in the living room. Mariel can see both fear and anger in her eyes.

"Mariel, why was Mutty even round the back of your bungalow exploring? When we're out it's your job to keep an eye on her. You should have shut her in the utility room if you were busy."

"I know, mam. Sorry, mam. I forget today." She remembers how her mind had been full of thoughts of presents for her family. "Jus' short time and then I notice she's gone."

"I'm so upset – Mutty means the world to me." Mariel can see her fighting back her tears.

"I sorry I make mistake, mam. Normally I so careful. I very sorry."

Mrs Laura turns to Mr Peter as he comes down the stairs and joins them in the living room. "What if we never find her? What if she's dead? I couldn't bear it." Tears start streaming down her face and she brushes at them angrily with the back of her hand. "Mariel, I'm not sure I'll ever be able to forgive you."

Looking taken aback, Mr Peter says, "Now, now, Laura, I'm sure there's a good chance we'll be able to find the dog."

*

Back in the kitchen, as she prepares the dinner, Mariel also swings between anger and fear. How can Mrs Laura be so angry with her when she herself made a mistake that led to Mariel being raped? 'I'm not sure I'll be able to forgive you', Mrs Laura had said. How many times has she apologised to Mariel for not doing as she was asked and driving to the police station straight away, and yet she expects to be forgiven? It takes every ounce of Mariel's self-control not to go out there and shout all of this at her boss, but her strength of character prevails – she will do everything she can to keep her job and protect her plan. *That damned puppy*, she thinks, *I knew it would bring ill fortune.*

Before dawn

The sound of the puppy's barking filters through Laura's consciousness, waking her with a start.

"Mutty. That's Mutty. She's come back," she whispers, more to herself than to Peter, who's in such a deep sleep he doesn't even stir as she leaps out of bed. The dog must have got back into the garden the same way she got out. Vijay had said he'd leave the hole in the fence just in case she tried to come back that way.

It's pitch dark except for the luminous glow of the little green numbers on the bedside clock announcing 5.07am. Gingerly Laura tiptoes out of the bedroom, always slightly fearful that the darkness might conceal a snake on the floor. Once on the landing she turns on all the lights and heads downstairs. In the kitchen she catches sight of a cockroach scuttling behind the fridge, but she doesn't even flinch. Her only thought is to open the back door in the utility room and let Mutty in. The door is locked, of course, and as her brain has become nothing but a sieve over these last few months, she can't remember where the key lives – Mariel normally unlocks it from the other side, on her way in from the staff bungalow.

Quietly she calls, "Mutty, Mutty, are you there? I'm coming, I've just got to find the key," and stops still to listen. Nothing, except the humming of the fridge – no barking, no snuffling. She looks around the room in a daze. And then she sees the little pot by the utility sink, between the pot with the washing-up brushes and the pot with the girls' paint brushes, where, she remembers, there lives a set of house keys.

Her sleepy fingers scrabble with the keys and finally she opens the door. But there's no sign of the puppy. Again, she calls her name quietly – so sure that she'd heard her barking. The garden looks ominous and foreboding – peering into the darkness her eyes spy monstrous shapes where she knows full well there are only trees and vegetation. The courage to go out and search eludes her. Perhaps Mutty's at the front of the house, where the cars are parked.

Laura heads back upstairs to the front door, which is bolted shut in two places. She knows this door – locks it herself at night before going to bed as she's always the last one up. Sliding the bolts back easily, she opens it and peers out. The cars and the parking area are well lit by the security light, but there's no dog. Again, she calls Mutty's name softly and checks around – even braves the edge of the pool of light, peering into the shadows at the base of the wall by the road. But no, nothing.

Disappointment engulfs her. She'd been convinced that Mutty had returned, had come home safe and sound from her little adventure, and that the agony of worry was over. Then, once again, anger briefly flickers through her grief. Why had Mariel been so careless? Why hadn't she shut the dog away if she'd been too busy to keep an eye on her? Why hadn't Laura shut the dog up herself before they'd gone out, knowing perfectly well that Mariel was busy? But more to the point, why hadn't Vijay ensured that the garden was dog-proof? That was clearly his responsibility as gardener and caretaker. Although, deep down, she knows that that would have been impossible without cutting down huge swathes of the garden.

Increasingly, Laura can't shift a fear that's been floating around her mind, that Mariel let the puppy out on purpose to get back at her and Peter for not going straight to the police station. Is she going insane to think such thoughts? Perhaps Mariel has finally told Vijay the truth. Perhaps they're both out for revenge. But Vijay hasn't seemed angry towards them. It's only Mariel whose servile manner is so clearly infused with rage. But would she really do something like this to retaliate? Mariel, who's so good and kind to the children – surely she wouldn't do anything to hurt them? Once more Laura's overwhelmed by the feeling that nothing works out for her in this land she finds so foreign, and again she senses herself sinking. Tears trickle down her face.

She bolts the door shut and creeps back to the bedroom, not caring that she's left all the lights on downstairs. She gets back into bed but sits up and leans against the pillows, pulls her knees up in front of her and rests her forehead on them. Now the tears really come, accompanied by slight shudders. What if the puppy is dead? She's still small enough to be eaten by a python. If she'd been hit by a car the driver would probably have left her, assuming she was a street dog. And she's still not very strong after all those transfusions for the parvovirus – she hasn't even finished her course of antibiotics. Laura thinks of the vet with his jowly cheeks and his obsequious smile.

"Yes, yes, madam, very good, very good. This puppy small small 'cos not enough nutrients. Has stunted growth. Can recommend this special food only available from veterinary surgery – will help puppy grow strong."

Laura knows perfectly well that the vet had charged her for every possible treatment he could, but what was she supposed to do? She knows nothing about animal health so she couldn't contradict him. And the whole family had fallen so in love with the little thing that she had to do everything she could to make her healthy. A loud, heartfelt sob accompanies this last thought.

Peter stirs. "Hmm… darling? Are you alright? What time is it?"

"It's about twenty past five. I heard barking. I was sure it was Mutty. I thought she'd come back…" Her words are muffled as she sobs into her knees. "Oh, Peter, how can she be lost? I was so happy to have her – I can't bear it. I was just beginning to get back on track and now I can feel myself slipping into the mire again." Another sob into her knees.

Peter sits up, wriggles next to her and wraps his arms around her, encasing the ball of sadness that her body has formed. "I know, darling." He pauses and then continues hesitantly, "Perhaps you should consider going back on anti-depressants. Just to stop it from overwhelming you. The children need you to be strong – we all do."

"I don't know, maybe you're right. But I can't think right now. All I want is to get Mutty back."

"Well, don't give up yet because I think there's still a chance we could find her. Last night, after you went to bed, I rang Jim to ask his advice about whether we should call the police." Laura turns her head sideways to look at him. "He said that dog-napping is common in KL. He suggested putting up posters offering a reward of five hundred ringgit to anyone who 'finds' her. He thinks that someone may have seen her on the road and taken her knowing that she belongs to wealthy Westerners and that now they're waiting for a reward to be offered. Apparently, this is a scam that happens all the time here."

"Oh God, that's awful. But I suppose I shouldn't be that surprised. They say kidnapping is also quite common here, which is why some of the super-rich Malaysian kids at school have bodyguards. Thank goodness Jim told you. He's right – we should print some 'lost puppy' posters." She wipes her tear-stained face with her hands and starts getting out of bed. "I'll find my camera – we can use that really sweet picture I took of her playing with her squeaky orange ball."

"Laura, wouldn't it be a good idea if we went back to sleep for another hour? We're going to need our strength today and I don't imagine you slept very well. And we both know that lack of sleep is one of the things that makes you feel wobbly."

"But I don't think I'll be able to get back to sleep. I just can't stop worrying about what might have happened to her."

"How about we get up and make the posters as soon as Aggie wakes us, which is bound to be within an hour?

251

She'll want to help in any case. Then I'll drive around and put them on every telegraph pole I can find in Bukit Tunku." He lies back on the pillows and pats her side of the bed invitingly, his eyes twinkling.

Laura knows it's a sensible suggestion, and both the bed and Peter do look appealing. But she has to fight the anxiety gremlin telling her that *something must be done now*. By the time she's crawled back into bed, Peter has already rolled over and drifted off. Trying not to be annoyed with him for falling back asleep so easily she wraps herself around his back, entwining her fingers into his sleeping hand, and breathes in his solid calmness.

*

As always, Mariel wakes on the dot of 6am and wonders whether she'll ever be able to sleep in. At least today is Sunday, no breakfast to prepare or floors to be mopped so she can lie in until it's time to get ready for church. It's a morning service this week. But then she remembers the puppy – gone, lost, run away whilst on their watch. If they don't find it today, she and Vijay will surely be fired and the life they have fought to build, the future they have dared to dream and made terrible sacrifices for, will no doubt shatter. She's never seen Mrs Laura angry the way she was yesterday.

Last night Mariel's dreams were filled with the sound of the dog's pitiful, nervous barking. Perhaps this will be a nightmare that will haunt her for the rest of time. She wonders if Tilly and Aggie are awake. She pictures them skipping down the stairs, like the fairies embroidered on their English nightgowns, to check if the puppy has returned, and she wishes she could save them from their disappointment and sadness. If only Mrs Laura had bothered to learn Malay, she would have known not to choose the name Mutty. The puppy's probably dead already, hit by a careless car or swallowed whole by a python.

Vijay is still sleeping but she can sense him beginning to stir. He too is incapable of sleeping late after years of having to be up by dawn, six days a week. His routine is already so entrenched that sometimes on a Sunday morning, Mariel wakes to find him sweeping the jacaranda leaves and papery pink bougainvillea flowers that are scattered around their little bungalow and checking around the main house for snakes.

This morning he's lying on his side, his strong, dark back to her – she curls her body and rests her cheek on the broad, flat space between his shoulder blades. She breathes in his solidness and wills him to stay sleeping a while longer because she knows that the moment he wakes he'll start fretting again. In all honesty, she can't bear his fussing – it only makes her more anxious, and she's trying to stay calm and make a plan. But that's proving difficult.

Perhaps Mrs Laura will calm down and be understanding and not fire them, but that seems unlikely after her reaction last night. The more she thinks about it the more she realises that her only option is to appeal to Mrs Laura's good heart. Even though she's a spoilt and foolish woman who doesn't seem to appreciate how blessed she is, she does appear to have a kind heart. Last night, in her distress, she'd seemed to have her priorities all confused, but Mariel knows that she feels terrible about what happened at the police station.

So, Mariel decides that she'll tell Mrs Laura all about her and Vijay's plan to live in the house that she's built in her village with its three rooms for sleeping, so plenty of space for her daughter and son-in-law, Rosa and Luis, and the baby too, plus her plans to expand the bakery to sell not only bread but cakes and cookies – the Western ones that she's learnt to bake since being a maid. Mrs Laura is always saying that Mariel's chocolate-chip cookies and brownies are the most delicious in the world. And she'll explain to her that all these wonderful plans will be ruined if she and Vijay are dismissed. Maybe Mrs Laura doesn't realise that they'll be deported if they're fired, and that Mariel won't then be able to get her divorce? Mariel will ask her to let them stay at least until August. Surely Mrs Laura will be kind enough to agree to that? Again, she thinks, she can't be certain. If there's one thing that nearly twenty years in service has taught her, it's that you can never entirely trust the boss.

A mosquito whines close to her face and suddenly exasperation overwhelms her. Why wasn't the puppy kept in a kennel or on a chain like a proper dog, not pampered like a spoilt child? She rolls away from Vijay and gets out of bed, her wide, strong feet enjoying the cool of the white tiled floor. She walks silently across the room and switches on the kettle. She knows its noise will be the final thing to pull Vijay from the last remnants of his dreams so, to apologise, she makes him a coffee. Tearing off the tops of the two Nescafe 3 in 1 sachets, she tries unsuccessfully to focus on what she will wear for church. If she and Vijay are fired for not watching the puppy, will that be God's punishment for her wavering faith, for living in sin and for planning to get a divorce? Vigorously she stirs the coffee powder into the hot water, making sure all of it dissolves. She hates the bitter taste of granules that haven't melted.

By now Vijay is fully awake and is talking to her, but she's trying not to listen because she knows he's talking about the dog, and she feels she might explode if her anxiety levels rise any higher. He's propped up in the bed with one knee up and the other tangled in the sheet. The rising sun is making dappled patterns across the bed as it peeks in through the thin curtain. She hands him the coffee and doesn't answer even though she knows he's asked her a question. Eventually his anguished expression penetrates her armour, and she tells him that she will pray for help in church and that, even though it's his day off, he must search the entire neighbourhood again, asking every guard at every property whether they've seen a skinny little street dog with a bright blue collar. She knows they will roll their eyes and laugh – only crazy *mat salleh* would be stupid enough to adopt one.

A reward

Breakfast on Sunday morning is a solemn affair. Laura makes pancakes to try and cheer them all up. Pancakes are one of her specialities and, although the girls eat them gratefully, they don't devour them with their usual delight.

"I want to give Mutty her breakfast. It doesn't *feel* right." Aggie looks so forlorn Laura struggles not to cry again. Tilly is pushing the last quarter of her pancake around her plate, anxiety etched across her face and seeping into her mannerisms.

"I know, sweetheart, the house feels horribly empty without her. But hopefully putting up these posters will help us find her." She walks to the kitchen doorway and, looking across the living room, sees Peter through the playroom door leaning over the printer. "Daddy should be finished making the posters soon and then he's going to put them up all over Bukit Tunku." As she finishes speaking Peter straightens up, collects the stack of papers from the printer tray and joins them in the kitchen.

"I've kept the wording simple in case some people don't speak good English."

Under an eye-catching yet endearing picture of Mutty sitting with a ball between her paws, looking not unlike Anubis the Egyptian god, are the words:

DOG LOST RM500 REWARD
CALL 012 210 4498

"Can I have that spare pancake? I'm just going to eat quickly and then go straight out and put them up." The girls gaze at their father with both adoration and trust as he wolfs down the pancake and then heads for the front door.

The sombre mood quickly returns, and the rest of breakfast drags on. They clear away the dishes and head upstairs to get dressed and clean their teeth, but the minutes continue to crawl by. Painfully aware that they need to do something to distract themselves, Laura suggests a swim, which the girls agree to but without much enthusiasm.

Tilly and Aggie have just jumped into the water and Laura is about to follow suit when Mariel comes out of the staff bungalow and walks towards the swimming pool. Laura immediately feels her neck tense and her shoulders stiffen. The idea that Mariel has done something underhand to exact her revenge is still haunting her.

Apart from the night at the police station when she was wearing a simple dress, Laura's rarely seen Mariel dressed in anything other than the T-shirt and long brushed-cotton shorts that she always wears for work. So, she's taken aback by how different she looks wearing a black pencil skirt and a red blouse – like a businesswoman on her way to the office. This complete transformation makes Laura wonder if there are, in fact, many different Mariels.

Mariel walks down the steps and approaches them, looking very serious. "Morning, mam. I jus' going to church but I send Vijay off to search neighbourhood again, mam."

The girls both swim up to the end of the pool, hold on to its edge and, looking at her lovingly, chorus, "Hi, Mariel."

Laura crouches down to steady Aggie, who's struggling to hold on. "Morning, Mariel," she says in a curt tone. "Peter's gone out again – we've made some 'lost puppy' posters offering a reward for her and he's gone to put them up."

"Is a good idea, mam. There lot of bad people in this city – somebody maybe take dog." She glances at the children and briefly an encouraging smile attempts to break through her grave expression. She retreats up the steps to the front gate and her waiting taxi. And again, Laura notices how different she seems – walking in court shoes – for, when she's at work, she's always either barefoot or wearing flipflops.

She knows it's unfair of her to be quite so cross with Mariel and Vijay, but she can't help it. Somehow, it's easier to deal with the sadness of losing the dog if she can blame them. Again, the demon in her head asks, did they let the puppy loose on purpose? Is Mariel *that* angry with her? Perhaps she should have kept Mariel and Vijay's passports – Arpana's been on and on at her that it's a necessary thing to do. What if Mariel's already finished her ten-year separation period? Laura doesn't know when the exact date is. If she has, she might suddenly leave without any warning, just like Arpana's maid left in the middle of the night.

Sitting on the edge of the pool, Laura slides herself into the water, sinking down until it covers her head, which she tilts back gently, letting her hair splay out behind her. The water is warm but soft and it soothes her anxiety. She opens her eyes and can see the girls' legs kicking under the water surrounded by myriad shafts of light, painting a constantly changing tortoiseshell pattern on the pool floor. Pushing off, she swims towards them, coming up for air just as she reaches them and making them laugh with surprise. An arm around each, she pulls them towards her and the three of them hold each other tight, bobbing in the water.

Tilly says, "I really hope we find her."

"Me too, sweetheart."

And Aggie concurs with a soggy little nod of her head.

The sudden sound of Peter's voice startles them. "What's all this hugging? You're meant to swim in swimming pools, not hug!"

"Daddy! Did you do it? Have you put them up?"

"Yup, all done. I don't think anyone living in Bukit Tunku will be able to miss them."

Leaving the girls to play, Laura pulls herself out of the side of the pool and squeezes out her long hair. Quietly, Peter says to her, "If she has been dog-napped, the perpetrator will be looking out for the reward posters."

"Let's keep our fingers crossed." She lies down on the towel-covered sun lounger and concentrates on taking slow, deep breaths – trying to get a grip on her nerves.

Peter dives into the pool and swims a couple of lengths before helping the girls onto the back of the crocodile lilo. Then he joins Laura and sits on the other lounger.

"God it's hot! I saw Vijay walking down the street searching for Mutty. He looked ready to pass out, so I told him to get in the car and come and help me with the posters. They both clearly feel terrible about what's happened."

"I know, but it *was* their responsibility to keep an eye on her. Although, I realise I did get a bit too cross with Mariel last night. But we do leave the children in her care, so we need to be able to rely on her." Laura pulls at the towel under her legs, straightening it out. "Maybe we were crazy to think that a street dog would actually want to be domesticated?"

"I don't know, I think all puppies are adventurous and want to explore. She certainly seemed very happy to be domesticated – I've never known such an affectionate dog." Laura looks up at him and again struggles not to cry. Clearly hoping to distract her he adds, "Anyway, I was thinking, why don't we go to the Shangri-La for their fancy buffet Sunday lunch? It might cheer us all up."

"But what if someone calls?" She fiddles nervously with the ring on her little finger.

"We'll come straight back – we can't just sit here all day anxiously waiting." But just as he says this, Laura's phone rings, making them both jump.

"Hello?"

"Hello, I find dog."

"Where? Where are you?" Her heart is pounding with a mixture of elation and anger – she knows she's talking to the dog-napper.

"Outside house."

"Outside my house? Are you outside my house now?"

"Yes, madam."

"Please wait there, I'm coming." She hangs up the phone. "Quick, girls, get out of the pool. There's a man at the front gate and he's got Mutty."

Tilly and Aggie scramble out of the pool squealing with joy and run through the house and up to the front door leaving puddles of water and a stream of excitement in their wake. Peter and Laura follow, Laura trying to control her wobbling legs.

Laura pushes the button and the front gate swings open agonisingly slowly, revealing a youngish man dressed in the uniform of a security guard holding Mutty on a piece of string. As the family walk together towards the gate, Mutty yelps and whines and pulls in their direction, but the man holds her firm. The children hide behind their parents, sheltering in Laura's shadow and holding hands tightly, clearly nervous of this slightly threatening man who's taken their dog.

He looks at Laura and Peter with a blank expression. "I find dog on street. You pay reward?"

Suddenly Vijay appears behind them, at the top of the steps that lead down to the staff bungalow. He shouts at the man in broken Malay, startling Laura so much she grabs Peter's arm to steady herself. The security guard looks embarrassed and drags Mutty closer to him still.

Peter turns to Vijay and asks in a suspicious tone, "Do you know this man, Vijay?"

"Yes, sir, this man security guard from condo up hill. He know me 'cos I walk there with puppy. I think he take her to get money."

"Yes, we'd guessed something like that had happened. I've a good mind not to give him the reward."

"Oh, Peter," Laura whispers, relief flooding through her, "let's just pay him the money and get her back. Go into the house and get the five hundred ringgit, *please*?"

"You're right, let's get this over with."

Peter strides back into the house and Laura says to Vijay, "Vijay, I think we should pay him the money now. I don't want any trouble. I just want my dog back." Vijay says nothing but continues to stare furiously at the man, his lip almost curled back in a snarl, and Laura feels terrible for thinking he could ever have been in cahoots with him.

Peter reappears with the five hundred ringgit rolled up in his hand. Laura snatches the notes from him and marches up to the security guard. "How dare you take my dog? Here's your bloody money!" She thrusts it at him, her hand shaking, then grabs the string lead and with a fierce tug pulls Mutty out of his grasp. "Don't you dare come near my dog or my family ever again!"

He looks genuinely alarmed by her anger and recoils, holding the ringgit notes close to his chest. Then, with a sudden bow of his head, he puts the money in his pocket and walks away. Vijay shouts after him and, even without an understanding of Malay, it's obvious he's not being polite.

*

Later that afternoon, having had a very happy and celebratory lunch at home, with Mutty enjoying hugs, kisses, treats and titbits (in fact, Aggie had fed her a significant proportion of her spaghetti Bolognese under the table), Laura and Peter are relaxing on the veranda, lying on the two teak and rattan sun loungers that they'd bought before Christmas from the elegant furniture shop in Bangsar Shopping Centre. They're watching the children and Mutty play tug of war with the dog towel when Mariel appears. She knocks awkwardly on the doorframe of one of the open French windows. This seems strange to Laura because normally she wanders freely about the house, only knocking on the bedroom door or saying, "Excuse me, mam," if she needs to disturb her at her desk or on the veranda. But of course, it's a Sunday and the rules are different on a Sunday because Mariel's not working. Laura realises that in the ten months she's been with them Mariel's never come into the house on a Sunday.

"Ah, Mariel, come in. As you can see, thankfully Mutty is back. Did Vijay tell you what happened?"

Mariel is still wearing the smart outfit they saw her in that morning. She looks relieved and delighted, and Laura knows immediately that it was indeed insane of her to ever have thought Mariel had endangered the puppy on purpose. Why does she let anxiety push her around until she's catastrophising? Yes, Mariel is angry with her, and rightly so, but she wouldn't do something like that, something that would so clearly hurt Tilly and Aggie. It's this place, Laura concludes – she lets it play games with her mind, making her nervous and suspicious, until she assumes that things are darker than they are.

"Yes, mam. I so pleased puppy home, mam. Is very good. But I so angry with that security guard." Her face clouds over.

"Yes, can you believe it? From the condo just up the hill. He must have seen her get out onto the road and thought 'that's an easy bit of money'. Thank goodness Peter's colleague told us to offer a reward otherwise I don't know what would have happened."

She looks at Peter, who nods in agreement. "The man called Laura less than an hour after I'd put up the posters – he must literally have been watching and waiting. I've a good mind to make a complaint to the management company of that condo, but it's probably not a clever idea to make an enemy of a security guard who's been monitoring our house for the last few weeks."

"Yes, sir, lot of thieves in this city – always best to be careful." Despite Laura's earlier invitation to come in, Mariel's still hovering on the threshold, shifting her weight occasionally from one leg to the other. "I think security guard was walking puppy at night-time along road. I heard her barking, but I thought was jus' in my dream. But now I know was real."

"Of course! That makes sense, I heard her barking too. I got up and went to let her in, and when she wasn't there, I also thought I must have dreamt it. Poor little thing was obviously trying to attract our attention."

"Yes, mam, she a clever dog. She know she want to live in good and comfortable home and she know you love her. I think maybe she won't run away again – she a clever dog."

"I hope you're right." Laura turns to look at Mutty, who, now playing ball with the girls, is indecisively eyeing Tilly, who repeatedly tells her, "Drop it!" Head down, bottom raised, tail wagging, it's the sparkle in the dog's eye which gives away the sweet agony of choosing whether to keep the ball and be the winner or let it go for the pleasure of another chase. Laura continues, "But I still think we should be careful and not leave her unattended in the garden. We can always just shut her in the utility room – she's happy in there."

"Yes, and Vijay better fix that hole in the fence," adds Peter. "Could you ask him to do it tomorrow?"

Mariel replies, almost passionately, "He already fix, sir. He do it straight after the puppy come home when I still at church. He make sure she not run away again, sir."

It's so obvious that she's keen to make amends that once again Laura feels guilty for mistrusting her and getting quite so angry. So, with a friendly smile, she replies, "That's good of him to do it on his day off, please say thank you to him from us. And thanks for coming over – you must go and enjoy the rest of your day off now. We'll see you in the morning."

Mariel, clearly realising that the conversation is over, seemingly places her shy, deferential facemask back in position. "Yes, mam. See you tomorrow, mam, sir." And she walks away towards the kitchen and the back door leading to the staff bungalow.

Laura leans back and stretches her legs out on the sun lounger, and as he refills both their wine glasses from the bottle on the table, Peter says, "I've never seen anyone look so relieved in my life – I think she thought they were going to get the sack."

"Well, I was furious with them, but I don't think I would have gone that far. I guess Mariel was terrified of being sacked, particularly if it meant she had to return to the Philippines before the ten years are up. I'm not quite sure when that is exactly. But of course, we wouldn't do that to her, not after everything she's been through." She takes a sip of her wine. "But I am worried that she's showing signs of not being as reliable as we'd believed – maybe she's just distracted by the thought of seeing her family after such a long time."

"Who can blame her? Can you imagine how weird it's going to be? They must be terribly hurt by what's she done. It is ironic when you think what a great job she does looking after Tilly and Aggie."

"I know – I think she has no idea what a difference it's made to our lives having her and Vijay working for us. I don't think I could bear it here without her help. Thank God I've managed to book our holiday in Langkawi for the same two weeks that she's going to the Philippines. It's going to be chaos here without her, even with Vijay still around. The cockroaches will march straight back in the moment she goes."

Laughing, Peter replies, "Well, you'll have to call up your young reserves again. Perhaps you should get them back into training before she leaves."

Laura gazes across the garden thoughtfully. "I've been thinking about what you said this morning. You're right, I really need to do more to arm myself against getting depressed. I was so distraught when I thought we'd lost Mutty, the blackness just came rushing at me straight away. I know I've got to find something to do that gives me a sense of purpose – it's just not that easy in this bloody place."

*

The phone alarm plays its pretty tune and startles Mariel out of a deep sleep. She sits up abruptly and looks around her, trying to get her bearings. It's Monday morning, she must get up for work and for the first time in years she hasn't woken before her alarm. She leans back against her pillows in amazement and can't believe how well she's slept. The puppy is home safely, she and Vijay haven't been fired, and Mrs Laura seems happy again. A wave of excitement washes over her, and she has neither the power nor the inclination to halt it. Soon she'll be going home for the first time in ten years. She'll have a month's holiday in her village getting to know her children and her little granddaughter, and then, on her way back to KL, she'll go to Manila to meet with a lawyer and start divorce proceedings.

"Vijay, wake up. It's time for work." Mariel gently caresses his shoulder.

Vijay rolls over, stretches and smiles at her sleepily. "Puppy home, everything OK."

"I know, I feel so happy. Can't believe it." When he reaches over to pull her towards him, she says, laughing, "No, no! Is 6.15, mus' get up. Children got school today – mus' get breakfast for them." And then she wishes that they had woken earlier because, for the first time since the rape, she actually feels like she could bear to be intimate.

She jumps out of bed and into the bathroom, and within moments she's dressed and heading out of the little bungalow towards the main house. There's been a heavy rainstorm and the garden smells damp and slightly

267

mouldy, and there's a chorus of raindrops dripping from the leaves. The utility-room lights are on, and this morning both Aggie and Tilly are sleeping under the counter with the puppy. Looking at them, Mariel feels another surge of contentment. She knows that, despite her best efforts, she's failed to stop herself from growing to love these little girls, even when their mother is being unreasonable and sending her into a nervous tailspin.

*

When Mr Peter has left for work and Mrs Laura and the children have left for school, Mariel and Vijay settle down at the table in the utility room to eat their breakfast.

"I so angry with security guard. He jus' greedy for money. He nearly ruin our life." Vijay looks up from his food, which he's eating with his right hand, using the tips of his fingers, fiercely squishing the rice and curry into bite-sized balls. "I go up there today and I fight him!"

"No, Vijay! Mus' not. Don't want trouble." Mariel's eating her rice and curry with a spoon and fork, which she sets down with a clatter. "That security guard is Malay, is *Bumiputra*. If you have fight with him, *polis* will always take side of *Bumi*. Cannot have trouble with *polis* – they will use it as excuse to send you back to India." The look of fury on Vijay's face intensifies as he digests the truth of Mariel's words. She adores him for his loyalty and protectiveness, but she fears his rash reactions and lack of wisdom. She must think of a way to get back at the security guard without any dangerous repercussions. "Everything good now. Puppy back. Not long till I go home and start divorce. Don't want any more problem." She looks at him beseechingly and he utters something between a growl and a murmur. Mariel continues, "Mrs Laura say she go out today. When she out, I go with you to condo. I have idea." As the perfect solution dawns on her she gives him a conspiratorial grin. "Instead of fight with security guard, we trick him. We pretend Mr Peter very important *mat salleh*, tell him he know government minister, tell him Mr Peter very angry. Then security guard frightened. That will be good revenge for us – better than punch and fight."

Vijay looks at her with unadulterated adulation. "You clever, Mariel. You are my woman!"

*

The heat of the day is at its most intense as they walk together slowly up the hill towards the condo at the end of the street. Mariel has checked twice that the puppy is securely shut in the utility room. The condo is a large, ungainly building, painted salmon pink and designed supposedly in the style of an Italian villa with the odd Corinthian column placed randomly about and on either side of its overly elaborate entrance. But Mariel and Vijay go no further than the grand metal gates decorated with brightly painted gold leaves and swirling patterns. Two pots of the ubiquitous pink bougainvillea stand in front of the small square guardhouse.

As they approach, the security guard comes out and walks towards them. He looks defensively belligerent and barks at them in Malay, "Why've you come back? Your boss offered a reward. I found the dog and returned it."

Vijay retorts in his poor Malay, "You not find dog, you take."

Mariel squeezes his hand gently and continues, her Malay more fluent, "It's OK, we just come to warn you that our boss think you take the dog. He's very angry." The security guard snorts as though he couldn't care less. "Mr Peter is important British man, he does work with Malaysian government, I think with Minister of Trade, import/export." As she watches the colour drain from the man's face, she smiles inwardly, realising that she hasn't actually got a clue what the nature of Mr Peter's business is but she's 100% certain that he doesn't work with the Malaysian government or have any contacts there. The driver, Prakash, would have told them if their mutual boss was that important.

At that moment a large Honda SUV approaches the gates, and the security guard stands to attention, greeting the Chinese lady driving the car with a sycophantic smile, while his colleague, still in the guardhouse, opens the gates. The car drives into the compound and he turns his attention again towards Mariel and Vijay.

"What do you mean he works with Minister of Trade? I thought he was small time *mat salleh*. Why does he live in that old house if he's big shot?"

Fearing she's been caught out, Mariel's stomach muscles clench. "Err… it's for Mr Peter's wife – she, err… likes to study jungle, the plants and the birds, so she needs that big garden." He looks at her suspiciously and she forces herself to laugh. "You know these *mat salleh*, they're a bit crazy, always like to study jungle!" She can see Vijay looking confused by the direction that the conversation is taking so she turns it back to Mr Peter's anger. "Last night we heard boss. He was very very angry. He was talking with his wife, and he said he was going to make phone calls. We just want to warn you. Maybe good idea for you to look for new job quickly, before any trouble starts."

The security guard scoffs again and kicks aggressively at some free stones on the tarmac, but Mariel can sense he's thinking about her words and that his discomfort is increasing. She turns on her heels, indicating to Vijay to follow, and as they start to walk down the hill, she calls back over her shoulder, "Just wanted to warn you. Have a good afternoon."

And Vijay reiterates, copying her phrase, "Yes, just wanted to warn you."

They walk away slowly. The heat is practically sitting on their heads and they're both dripping with sweat. As they reach the frangipani trees and the large white wall, Vijay points the remote control at the gates and Mariel steals a glance back up the hill. She can still just see the guardhouse but there's no sign of the man.

"What you think?" she says.

"I laugh laugh laugh all day," he replies with a chortle.

Once back in the house they settle themselves on the veranda's sun loungers with a couple of cans of 100Plus. They like to sit out there when they've got the house to themselves, and they know that the family won't come back unexpectedly. And they need the energy drink to revive and restore them after such a hot and heated exchange. They sit quietly, too depleted for conversation, and gaze out at the garden below. As always, Mariel looks out for the golden oriole and eventually spies it shading itself amongst the leaves of the rambutan tree. Gazing at it, she fancies that it nods at her, wishing her well for her trip to the Philippines and congratulating her for tricking that wicked security guard into thinking that he's going to lose his job.

A big decision

Laura leans back in her chair and looks at her friend Evi, a slightly self-conscious smile on her face.

"I know I've said time and time again that it's not for me, but I've decided that I would like to help out at your Burmese refugee school."

"Wow, that's great news! I wasn't expecting you to say that. What made you change your mind?"

They're having lunch at Alexis, Laura's favourite restaurant in KL. She loves that you can order either authentic Vietnamese beef pho or a delicious homemade burger with perfect French fries. And the New York warehouse-style interior reminds her of the Nicole Farhi store on Westbourne Grove, one of her old favourite haunts.

"To be honest, it was what happened to Mariel – I feel so responsible and guilty. I can't just go on sitting around living the life of a spoiled princess. I have to do something. And Mariel's so angry with me. I know I can never make it up to her, but I feel like I need to do something to atone for what happened. Also, I think I need to prove to myself that I have it in me to do something worthwhile. So, even though I've no teaching experience, I'm hoping that I can be useful at your school in some way. You can always just give me admin jobs."

"If you could come in and effectively do conversation classes with the kids, that would be fantastic. There are a couple of proper teachers from the refugee community who speak excellent English, but their time is already stretched. If the kids could talk with a native English speaker that would be such a help. As I think I said before, you can always just sing songs, read stories and play games with them, and maybe oversee them studying their workbooks." A huge smile lights up Evi's face. "Wow, Laura, I'm so pleased. This is really good news and I think it'll be good for you too."

"I hope so. Mariel getting raped has really put things into perspective for me. Here I am worrying about losing my self-worth because I haven't got a job and yet she's being told she has to have sex with a policeman if she wants to get her identity papers back. When Peter suggested to his boss that we should make a complaint, he said he thought that would get her in even more trouble. So basically, she's got no legal protection in this country at all."

"I know, I know, it's insane."

"Talking of the law, have I told you about Mariel's plan to get divorced? She's discovered some loophole which means that because she's been out of the country for ten years, she can get a divorce."

"Really? That seems unlikely. Are you sure?"

"Yes, totally. She consulted a lawyer here in KL and in August she's going home to file the papers." Taking another bite of her burger she's doesn't notice Evi's sceptical frown. "It's incredible how strong and resilient she is. If I was raped, I would have a complete collapse and yet she seems resolved not to let it break her. She won't talk about it. When I ask her if she's OK, her expression becomes fierce, and she says she just wants to look forward to getting her divorce and marrying Vijay. It's like she's a different woman. I mean, she used to be so reticent, always looking at her feet. Now the determination in her is palpable, not to mention her anger. I was so convinced she'd ruined the dinner party on purpose, but afterwards she was genuinely apologetic – she'd just misunderstood my instructions. But, as she explained herself, she was strong and resolute, not nervous and uncertain like she used to be. So, anyway, that's why I've changed my mind – I want to do something good, something worthwhile."

"Well, you'll certainly be doing something worthwhile if you help out at the school. We'd need you to commit to one or two days a week. So, I'd recommend you come for a couple of trial days to check it out and make sure you're definitely up for it." Evi leans over and steals a few of Laura's French fries. "It'd be great for them to have an English English speaker. My English is fairly fluent, but I'm Dutch – there's no point in me teaching them Dutch nursery rhymes! We do have an American volunteer helper called Betsy, but she can only do one morning a week."

Hearing all this suddenly makes the whole thing seem terribly real and Laura starts to panic that she's made a mistake. "What if I turn out to be hopeless at it and fail to teach them anything? I mean, it's only since we moved here that I've started helping my own children with their homework."

"To be honest, the more opportunity they get to hear English being spoken the better. And it's helpful for them to get to know another Western person because if they manage to get resettled it's likely to be in the West. Don't forget, you're a capable woman with thinking skills and management skills. It's just a question of adapting them."

The waiter appears and clears away their plates. "Ladies, would you like dessert?"

Smiling conspiratorially at Laura, Evi turns to him and says, "We'll have one of your warm chocolate brownies with vanilla ice-cream and two spoons, please."

They also order coffee and then, feeling distinctly embarrassed by her lack of knowledge, Laura asks, "So, tell me more about your school. Why are they refugees? I'm afraid I don't know much about Myanmar beyond the fact that it's run by a military junta who keep Aung San Suu Kyi under house arrest. She's campaigning for democracy, right?"

"Yes, that's right. The children that come to my school are from the Chin State. The Chin people are one of the ethnic minority groups in Myanmar that are persecuted by the military government – mainly for being Christian. In fact, the junta aren't that keen on any of the ethnic minorities. But the Chin are a devout and strong community. They've set up various well-organised refugee groups in KL which help people find housing and work (even though it's illegal) and provide schooling for both kids and adults. They also run a great charity business selling traditional handicrafts like bags, bedcovers, bookmarks, etc. It's beautiful stuff – I'll show you some. Perfect presents for family back home."

"Oh, right, that sounds good. I'd like to see them. But tell me more, how are they persecuted by the Burmese authorities?"

"Well, for starters, they're made to convert to Buddhism. But also, the government forces them to do terrible jobs like human mine-sweeping – they make them walk through the mine fields to detonate them. And many of the women are forced to become military nurses – and then they're routinely raped by the soldiers. It's grim."

Their pudding arrives and Laura stares blankly at it, trying to absorb the horror of what Evi has just told her. Does she have it in her to work with children who've had to flee such cruelty?

"I know it's hard to hear this kind of thing. But the refugee organisation is really worthwhile and deserves support." Evi hands Laura one of the spoons and looks at her encouragingly. "Recently, I've started talking to some of the kids, the ones that want to tell their stories. Not so much *why* they had to escape but *how* they escaped. One of the Chin teachers has been helping me translate when the kids struggle with their English. In fact, I've just typed up the transcript of my first interview, with a lovely boy called Kung Bik, and I've got it with me. Would you like to read it?"

"What, now? Do you have time?" The sweet

deliciousness of the brownie and ice-cream has settled Laura's nerves.

"Sure, why not? It's not very long and I'll be happy drinking my coffee while you read it." Evi rummages in her bag, pulls out an A4 document in a clear plastic folder and hands it to Laura. "It's quite a story."

Transcript of interview with Kung Bik
Date of interview: 10th May 2007
Date of escape: c. 2006

Kung Bik is fourteen. He has been in Malaysia for one year. He came here with his brother and his mother. His father was already in Malaysia – the rest of the family were travelling to join him.

In Myanmar, Kung Bik lived in a small village in the Chin State. He went to a good school. He was in the eighth grade and his brother was in the sixth grade. They were happy at school and both had a lot of friends. Their father had been in Malaysia for five years. Kung Bik could hardly remember him. Life had been difficult for his mother with her husband in Malaysia, having to bring up her two boys on her own. And they had had to wait five years to save up enough money to travel because the agents who arrange these journeys charge such high fees.

One day Kung Bik's father rang his mother and said that the time had come for them to leave. So, they had a family meeting and his mother packed up a change of clothes for each of the boys. Otherwise, Kung Bik took nothing with him.

Using different names, the three of them booked bus

tickets to Yangon via Mandalay. At the time of travel Kung Bik was thirteen and his brother was eleven.

The journey

Kung Bik told some of his friends where he was going but he told them they must keep it secret. He was very sad to say goodbye to his friends and the rest of his family, especially his grandfather. The bus journey to Yangon was long and boring, but he wasn't scared. His mother was with him – she's a strong woman and she gave him confidence.

When they arrived in Yangon they went straight to the house of the agent who was a good man and who was kind to them. They spent two nights there. Kung Bik was amazed by the large and busy city – everything was so different. He particularly liked the cars, the roads and the big buildings.

At the agent's house they all slept together on the floor. After two days they started the next part of their journey. The agent arranged bus tickets for them to Mawlamyine, the capital of the Mon State. It was not that long a journey and Kung Bik slept on the bus. They arrived at night and had to wait for a while. By now there were about fifteen refugees in their group. They were told they had to travel into the jungle by motorbike, two at a time. The first people to go were a woman from the group and Kung Bik's mother. Kung Bik and his brother were left behind with the other adults. They were very frightened watching their mother drive off into the night towards the unknown jungle. Then it was Kung Bik and his brother's turn – they were able to travel together on one bike, which was some comfort. They had to follow a man in front of them and the journey took more than four hours.

Kung Bik found the bike journey very gruelling. He wasn't very practised at driving a motorbike and he felt very responsible for his little brother. The journey was along dirk tracks and the boys found it very difficult, having to cling on for such a long time. When they arrived their limbs were rigid, they were aching all over, and they were very hungry and thirsty.

It took the entire night to ferry the whole group of refugees into the jungle. Then they had to wait for a while before starting the next part of the journey. There was a tent for them to shelter under – a big one with just a roof and no sides, but there was enough room to lie down and rest. They were given food. Kung Bik was so hungry that the food tasted delicious even though he thinks it probably wasn't.

Then a large truck arrived and took all fifteen of them to another part of the jungle. They had to hide in the truck. They were able to sit but they were covered by a huge piece of plastic. Kung Bik was very frightened. He knew that if they were stopped by the police they would be in serious trouble. They travelled for one night. They didn't stop at all. [Having been pretty composed up until this part of his story, KB became quite emotional as he described this truck journey – his voice faltered as he spoke.]

It was not until they arrived that they were able to go to the toilet and have something to eat and drink. The agent provided the food and drink.

For the next part of the journey they had to walk through the jungle. They didn't have tents but they did have plastic sheets which they lay on when they were sleeping. When it rained they put the plastic sheets over their heads and tied them on.

The agent provided about seven porters who showed them the way and carried food for them. They had to walk through terrible thorns which cut their legs and feet. Kung Bik didn't have proper shoes, just flipflops which broke on the first day, so he had to walk in bare feet. It was terribly painful. They walked for a whole week. [Again, here KB struggled to speak of this. He was silent for quite some time before he continued.]

Luckily, they didn't see any snakes but it was very difficult to sleep at night because of all the jungle noises, the pain of their aching limbs and scratched feet. Often Kung Bik was just too frightened to sleep.

Kung Bik admires his mother. He thinks she was very strong and brave to walk through the jungle for a week with her two young boys. The boys were also strong – they walked the whole way without any help, but it was the worst part of the journey. Everything hurt – their feet, their legs, their groins.

Finally, they reached a place where they stopped. Three jeep cars arrived, driven by Malaysian people. In the jeeps the refugees had to hide in boxes. Kung Bik was in a box with two other men – he thinks there were about three people to each jeep. He knew these men – they were good to him, but he was still frightened and didn't like being separated from his mother and his brother. In the box it was terribly difficult to breathe – there were only a few air holes. It was effectively the shape of a wide coffin – they could only lie down, there was no room to lift their heads; it was very claustrophobic. They travelled through the night, arriving in KL in the morning. He was so relieved when they arrived.

Although his mother and brother travelled in a different jeep, also hiding in a box, they all arrived in KL at the same time. They were taken to the agent's house.

When Kung Bik first saw KL, he thought it was wonderful.

The agent contacted Kung Bik's father to tell him they had arrived. When he first saw his father he was overwhelmed. He was so happy he wanted to cry, but he also felt sad and relieved and excited – lots of confusing emotions.

Luckily his father had an apartment and a job as a waiter in a restaurant, so Kung Bik and his mother and brother were able to go home with him straight away – a happy ending. Although they have somewhere to live and some money coming in, the family are not officially allowed to be in Malaysia – the father is working illegally, and the boys can't go to a real school. But they like going to the refugee school. They have good friends there.

Laura puts the document down and takes a sip of her cappuccino. It's gone cold.

She's completely astounded by the awfulness of Kung Bik's story and the boy's strength of character. She had, of course, known that the term refugee meant that these children and their families had had to leave

Myanmar. But she hadn't really thought it through and not for one moment had she imagined that the Burmese authorities would use people as human mine-sweepers just because they were from an ethnic minority, and she certainly hadn't thought to visualise their escape journeys.

She remembers how much Tilly and Aggie had whined when they'd gone for a weekend walk at Bukit Gasing: "Mummy, it's too hot! My legs are hurting." "Mummy, the mozzies are biting me everywhere." She'd been sympathetic because it had been extremely hot, even at nine in the morning, and there were hundreds of insects. How they all would have coped walking for a week with bare feet is inconceivable.

"It's shocking, isn't it?" Evi's words startle Laura – she'd almost forgotten she was still there.

"It's just terrible. Makes me ashamed of my privileged life."

"I know what you mean. And Kung Bik's isn't even the most disturbing of the interviews I've done. The mother of one of the little girls was drowned when the boat she was in capsized. She was hiding in a crate and couldn't get out – just horrific." Evi shifts in her chair and re-crosses her legs to the other side. "I should warn you that when the children first arrive at the school they're often in severe shock. Their lives have been turned upside down and they've had to endure these terrible journeys. But normally after a month or so they start to settle in. I think it helps that they've generally all had similar experiences. As I said, the Chin community here is very strong and supportive."

"I really understand now why you want to help them so much. I'm going to do my best to be as useful as I can, but I'm still concerned that I won't be much help."

June 2007

Batik painting

The smell of the hot wax tickles at the back of Mariel's throat. It's not an unpleasant sensation, just very distinctive, and one that she's only ever had here in this traditional Malay hut where she's spent many pleasant afternoons, over the years, batik painting with the children in her care. Mrs Laura has left her to mind Tilly and Aggie at the Kompleks Kraf in downtown KL. And of course, because it's one of the nicest activities for young children to do, they have come to the little Malay house at the back of the complex, where two patient and kind ladies, Nur and Farah, have been teaching the art of batik painting since before Mariel came to Malaysia. On Saturdays Mariel often accompanies Tilly and Aggie on outings. They've been a couple of times to the aquarium and to the pottery-painting place in Megamall, but for all of them their favourite is batik painting.

Mariel thinks it's a brilliant activity for children because it's effectively colouring-in. They stencil a copy of the picture they want to paint onto a piece of silk or cotton, and then either Nur or Farah goes over the outline of the drawing in wax using an instrument that looks like a Chinese pipe. Then, all the child must do is to dip a brush into the watercolour paint and touch it gently to the silk – the paint will spread out like a wave reaching as far as it can across the sand. The wax lines act as a row of sand dunes, stopping the wave in its tracks. So, even a child as young as four can produce a beautiful painting on silk without smudging over the lines. Once she's moved back home to the Philippines, Mariel thinks, she will find a batik artist in the village who might be willing to give lessons to little Gloria and of course any other grandchildren she might have by then. She smiles at the thought that she'll be wealthy enough to afford such luxuries for her family.

Aggie, wearing an apron that's far too big for her, has chosen a childish picture of a butterfly and Mariel helps her trace it onto the silk. Tilly's choice is an elaborately decorated Indian elephant. As they start to paint, Mariel contentedly watches the two girls concentrating hard on their work. Aggie, her little tongue poking out slightly, is focusing on mirroring the colours of the butterfly – for they'd learnt all about this at school in their project on 'mini beasts' – and Tilly is painting her elephant's blanket, bells and tassels in as many bright colours as possible. Mariel particularly enjoys seeing, every once in a while, each child stop and admire with great pride how well they're creating their art. She's pleased with herself for suggesting this visit to the Kompleks Kraf to Mrs Laura, who'd wanted a Saturday-afternoon activity for the children to keep them occupied while she went to Kinokuniya in KLCC, the bookshop in the mall below the Twin Towers.

For the last few days Mrs Laura has been in a great state of agitation because on Monday she's starting some voluntary work teaching at a school for refugee children from Myanmar. Indeed, her apprehension has been getting on Mariel's nerves. Why has she been working herself up into such a fret? They're just children, like all other children, and all she must do is teach them some English words. Surely she can do that. After all, she has a university degree. But no, she's done nothing but worry about the fact that she's never taught before and now she's gone off to buy books on how to teach English as a foreign language.

On the way to the Kompleks Kraf they'd driven over the bridge with the view of Masjid Jamek and Mrs Laura had stopped the car and they'd got out briefly to admire the mosque's delicate white domes. She'd explained to the kids that the mosque had been built at the point where the River Klang meets the River Gombak and that's why the city was called Kuala Lumpur, which means 'meeting of muddy rivers'.

Tilly had said, giggling, "They should have called it 'meeting of smelly rivers'." And they'd all laughed.

Now Mariel thinks of the muddy river running through her village back home which is always smelly but gets even worse when the rains come and churn up all the stinking rot resting on the riverbed. It's now only a few weeks until she goes back for her visit, and as the day approaches, she's getting more and more apprehensive.

At least Rosa has stopped going on about there not being enough work for them all at the bakery. But generally, Mariel's not getting a great sense of welcome from her children, except perhaps from Vito, who's very excited about the flat-screen TV she's bringing. Maybe, like her, they're all just nervous. It will certainly be strange trying to build a relationship after such a long time apart. She knows they're hurt that she chose Vijay over them. They obviously think that if she was prepared to sacrifice seeing them for so many years in order to marry him, she loves him more. But of course, it isn't as simple as that. Working abroad meant that she was never going to be able to spend more than a few weeks a year with her children so they would never have had much of a relationship. Her friend Faye has been home every year for a month's holiday for the last twenty years, and she still complains that she's not close to her children. But she does say that, even now they're grown up, it's still agony to leave at the end of the visit. Mariel can well remember how difficult these farewells were from the time before she stopped going back. Mila in particular used to beg and beg her to take her with her to KL. At least these years of separation have meant all that heartbreak has been avoided and they've learnt to be without each other.

As if reading her mind Aggie looks up from her batik painting and says, "Mariel, is Vijay going wiv you for your holiday to your home?"

Despite its lack of air-con, the little wooden hut is cool, its square latticed windows all open and shaded by the wide overhanging roof, and in amongst the many batik paintings on the walls there are also two electric fans.

But, with Aggie's question, Mariel feels a hot flush spread across her face.

"Not this visit," she replies. "He need stay and look after the house and Mutty, especially as I think maybe you and Tilly and Mummy and Daddy will also go on holiday."

"So, we're all going on holiday at the same time?" Aggie seems particularly delighted by this idea.

"Yes, I think so."

Tilly, painting her elephant's headdress a brilliant red, says, "But don't you want to introduce Vijay to your family?" And Mariel's face burns hotter.

Of course, that is the thing she's most nervous about, particularly the thought of introducing him to her mother. Her kids, she hopes, will eventually get used to the idea of them as a couple, especially Mila and Vito, with their more modern views. But her mother's traditional attitudes are firmly entrenched. She'll never accept an Indian Hindu into the family even if he converts to Catholicism. And then there's her grandmother. Mariel has begged her mother and children not to tell her grandmother about Vijay. She's so old that Mariel worries the shock might kill her. Indeed, the chances are she'll have passed away by the time they move back for good.

"Of course, I want introduce him to my family, but we wait for another time – maybe after we're married. Now come on, you mus' keep going with painting otherwise Mummy come back before finish. Still mus' do body of elephant. What colour you choose?"

"I'm going to make the body blue and the background purple."

Suddenly Aggie says, as though the injustice has only

just occurred to her, "But s'not fair on Vijay if we all go on holiday and he doesn't. Doesn't he want to see his mummy and daddy in India?"

"Is OK, he say he don't mind. He like stay, look after Mutty."

Aggie smiles at this. And Mariel reflects that in truth it's because he doesn't want to return to India and will probably never dare to tell his family of their relationship.

Another thirty minutes of quiet painting passes before Mrs Laura returns. In fact, the children are both so engrossed in their art that neither of them notices her enter.

"Oh my goodness, girls, those are beautiful!" The children look up and beam at their mother and then look back at their art. The magic of the wax lines really has enabled them to make something special.

"Look, Mummy, the butterfly's wings are the same on both sides. Although I got a bit muddled on that bit. I did it pink instead of purple."

"Oh, it doesn't matter, it still looks lovely."

"Did you get the books you wanted?" Tilly asks, adding the final touches to the background of her picture.

"Yes, but I'm not sure how much use they're going be. Tomorrow, I want you both to help me practice lots of songs like 'Head, Shoulders, Knees and Toes.'"

Aggie responds by immediately singing the song and doing the actions, but when she moves her hands from her head to her shoulders and then to her knees, she knocks over the little pot of water by her side. There's almost a terrible disaster as the spill moves rapidly towards her batik. But luckily Nur, having had years of experience of batik painting with young children, moves with the speed of light and whisks away the precious artwork before any damage is done.

Mariel looks at Nur. Smiling with gratitude she says, "*Terima kasih*," and Nur responds with a look of friendly understanding.

Then they all pack everything away carefully and drive home via the meeting point of two Malaysian muddy rivers.

The lesson

The Burmese refugee school is in Cheras, a district of Kuala Lumpur that Laura's never been to before. Prakash has driven her there as she was nervous of finding the place on her own. He pulls the car up in front of UNIPRIN, a scruffy-looking photocopy and printer shop. At first Laura thinks they must be in the wrong place but then she remembers Evi saying that the 'house' was the first and second floors above a shop. She can't quite believe how nervous she is and keeps having to remind herself that throughout her career she's had to deal with many stressful occasions. Like the time she'd been to interview Alexander McQueen at his studio in Clerkenwell and she'd arrived just as he was having a furious row with his team. The interview had been terrifying, he'd sat there growling and she'd been so intimidated she'd failed to ask any decent questions. So really, by comparison, singing nursery rhymes to a roomful of eleven- and twelve-year-olds shouldn't be nearly as daunting. And yet that morning it had taken her a ridiculous amount of time to decide what to wear. It was a question of finding something that wasn't too fancy, that was respectable, cool and comfortable, and which she didn't mind getting grubby because she assumed that the house where they held the school would be run-down and dirty. She'd finally decided upon a simple cotton dress that was an old favourite. With its pretty blue and pink flowers, she felt it was the epitome of Englishness. Evi had said that it was helpful for the children to learn about Western culture as they're most likely to be relocated to the West, so Laura had decided that looking typically English would be a good start.

Evi had also asked her to take a good amount of bread, milk and fruit to the school – supplies for the children's break-time snacks during the week. Luckily Laura had mentioned this to Mariel just as she was heading out to the supermarket.

"Mam, I think you mus' buy UHT milk," she'd said. "I think maybe they don't have fridge." Laura had felt foolish because this hadn't occurred to her, and as soon as Mariel had said it, she knew she was right. How awkward it would have been if she'd turned up with several pints of fresh milk which would have gone off quickly in the heat. "And Gardenia white slice bread, mam. I think that the one they like."

This was the bread that Mariel and Vijay liked, and again Laura had realised that Mariel was right. But what was most telling and inwardly embarrassing was that Mariel had immediately guessed that, as well as the fresh milk, Laura would have bought fresh country loaves from the bakery counter, the ones that she normally bought for the family, which would of course have been completely unsuitable. The incident had once again made her very aware of how disconnected she is from the reality of people's lives in Asia – that sense of being in a gilded cage.

So now Laura's standing in front of the printer shop with a large box of UHT milk cartons in her arms and Prakash beside her – a bag of watermelons in his left hand and a bag of several loaves of sliced white bread in his right. The road is wide and clogged with traffic – cars and motorbikes and ancient trucks belching out filthy fumes. The row of shops, all as scruffy as the printers and all with 'houses' above, stretches far to the left and right.

There's no front door to the school but rather a metal grilled gate to the right of Uniprin's shop window and, having been told it would be unlocked, Laura steels her nerves and pushes it open. The concrete stairwell is dark and vaguely cave-like, but as she reaches the first floor it opens out onto a hot, sunny courtyard built above the back room of the shop below. Evi is standing in this courtyard talking to two Burmese ladies who are busily cutting up apples into large red plastic bowls on a wooden trestle table. The sound of children chattering loudly is coming from both the room at the back of the courtyard and the room at the front which overlooks the street. And then, looking up, Laura realises that there's another floor above, again with a room at the front and the back, and with a balcony passageway connecting the two and overlooking the courtyard. The building is indeed run-down – the exterior paint, once white, is now grey with mildew; the doors and windows looking out onto the courtyard are dilapidated. And yet it is cheerful, and the school exudes a vibrant atmosphere generated by the noise of so many excited children. After reading the harrowing tale of Kung Bik's escape from Myanmar, Laura had expected the refugee school to be a sad place. But far from it – there is energy everywhere.

"Hi, Laura! Welcome! Come on in." Evi takes the box of milk cartons from her and places it on the table. Prakash does the same with his bags of groceries and then retreats down the stairs inconspicuously.

"This is Stella and Malawm, they're both teachers here teaching math and English – which they speak very well." Evi looks from one to the other, smiling, and the two ladies giggle. "And this is my English friend Laura who I told you about." Laura shakes hands with them both and feels as shy as they look.

Then Stella says, "Thank you, Teacher Laura, for coming to help us."

Embarrassed, Laura replies, "Well, I'm not actually a teacher but I'll do my best to help."

"Come on then, I'll introduce you to the class you're going to help with." Evi takes her arm and leads her towards the room at the front. "You're in here and this class is called P3."

As they walk into the classroom the children immediately stop talking and stare at Laura, clearly intrigued.

Evi directs a confident smile around the room. "Good morning, children, this is Teacher Laura. She's from England. Please say hello to her." Nearly all the gawping faces break into huge, welcoming smiles – Laura thinks she's never seen such a sea of warmth. Those children that were sitting down stand up and the girls that were at the front of the class come towards Laura, and two of them take her by the hand and just stand there gently holding on to her. The rest of the class clap quietly as they say, almost in unison, "Hello, Teacher Laura, welcome to our school!" And Laura feels her heart melt. It is an extraordinary greeting – one that has both gratitude and love bundled up into it – and Laura is immediately aware of how determined the children are to learn so that they might have a better future. Their faces are round and animated, and their skin incredibly smooth and beautiful. Their feet, she notices, are wide and splayed like Mariel's – gaps between each toe.

Evi looks encouragingly at Laura. "Now, as we discussed, I'd recommend starting with 'introductions', then help the kids to get on with their workbooks and maybe finish by teaching them a song. After lunch they'll be having their proper English lesson with Stella." Laura smiles at Evi weakly. "I'll be in the classroom on the other side of the courtyard so you can always come and get me if you need me."

Evi leaves the room, and although the warmth of the children's welcome still lingers, Laura suddenly feels terribly alone. The children are all now sitting cross-legged on the floor – there are no desks or chairs. Indeed, there is no furniture at all – just a light brown linoleum floor, peeling away in places, a clock and a whiteboard on the wall behind Laura, and a series of maps and alphabet and number posters covering the other three walls. The students have settled into groups of girls and boys – the girls at the front and the boys at the back – and they're all now chatting quietly amongst themselves.

"Um... Err... Let's begin, shall we?" To her surprise they all fall silent.

As she stands before the children, she realises that her dress is entirely the wrong thing to be wearing. Sitting on the floor in front of her, there is nothing they can do to avoid looking directly at her bare legs, the whiteness of which she knows, from what Evi had said, will be a novelty to them. In fact, the kids in the front row will struggle not to inadvertently look up her skirt, if she doesn't keep as far back as possible. Laura realises that next week she must wear thin, loose trousers – ones that won't stick to her in the heat. The room is hot and stuffy, for there's no air-con, just a small open window, a wall-mounted fan and twenty-four enthusiastic, cross-legged children, who, she notes, are all sensibly wearing either shorts or trousers.

"Right then, children, I'd, err... like to go round the room and for everyone to tell me their names and how old they are." She tries to put on her most confident, teacher-like expression. "My name is Laura and I'm thirty-seven years old." She looks towards the girl on the far left of the front row and recognises one of the two that had held her hand. They smile at each other – the bond of teacher and pupil somehow already formed.

"My name Elly Sui, teacher. I am ten year old."

"Hello, Elly Sui, very nice to meet you."

As she continues along the front row, she wonders how she'll ever remember all their names: Centenary Par, aged ten; Nung Men Tial, aged ten; Sang Chin Pui, aged thirteen; Tha Hlei Sung, aged twelve. And then, at the end of the row, there's a small girl with a haunted look upon her face who's staring vacantly at the wall. Her feet and lower legs are entirely covered in lacerations as though she's been whipped by thorny bushes.

Laura feels the sweat on her back go cold as she remembers Kung Bik's story – how he and his brother had walked barefoot through the jungle for a week during their escape from Myanmar and how the pain of the cuts had kept them awake at night. She knows she's now staring at a girl with a similar story etched upon her legs. And she remembers what Evi had said about the children being in shock when they first arrive. Laura forces herself to look smilingly into the girl's eyes and says, "And what's your name?"

At first the girl seems unaware of Laura and then she jumps with a start before lowering her head so that her chin practically disappears into the dip at the base of her neck. She mumbles something incomprehensible. Laura hesitates and inwardly berates herself for her own awkwardness before finally saying, "Well, it's very nice to meet you." Then she quickly moves on to the second row who are all boys (as is the third) and she wonders if there's a significance to this gender imbalance or whether it's just a coincidence.

The boys' names are equally difficult to understand and remember: Ceu Lian, Josep Ram Bik Ceu, Lal Kung Uk. And then, sitting in the middle of the second row, a boy wearing a blue polo shirt with a dark red collar that's almost the same colour as his wide beautiful lips looks at Laura with dancing eyes and says, "Hello, teacher, my name is Kung Bik. I am fourteen year old."

And at that moment the joy of being able to help these children floods through her, of being able to do something truly meaningful and not just encourage entitled British women to be up to date on the latest fashions. For she knows that only a year ago Kung Bik would have been sitting here, his legs and feet crisscrossed with cuts, feeling displaced and confused and wondering why his life had suddenly been turned upside down. And yet now he is smiling at her, the happiness and determination discernible in his eyes, lapping up the opportunity to learn and to head towards a more positive future.

"Hello, Kung Bik, it's very good to meet you."

The rest of the lesson passes much more easily than Laura could ever have imagined. The children work conscientiously on their workbooks. The topic is 'Question Words' – why, who, what, when – and Laura is surprised how easy it is to help the kids who get stuck. But what strikes her the most is how keen and hard-working they all are. Of course, there's some chat, particularly amongst the boys, but it's certainly not disruptive and her concerns that she wouldn't be able to keep the class disciplined are completely unfounded, for they keep themselves under control as a matter of course.

At eleven o'clock they stop for a break – the Chin teachers are back at the trestle table handing out pieces of apple and a mug of milk to all the students. As the children mingle, chatter and buzz, the building reverberates, as though purring with satisfaction. Laura, desperate for a pee, finds the loo, which is basic but clean. She's not surprised that it's a squat version; after nearly ten months in Malaysia she's now used to them, but as there's no light other than that which comes through the gap at the top of the door, she has to concentrate on her aim. She's also not surprised to find no loo paper, just a bucket of water and a ladle. She's learnt to keep a packet of tissues in her handbag for just this type of emergency.

After the break, following the guided suggestion at the end of the workbook chapter, she practises a series of questions with the children. Where is your school? Who is your best friend? What is the capital city of Malaysia? Why do you go to school? They don't know the answer to the third question, and she struggles to explain the concept of a capital city in simple English. But they all have an answer to the last question, and it is: 'to study and to learn English'. And again, she's struck by how driven they all are to arm themselves with this valued weapon that will help them fight the trials and tribulations of their lives, a weapon she realises she was given for free by the fortune of her birth.

And then it's time to teach them 'Head, Shoulders, Knees and Toes', and suddenly she wishes that Tilly and Aggie were with her, infecting her with their joy and lack of inhibition when singing this song.

"OK, children, please stand up. I'm going to teach you a song." They all look a little surprised by this announcement. "I will sing and then I want you to repeat it with me." She places her hands on her head and the children immediately follow suit but start giggling, and so, before her courage falters, she launches straight into it: "*Head, shoulders, knees and toes, knees and toes.*"

They all copy the actions, and the giggling intensifies. Above the laughter she says, "Now sing with me... *Head, shoulders, knees and toes, knees and toes.*" And the giggling gradually subsides as they all do their best to sing the words. By the time she gets to, '*And eyes and ears and mouth and nose*', the entire class is completely engaged in the song and loving its ridiculousness.

When they finish, there's a chorus of, "Again, Teacher, again!" but looking up at the clock Laura realises that it's 1pm.

"I'm sorry, children, but it's time to stop now. I'll see you all again next week and then perhaps the week after that I'll come on Monday *and* Wednesday. Thank you for working so hard. I've really enjoyed meeting you all."

As they start packing up their bags there are individual calls of, "Thank you, Teacher." and, "Thank you, Teacher Laura." And the children start to cluster into their friendship groups as they leave the room and congregate in the courtyard. Laura smiles to herself with a true sense of inner happiness as she watches Kung Bik drape his arm across the shoulders of his friend, the friend do the same in return and the two of them lean on each other in a display of sincere youthful camaraderie. But her joy is dampened when she notices that the girl with the lacerated feet is still packing up her bag, moving very slowly, and is the last to leave the classroom. Just as Laura is wondering whether to approach her, Stella, one of the Chin teachers, comes into the room and helps the girl with her last few things whilst talking to her in their dialect, her voice quiet and gentle. Laura walks towards them and Stella looks up, but the girl's eyes remain firmly downcast.

Gently, Laura says, "Thank you for coming to my class. I hope to see you again next week." The girl raises her head very slightly and Laura can tell she's doing her best to smile.

Stella puts a comforting arm around her shoulder. "I

tell her I will give her extra help with English so everything not so confusing."

"That sounds like a great idea." Laura hopes her encouraging tone doesn't appear too forced. "I'll see you both next week. Bye… and thank you, Stella, this school is wonderful." Stella's face lights up with pleasure and pride, and the girl's gaze is drawn up towards it as if by a magnet. She looks forcefully at Stella as though trying to drink in her strength and confidence.

Looking back at her, Stella tightens her arm around her, and then turns to Laura and says, "Thank you, Teacher Laura. Goodbye. See you next week."

*

Arriving home, hot and sticky, Laura quickly exchanges her dress for her bathing costume and flops into the cool of the swimming pool. She's utterly exhausted and yet filled with an extraordinary feeling of satisfaction and well-being. She dips her head back, not caring that she'll have to wash the chlorine out of her hair yet again, and floats on her back, gazing up at the sky, too tired to swim. The water feels wonderful as it laps around her. In fact, everything suddenly seems rather special and luxurious. She looks up at the house, which appears so much prettier and less dilapidated than it did yesterday.

Feeling cooler, she gets out of the pool and collapses onto the sun lounger underneath the jacaranda tree. Moments later Mariel appears from the back door carrying a tall glass of her homemade lime juice and a bowl of cashew nuts.

"Thanks, Mariel, you're a lifesaver." Taking a sip of the drink Laura turns to her and asks, "Mariel, when you were a child, did you *want* to learn English?"

"Of course, mam. Mus' learn English if you want to make good money. All good job need English. My daughter she is now qualified nurse and 'cos she speak English can now apply job abroad and get top, top salary. Same for my son when he qualify as veterinarian." She looks down and studies her feet. "If I not learn English then I have to stay in Philippines – stay with my husband, not come to KL, never meet Vijay." And then she looks up again. "Mam, shall I make chicken curry for dinner tonight? Today I buy from Van Man very nice *ladies finger* – very good in chicken curry."

"That sounds delicious. Thank you, Mariel."

Mariel returns to the kitchen and Laura lies back and looks up at the branches above her. She ponders the profundity of what Mariel has just said – how she'd determinedly mapped out her pathway as a mere child and how the act of learning the still-dominant language of the world had eventually opened for her the gates to love and freedom. But will it be the same for those children from Myanmar? Will learning English be enough to enable them to survive even if they are repatriated to another country? Will it be enough to help them find work as adults, let alone love and freedom, or will they always be stuck at the bottom of the pile? As she watches the light dancing and twisting around the mass of lilac-coloured flowers, an idea comes to her, and the more she thinks about it, the more excited she becomes. What if the little girl with the lacerated feet were to come and live with them for a while? That way she'd have a safe and secure home, and plenty of healthy wholesome food to help her get her strength back. Laura could take her to the doctor to check her cuts for any infection and for any other problems. She could have the guest room all to herself so that she'd have some privacy. And she'd be able to learn English quickly, having Laura and the girls around all the time to help her. It feels like a wonderful idea. Laura tingles all over with anticipation.

She'd like to run into the kitchen and tell Mariel of her plan. Mariel loves children – she'll surely want to help this little girl as well. Maybe now she won't think so badly of Laura. Maybe she'll finally decide that she's a good person, and that she was only trying to do the right thing on that terrible night. But, Laura realises, she must talk the plan through with Peter before discussing it with Mariel and Vijay or, indeed, the girls. Sitting up to finish her drink, she looks down at the glass and swirls the ice thoughtfully.

Before long she's too hot again and decides to retreat to her bedroom and the air-con. Walking through the kitchen, she sees Mariel skilfully cutting up a whole chicken into pieces, ready for the curry. Putting all thoughts of the little girl to the back of her mind she says, "Oh, Mariel, I forgot to tell you that I've managed to book the hotel that I wanted in Langkawi. So, we're definitely going to be away for the same two weeks that you're in the Philippines which I must confess is a relief!"

"But, mam, I go to Philippines for whole month, not jus' two weeks."

"What do you mean a whole month? You never said – you said you were leaving on 1st August. I'd assumed you were just going for two weeks…"

"I did tell you, mam. At interview. You agreed I can take my leave in August – go to Philippines for whole month." Mariel has stopped cutting the meat and is standing there awkwardly holding the knife.

"I remember you said you wanted to take your leave in August, but I don't remember you saying all four weeks in one go. Oh God, this is bad timing. I'm not sure I'll be able to cope without you." Immediately the idea of looking after the little Chin girl as well as Tilly and Aggie, not to mention keeping the house clean and managing all the washing, seems utterly overwhelming.

"Sorry, mam." Mariel looks down at the knife and places it carefully on the chopping board. "At interview you agree that my salary package include you pay my flight home one time per year. I thought you understand that I take leave for whole month 'cos flight expensive. Cannot afford a second flight, mam."

Laura is taken aback by this logical explanation, but it doesn't do much to reduce her shock at the unwelcome news that's been sprung on her. The sweat on her lower back is making her sarong stick to her, adding to her discomfort.

"Oh, right, yes, I see. Well, perhaps you could help me find a temp maid for those two weeks?" she asks irritably.

"Yes, mam, of course." A silence hangs between them. "Mam, I *need* one month back home – mus' get to know my family again."

Shamefaced, Laura looks down at her feet. "Yes… of course you do, I'm sorry. You've been apart for a long time, a terribly long time, of course you must spend a month with them." And awkwardly she leaves the kitchen and

305

heads off to her bedroom, hoping that the cool of the air-con will restore the benevolent and inspired Laura of earlier that afternoon.

The teacher teaches

The next day, Tuesday, Laura is desperately trying to make the morning pass quicker. She's taken the girls to school, picked up the dry cleaning, swum twenty lengths, had a shower and washed her hair. She's rung Mrs Faridah at the maid agency, who said there should be no problem finding a temp maid in August, which has calmed her nerves considerably. She's also checked her emails and sent a few replies. But still, it's only ten thirty.

She's decided to go and talk about her fostering idea to the Chin teachers, Stella and Malawm, after the refugee school's morning classes, during the lunchbreak, when many of the kids go home for their meal. She's planning to leave the house at twelve, to give herself an hour to find the school in Cheras, as this time she won't have Prakash to take her.

So… what to do for the next hour and a half? She gets up from her desk, takes her book from the bedside table and wanders downstairs to the veranda. She's reading a detective novel, set in Edinburgh. The detective is a complicated and cantankerous character, but deep down he has a heart of gold and Laura has a bit of a crush on him. But today he holds no power over her. She can't concentrate on the story at all and puts the book down after five minutes of staring at the words. No monkeys at the bottom of the garden this morning – just when they might have been some sort of distraction. Perhaps, if she sits quietly, the beautiful langurs with their round white eyes will come for the flowers at the top of the jacaranda tree – they're so composed and reserved compared to their more aggressive cousins, the macaques.

She and Peter had discussed her idea last night over dinner. He'd agreed that it was a lovely suggestion, that it would be a great way of giving direct help to the little girl if Laura felt ready for such a commitment.

"It's a joy to see you being your happy and motivated self again, my love," he'd said, leaning over to give her a kiss. "Obviously you must talk it through with Evi and the Chin teachers and whoever else in the refugee community you need to consult with – she may have family members here with her. And we must make sure that Tilly and Aggie feel completely included in the plans so that they don't get jealous."

Laura had rung Evi there and then, who'd surprised her by being quite reticent.

"I thought your visit to the school would inspire you, but this is quite an extreme U-turn, Laura. Only a few days ago you were worrying about not being good with kids."

"I know, I know, but I was just down in the dumps and low in confidence. There's so much we could give that little girl and she could be fluent in English in just a few months. Just think what an advantage that would give her once she's resettled in another country, which will probably be America. When she starts at school there, she could get stuck in straight away to full-on learning and not be held back by any language barrier."

"I think her name's Esther Sui Hliang Sung. Hang on a minute and let me check my lists…" While waiting for Evi to check, Laura had whispered to Peter, "*Her name is Esther, like my grandmother – that must be fate talking.*"

"Yes, I'm right, it's Esther Sui Hliang Sung. Bit of a mouthful. The Chins often don't shorten their names but use the entire thing. But she might well go by just Esther, eventually. The notes do say that she came here without her parents, but you must talk to Stella and Malawm. We've never had a situation like this before, where one of the children is looked after by someone outside of the Chin community."

"Yes, yes, of course I will. If she's here without her parents, that's all the more reason why she needs lots of love and care and a safe place to live. Is she an orphan?"

"It doesn't say in her notes. But not necessarily. Sometimes children do travel ahead with other family members and then the parents follow later. Either way, Laura, it's a big responsibility you're thinking of taking on, so you mustn't rush into it."

Evi is right, of course, it will be a huge responsibility. But Laura is just so thrilled at the idea of being able to do some good. Her heart is soaring.

Unsure of where she's allowed to park Laura drives down a couple of the side streets off the main road in

Cheras until she finds a spot that doesn't seem to have any restrictions, and then walks slowly to the school, attempting not to get too sweaty. From the other side of the road she sees children pouring out of the metal grille gate, heading to the various places where they're living, to have their lunch. She looks for little Esther but doesn't spot her, although she does recognise some of the other children and a couple of girls smile and wave shyly at her. Hanging back, she waits for all the kids to disperse before she crosses the road, opens the gate and walks up the creepy staircase.

The courtyard is empty but almost immediately Stella appears from the back room where there's clearly a group sitting on the floor having their meal. She's wiping her hands on a tea towel.

"Teacher Laura! Hello, what are you doing here? Is good to see you again."

"Hi, Stella, sorry to drop in like this but there's something important I want to talk to you about."

"Of course, no problem. Would you like some food?"

Laura flushes with embarrassment. "Oh, no thank you, that's very kind of you but I'm fine. I'm sorry to interrupt your lunch."

"Is OK, really. Come, let's sit in other room." Stella leads the way to the front classroom, the one where Laura had taught. "Is there something wrong? You look bit stressed, Teacher Laura."

"Oh no, there's nothing wrong. It's just that I've had an idea I want to talk to you about." Stella sits on the floor, crosses her legs and pats the linoleum next to her. Laura joins her and continues, "I know that the little girl called

Esther Sui Hliang Sung has just arrived from Myanmar and is having a difficult time. I was wondering if I could help. I thought maybe she could come and stay with us for a little while and we'll make sure that she's really cared for and well looked after and gets whatever medical attention she needs. Obviously, we'll cover all the costs. And we'll bring her to school every day and make sure that she's got whatever clothes she needs." Laura's conscious she sounds breathless and also very aware that Stella's no longer looking at her but has her eyes cast down, apparently staring at a worn patch of flooring.

"Ah… Teacher Laura, I know you are very kind lady, but I think perhaps you don't understand." Raising her eyes, Stella smiles gently. "It would not be good idea for Esther Sui Hliang Sung to stay with you and your family. I know you would care for her very well, like your daughter. But would be frightening for her to be away from people she knows, to be with people who do not speak her language. She would feel alone with your family even though you try to make her happy." Laura feels suddenly deflated, all her excitement dispelled. "The Chin community in KL is very strong. Esther Sui Hliang Sung travelled here with small group that now are all staying in our school till they find apartment they can stay in. One of the aunties is her mother's cousin. She has been caring for her as well as her two small children. And Esther Sui Hliang Sung has been helping with the babies. So, even though she is finding class difficult, she has family that would be best for her to stay with. They will help each other. And soon she will not find school difficult. Maybe if you have English storybooks for young children, you can bring them to school, and you can read them with Esther Sui Hliang Sung and some of other children that need more help. That would be a good thing to do, Teacher Laura."

There are a couple of moments of silence, as it takes Laura time to digest what Stella has said: that the situation is much more complex than she'd realised; that even though Laura and the family can offer love and care, it isn't a love and care that the little girl either wants or needs. And, as Laura thinks it through, it makes perfect sense, and she feels foolish for not understanding before.

"I see what you mean, Stella. She needs to be with people who understand what she's been through and who make her feel less isolated. I'm sorry, you're right, I made a mistake. I just wanted to do something to help."

"But you will help if you come to school one or two times every week and help children with speaking English and workbook study. We have so many children coming to school now, and is very difficult for Malawm and me to do all teaching, so if you can help us like this then it will be very good."

Laura's eyes smart with tears. She swallows hard, determined not to embarrass herself further. "That's a deal then. I'll come and help out twice a week, and every week I'll bring some reading books to share with the children." They stand up and Laura puts out her hand to shake Stella's – Stella takes Laura's with both of hers and clasps it with kindness.

"Thank you, Teacher Laura, I will see you again next week."

The Queen's birthday party

As they walk into the gardens of the British Embassy Laura marvels at the number of British people there are living in Kuala Lumpur but, to her dismay, recognises none of them. She guesses there must be about two hundred people milling around chatting, eating and drinking – some Malaysians but mainly Brits.

They're all there to celebrate the Queen's official birthday. When the rather grand and formal invitation had arrived in the post, Laura had been amazed. It'd seemed so old-fashioned to be having a party for such an occasion, and why on earth were she, Peter and the girls invited? Come to think of it, how did the embassy know where they lived? And then she'd remembered that when they'd first arrived in Malaysia they'd registered with the British Embassy and had given their address. Laura had met the High Commissioner's wife a couple of times through school – her daughter was in the same year as Tilly. They'd got on well and the girls were friendly with each other, so Laura figured that had been enough to get them on the invite list. But still she can't help thinking what an extraordinary thing it is to be asked to such an event purely because they're four of the Queen's subjects living in a foreign country. They certainly would never have been invited to any of her official birthday parties back home.

"Is the Queen going to be there?" Aggie had asked. And when Laura said she wouldn't Aggie had quite understandably wondered, "But why? It's her birfday party. Who's going to blow out her candles?"

Of course, being birthday party pros, it's the girls who settle into the occasion quickest, rushing off to play with their hostess, the High Commissioner's daughter, and a bunch of other friends from school. They seem completely at ease with the size and grandeur of the gathering, significantly less bothered than Laura by the sticky heat and delighted to be joining in with a game of '40 40 Home'. Laura and Peter, on the other hand, hover uncertainly at the edge of the crowd, gratefully accepting a glass of wine from one of the many waiters, Laura wishing that Evi was British rather than Dutch.

"Ah, look," says Peter, "there's Jim and Susan. Let's go over and talk to them." And Laura smiles to herself, thinking that she'd never imagined she'd be so pleased to see Susan. Since the disastrous dinner party she'd been avoiding her even more than usual.

"Laura, Peter! Hello, good to see you. So glad you were able to make it," Susan says, as though she were the hostess, and Laura wonders whether she'd had something to do with getting them on the invite list. "I see you've been given a drink. There's plenty to eat too – lots of tables laid out in the main reception room serving a wonderful assortment of Malaysian specialities. You *must* try them." Susan looks as though she's about to herd them towards the food when Jim cuts in with, "Hello, you two. How are things?" He smiles at Laura. "So glad to hear you found your puppy."

The conversation turns to the story of the dog-napping, and the mission to taste all the Malaysian specialities seems forgotten. As the party continues, Laura's feet begin to ache, swelling in the heat. The dress code is formal so she's wearing proper heels for the first time in ages with a pair of well-cut cream linen trousers and a floaty silk blouse. Some of the other women are even wearing hats as though it were a garden party at Buckingham Palace. The men are all in suits except for a few in military uniform – the latter appearing even more determined than the former to ignore the heat. Laura looks around, shifting her weight from foot to foot, trying to ease the ache, and once again finds herself wondering if she's stepped back in time.

There's a call for quiet as the High Commissioner steps up to a microphone on a small podium and starts to make a speech. As he drones on about the 'relationship of partnership and collaboration between Britain and Malaysia', and the 'journeys they have made together from colonial to post-colonial reality', Laura can hear all the children still playing at the far end of the gardens, which are now beautifully well lit, for, as usual, darkness has fallen suddenly. She wishes she could throw off her shoes and join them. Their laughter makes her think of the children from Myanmar and the school. Indeed, she's thought of little else since her talk with Stella on Tuesday. The roller-coaster of her emotions now seems to be slowing down and she's finally beginning to understand what her purpose is for being in Kuala Lumpur beyond that of supporting her husband and children.

When she'd told Peter what Stella had said, he'd been taken aback at first but then agreed that, when you really think about it, her point makes perfect sense. But, as they'd talked it through, they'd both confessed to each other that there was still a part of them that wished they could foster her as they felt they had so much to give.

"I guess it's just hard to accept that what we have to offer isn't what she needs," Peter had said.

"I know, and now I understand it seems so obvious, although I keep wondering why it didn't occur to us before."

She'd also called Evi, who'd said she'd wondered whether that would be Stella's response but hadn't wanted to pre-empt her.

"I'm sorry if you're very disappointed," she'd said kindly to Laura.

"No, it's fine. I just want to do something to help, but Stella's explained that it genuinely does help reading to the kids and chatting to them."

So, Laura had confirmed to Evi that she'd like to help two days a week and Evi had given her advice on how best to use the workbooks and mentioned that there are actually some teaching materials available online if you know where to look for them. Although, as the internet at the house is so unreliable and slow Laura doubts she'll ever be able to get online long enough to find them.

Now, looking at the High Commissioner's animated face, she wonders whether any refugees from Myanmar are resettled in the UK and determines to find a moment to ask either him or his wife about this.

Then thankfully, before too long, he's asking everyone to raise their glasses to Her Majesty the Queen, to which there are hearty cries of, "The Queen!" and a soldier starts playing the national anthem on the bagpipes. The squeaky instrument seems so incongruous in the setting, not to mention the upright and respectable expressions across the faces of the other guests, especially Susan's, that it's everything Laura can do not to giggle. She controls herself by staring at her sore feet and imagines soothing them in the pool once home.

As the music finishes the High Commissioner says, "Now please join me in a toast for the good health and well-being of His Majesty the Yang di-Pertuan Agong, the success and prosperity of the Government and People of Malaysia." Laura looks up, wondering if the piper will now strike up with the Malaysian national anthem, but there's just a general raising of glasses and within moments the party is back in full flow, the guests chattering like sparrows.

"Come on, you two! I'm not going to let you get away without trying out these wonderful Malaysian dishes," announces Susan as she takes them both by the arm and steers them towards the food.

*

The following morning the family have Sunday brunch at one of the street food restaurants on Jalan Alor. Laura smiles inwardly at the thought of how much Malaysian food they've eaten this weekend and how a year ago she could never have imagined Tilly and Aggie tucking into these kinds of dishes. They would have turned up their noses at anything that wasn't pasta, sausages or roast chicken. Now all four of them are sitting at a round table in the middle of the street on red plastic stools, the girls' legs swinging slightly – enjoying their favourite, *roti canai*, a deliciously greasy flatbread which they're happily eating with their fingers, Malaysian-style, and which, to Laura's further amazement, the children are bravely dipping into a spicy dahl.

Everyone is tired – all quietly appreciating their food. Last night the girls had stayed up well past their bedtime, and both Peter and Laura had had too much to drink – Laura had felt it was the only way to get through the evening. Aggie had been very disappointed that there was no cake, not to mention candles (all eighty-one of them), and as they'd driven home Laura had placated her by promising brunch in Jalan Alor, knowing perfectly well that it would also be good for their hangovers. They've been there a few times in the evening, but she prefers the calmer, less crowded atmosphere during the day.

A waiter in a bright yellow T-shirt starts to clear away some of the empty plates on their table.

"Mummy, can we order some satay, please?" asks Tilly, finishing the last of her *rotis*.

"Sure, good idea. Let's get both chicken and beef."

But before Laura has had a chance to even look up at the waiter, Tilly says to him, smiling, "*Sate ayam, sate daging lembu. Terima kasih.*" And he nods, jotting down on his little pad before returning to the large grill standing on the pavement, where the satay is sizzling.

"Wow, Tilly, I had no idea your Malay was that good now!"

The delight of basking in her father's pride spreads across her face. "S'not really. I only know the food names and my numbers and colours and stuff."

"Well, I'm impressed."

"I know numbers too," says Aggie. "*Satu, dua, tiga, empat,*" but then she takes another big mouthful of *roti*, and so *lima, enam* and *tujuh* are garbled.

"That's also very impressive, sweetheart. I clearly need to improve my Malay to keep up with you two."

The waiter brings a big square plate piled high with chicken and beef on little wooden skewers and a bright orange plastic bowl full of the spicy peanut sauce. And once again they're all silent for a while as they enjoy the food. And then, looking up from his plate and surveying them all, a little like he's chairing a meeting, Peter says, "Girls, Mummy and I have been talking and we'd like to know what you think about the idea of staying here in Malaysia for another year or two rather than going back to England as soon as I've finished my big project at work. What do you think? Do you like it here?"

Looking very serious, Tilly replies, "Well… I still miss my friends in England, but if we moved back then I'd miss my friends here. I do really like it here – especially the swimming pool and the slide."

"I like swimming too! I can swim wivout my jacket now!"

"Will Mariel stay with us too?"

Laura helps Aggie with a piece of chicken that's

stubbornly refusing to come off its skewer. "Yes, at least for another year. She told me that once she and Vijay are married, they'd like to work for us for a bit longer before they move back to the Philippines. I think they want to save up some more money."

"I luv Mariel, I don't want her to go away." Aggie looks a little mournful.

"I know, sweetheart, Mariel is very special. She really looks after us all. I don't want her to go away either."

Still very serious, Tilly asks, "But what about you, Mummy, do you want to stay here? I thought you don't like the house – you're always complaining about it."

"Even though it drives me crazy, I must confess, I've grown rather fond of it. At first, I thought I wanted to move back to England as soon as possible so I could go back to my job. But now I'd like to stay here and help the children from Myanmar because they were made to leave their homes even though they didn't want to."

"Are they very sad?"

"Yes, I think they're sad when they first arrive, but some of the grown-up refugees who were teachers in Myanmar have set up the lovely school I told you about, and the children really seem to enjoy it there. So, I'm going to go there twice a week and help them to learn English. You remember I taught them 'Head, Shoulders, Knees and Toes'? Well, they loved it, so next week I'm going to teach them 'The Wheels on the Bus.'"

On cue both girls start singing the song and doing the actions. A few bits of chicken fly across the table because the wheels of Aggie's bus are still holding a stick of satay and they all burst out laughing.

August 2007

Going home

Mariel had forgotten how fantastic-looking Filipino jeepneys are, with their bright colours and words and pictures painted all over them – much better than regular buses. She remembers learning in school that the first ones were made from the US military jeeps left behind after the war, which is how they got their name, and now, of course, they're one of those special things that are part of the Philippines, her home.

She'd also forgotten how long and arduous the journey is. After the flight from KL to Manila she'd taken an airport coach to the bus terminal in Cubao, where she'd had to wait for two hours for the overnight bus to Maddela. She'd known she'd be too nervous to leave her bags unattended, so she'd planned ahead and had been to the toilet in the airport before baggage collection and had also brought food with her and a good romance to read. So, the wait at the bus terminal hadn't been too bad. And by the time she'd got on the Maddela bus she was so tired that she'd slept, despite the ache in her neck she always gets sleeping upright.

Waiting in the early morning in Maddela for a jeepney to take her to her village, she'd worried that she wouldn't be allowed to get on it because she had so much luggage. But luckily, when it pulled up to the bus stop, the driver and one of the other passengers had got out and helped her get her things up onto the roof rack and strap them on. Her two suitcases are both huge and the flat-screen TV in its box is now the size of a third suitcase after Vijay carefully wrapped it in some of the bubble wrap left behind after Mrs Laura and Mr Peter's fancy pictures had arrived from England. He'd made a handle out of string so that Mariel could carry the TV, but she'd still found it terribly hard to manage all her stuff. Luckily, the electric rice cooker had fit into one of the suitcases, otherwise she'd have had to carry that as well.

The jeepney is bright green with rainbow stripes and a huge Adidas logo painted on the driver's door. She thinks, with all the stops, the ride will take about an hour and then she'll be back in her village – finally, after all this time. She'd told Rosa that she'd SMS as she was approaching so the family could come down to the bus stop to meet her. The last time she'd seen them all had been at this very same bus stop – they'd been standing there, waving goodbye. Rosa was thirteen and Mila eleven. The girls each held on to one of their grandmother's hands and sobbed onto her shoulder. Vito, though only ten, bravely tried to control his tears like a grown man. Watching them, Mariel had felt as though her heart was being wrenched out of her – she'd turned around in her seat and not looked back. She hadn't wanted them to see her crying. She'd determined never to show them how hard she found it to leave. She wonders now if she'd made a mistake hiding her grief. Did they think her cold? At the time she'd been sure it was the best thing to do. As she'd turned away, she'd seen her mother gently nod at her as if to say, 'yes, you're doing the right thing'. But her mother hadn't known then, neither had the children, that she didn't intend to return for ten years.

Six months later she told them she wouldn't be back. Her mother refused to speak to her for about a year after that, and even then, only very occasionally and normally just to talk about money. At first the children didn't really seem to believe that she'd be gone for such a long time – perhaps they just couldn't comprehend it. But then, after about three years, it was almost as if they'd forgotten about her as a mother and she'd just become this distant person who sent money and who was always checking whether they were studying hard enough.

Looking out of the window now she recognises the neighbouring village – hers will be the next stop. On her handphone she types out, *Arriving just now*, and presses send. The patchwork of paddy fields spreads out until it reaches the base of the mountain range shimmering in the distance, and she remembers back to the years when she worked in the fields. How strong she was then – carrying one of those huge bags of rice on her head.

Her children are already waiting at the stop as the jeepney approaches. Even though she's seen photos over the years, she still can't quite believe how adult they are.

Her eyes well with tears and she swallows to control them. Mila is so pretty and holds herself with so much confidence – such a long way from the shy, frightened child she'd been. And Mariel hadn't realised from the pictures how unusually tall Vito is, like his father. She's become used to the man in her life being shorter than her.

Luis, her son-in-law, is a more regular height, and she's pleased to see that he's nice-looking – an honest, kind face. Rosa is holding the baby on her hip and the baby is attempting to wave at the jeepney. Mariel waves back briefly, but the bus is pulling to a halt, so she starts to push past the other passengers' knees, towards the open back of the truck. As it stops, Vito comes forward and helps her down.

"Hello, Mom."

*

Conscious that her mother hadn't come to the bus stop with the rest of the family, Mariel feels a further pang of hurt as they approach the house and still she doesn't come to greet her. But she's glad to see her house again. She must remember to take some photos to show Vijay. It's painted a bright turquoise green and is well built with its solid concrete outer walls and corrugated iron roof. Since she's been away the window frames have been painted navy-blue and they look nice, especially with the pale pink curtains on the inside. The kitchen is in the front yard, in a typical village-style bamboo and wood shelter, again with a corrugated iron roof. The gas rings and the barbeque grill are close to the open side – to let out the smoke. And there's a wooden table under the shade of the roof, large enough for big family meals. Two chickens are scratching around the table legs, pecking at the dirt floor. And a dog, like Mrs Laura's but white in colour and with pink ears and pale brown patches on its back, is fast asleep under the coconut tree.

The electricity cables running overhead from the road to the kitchen and the house hum constantly. The noise grates on Mariel's nerves, but she knows that soon she'll no longer notice it. Rosa starts to busy herself in the kitchen, shifting Gloria, the baby, from one hip to the other. The atmosphere is awkward; Mariel knew it would be. Greeting her off the jeepney, Rosa had returned her hug, holding her tight, but Mariel could sense a tension. Mila had been warmer, telling her how much she'd been missed, but she's always been the soft and loving one.

Rosa tips vegetables into a wok, and they hiss and spit, the steam billowing around her face. "Mom, d'you want something to eat? You must be hungry."

"Yes, thank you, dear. I'll be back out in a minute, but first I must say hello to your grandmother and to Lola."

"Sure. Good idea. Grandma's been waiting to see you for ten years; they both have. Mila, can you get some Cokes out of the fridge and put them on the table?"

Ignoring the jibe, Mariel leaves Rosa and Mila in the kitchen, and follows Luis and Vito as they carry her things into the house. Her mother is sitting expectantly at the small table in the central room, her lips pursed. Despite her scowl, she looks good for nearly sixty. Her skin is still relatively smooth, and her grey hair, tied back in a ponytail, is thick and strong. Behind her, Mariel recognises the bright yellow-painted dresser which she'd bought when the house was first finished.

"Hello, Ma."

"So, you came back? I thought maybe you'd never come again."

"Of course I came back. I told you, Ma, ten years and then I'll be back."

"I don't understand this divorce business. How can you get a divorce? Nobody gets divorced."

"It's different, Ma, if you're in another country for a long time. Anyway, let's not talk about that now. How's Lola? Mila says she's not so good."

"She's very weak now. Spends nearly all the time in bed. Sometimes Luis helps me get her into the chair but most of the time she just sleeps." Mariel's mother stands up and walks towards one of the small bedrooms. The rooms of the house are separated by thin bamboo walls and, even before they've passed through the hanging piece of batik that serves as a door, Mariel can hear her grandmother's laboured wheezing. She's shocked at the sight of her. The sprightly, twinkly-eyed old lady that she remembers is now lying on her mattress, her skin like that of a shrivelled walnut. She turns her milky-white eyes towards them as they enter.

Crouching down by the side of the wooden boards and roll mat that serve as a bed, Mariel takes her grandmother's hand and says, "Hello, Lola, it's me, Mariel."

The old lady squeezes Mariel's hand feebly. Her voice is faint and wheezy. "Mariel, is that you? That's good." They sit in silence for a moment. "How's your job? Do you remember to dance with the broom, like I told you?"

Mariel laughs. "Of course, Lola, always!"

Vito, appearing in the doorway, says, "Mom, can we unpack the TV? I want to see it."

Still laughing, Mariel replies, "Of course, son, glad to see that you still get excited about presents." She turns back towards her mother and grandmother. "I need to freshen up now and Rosa is preparing some food."

"Yes, good idea. We thought you could have my bedroom. I'll sleep in here with Lola. Mila and Vito will be in the living room."

Mariel's pleased. Her mother's room is the room she plans to share with Vijay when they move back. She can lie on the mattress and picture the time when they'll sleep there together as man and wife – free of bosses and immigrant worker regulations, running their own little bakery business, the bad memories securely locked away in the past.

"Thanks, Ma, that's kind of you. After I've got over the flight and had a couple of nights of good sleep, we can take it in turns. I'd like to help you take care of Lola." She squeezes her grandmother's hand again. "I'll come and see you later."

*

Two days later Mariel, her mother and Mila are sitting in the yard with little Gloria when Mariel's husband, Vincente, comes crashing through the front gate, roaring obscenities. The baby lets out a terrified howl. Mila takes one look at her father, gathers her niece up in her arms and runs into the house.

As he stumbles towards Mariel it's clear that Vincente is blind drunk. The memories come flooding back. From her years of experience she knows instinctively that he's so drunk he's beyond the most aggressive phase.

"Hello, wife…" he slurs. "Where the hell have you been? You owe me money, bitch!" He trips over the cockerel. They squawk at each other with equal fury. The bird takes refuge under the table and Vincente collapses onto his backside in the dirt.

Taking an arm each Mariel and her mother manage to help him up and out of the yard back onto the road.

"Go home, Vincente, and sober up. I'll come to your place this evening and we'll talk then. Go now. And drink some coffee."

*

Mariel arrives at his house just after six o'clock and is shocked by the sight and smell that greet her. Empty beer cans scattered everywhere, plates piled high with cigarette ends – more just stubbed out on the floor. And the stink of the place makes her think of the police station. She tastes bile in her mouth as it rises from her stomach. For the last three months she's worked so hard to lock away that memory. She'd feared that seeing Vincente would unleash it again, and sure enough, here she is just smelling him, and immediately the vision comes flooding back of that foul man huffing his stinking breath in her face, his arm pressed across her collarbone, as he forced his way into her, rutting like an animal. Feeling herself swaying, she swallows hard and clenches her fist. Enough! Enough of letting these pigs damage her life – they will stay in her past; she has nearly reached the future.

Vincente's roll mat has been left out, and even though the little bamboo house is dark and gloomy she can see a couple of cockroaches scuttling in and out of the hidey holes made by the bunched-up dirty sheet. He's slumped in a wicker chair in the middle of the room. It's the only piece of furniture other than an upturned crate. He has a cigarette in one hand and a cup of coffee in the other. His hair is grey and shaggy, and he's poorly shaven. As he drags on the cigarette, she sees he's lost several teeth. She steels herself.

"Hello, Vincente." He stirs slightly and grunts in response, without looking up.

Rosa had warned her that he'd been pestering for some of the bakery profits, so Mariel's not surprised when his opening line is, "I'm your husband so half that bakery belongs to me. You should be paying me half of the profits!"

She takes a deep breath, willing herself to stay calm. "The bakery doesn't belong to me, it belongs to the kids."

She'd known that if she bought the bakery herself it would legally be the joint property of them both, and so she'd bought it for the children, determined not to let him have a penny of her hard-earned money.

He stubs out his cigarette, immediately lighting another. "It's still your duty to give me money. You must give me some of your salary!" he says, looking up suddenly and jabbing his finger in her direction.

"It's not my duty to give you anything. You've already had this house. If you need money, you can go out and earn it like the rest of us!"

With that she leaves quickly and quietly, without looking back. She hadn't mentioned the divorce – there's still a piece of her that's frightened he might try to stop it. Walking back to her house she whispers a quiet prayer of thanks for Vijay – for his love and protection, his gentle soul and quiet manner.

*

Two weeks later, halfway through her leave, Mariel feels like she's had a proper holiday. She's hardly done any cooking, just a bit of cleaning. And she's spent every day looking after Gloria while Rosa and Luis have been at the bakery. It's been total joy. The little girl is lively but sweet-natured and generally easy. She reminds Mariel of Rosa as a baby. Mariel was worried that her mother would mind having the role of childminder taken from her, but she seems to be enjoying spending more time chatting with her friends and Mariel has enjoyed helping her take care of Lola, which, in turn, seems to have helped soften her mother's attitude towards her. Mariel was sad to say goodbye to Mila and Vito, who'd both had to return to Manila after a week, but she's given them the money for the bus journey so they can come home again the weekend before she leaves for KL.

Despite the luxury of being on holiday she's missing the comforts of her and Vijay's little bungalow in KL. The house here is so hot with no air-conditioning and only one portable fan, which they generally leave in Lola's room. The heat seems to build up under the corrugated iron roof like a layer of hot gas, and at night it creaks and groans as the temperature of the metal changes. On her next visit home, she must remember to bring another fan. The roll-out mattress on the wooden boards feels so hard compared to their mattress in Malaysia. But the bathroom is nice – she's pleased she'd spent that bit more having a proper one put in when she built the house; there's a handheld shower and sink as well as the toilet. There are no tiles, but with concrete walls and floor there's no need. However, she's not used to having to share the bathroom with so many people. Luckily Luis and Rosa leave for work before dawn so it's not so busy in the mornings.

Today she's going to leave Gloria with her mother and join Rosa and Luis at the bakery. She's already been there a few times during her stay, just to see how things are getting on, but now she's going over to make a batch of her American-style chocolate-chip cookies to test out how well they might sell. She'd discussed this with Rosa before leaving KL and had brought the chocolate chips with her, knowing full well that the local store wouldn't stock them. If, in the future, they decide to make them regularly they'll have to order the chocolate chips from the wholesalers in Maddela. Rosa is still being a little snippy about the idea of Vijay joining them in the bakery once they move back, but she seems excited to be trying out new things, so Mariel's hoping there won't be too much tension as they work together today.

It's only a ten-minute walk from the house to the bakery, but Mariel moves slowly. The bakery will be hot, and she doesn't want to arrive steamed up – at eight o'clock in the morning it's already stifling, even walking in the shade. Looking up, she watches the light as it dances around the wide leaves of a banana tree and bounces off a newly emerging bunch of fruit – it reminds her of the garden in Kuala Lumpur. Pulling off one of the smaller lower leaves she uses it to fan herself and reflects on how content she feels, that finally after all these years of battle everything seems to be falling into place. She can now envisage her life here with Vijay. Even though it won't be easy persuading the community and her family to accept him – that final battle will surely be better than the alternative of the two of them having to return to their respective countries. But coming home has certainly brought all that she's lost over the years sharply into focus – watching her children grow up, their first communions, confirmations, graduations and so many other milestones; and losing touch with old childhood friends, most of whom are too shy to approach her now that she's the wealthiest woman in the area.

Her return has been the talk of the village – every time she's been out, she's been aware of people staring at her – so she walks proudly and smiles pleasantly at everyone she passes on the way. There are many other women in the village who work abroad, either as maids or nurses, but most come home every year. Mariel's behaviour has intrigued and probably shocked many. She doesn't know what her mother and Rosa have told people, whether they've explained why she's been away for such a long time. But she's conscious that Rosa has shown off about their growing wealth, especially when the new house was built – still the smartest in the village – and when they took over the bakery. If Mariel now buys the nearby paddy field that will certainly cement her position as queen of the neighbourhood.

Walking along, she watches her neighbours preparing for their day – the woman who lives immediately next door is feeding her chickens while a couple of toddlers play in the yard. Mariel knows one is her son and the other her nephew who she looks after while her sister is working in Dubai. The couple that run the vegetable stall are already doing a busy trade. She thinks she'll stop on her way back and buy some red spinach and bitter gourd for dinner – her favourite vegetables and so much better here than in Malaysia. On the bend in the road, a man she knows to be Vincente's brother's wife's cousin is watering down his pair of pigs; in fact, he's squirting the hose directly into the mouth of the bigger sow, who's gulping it down with glee. Just before she gets to the bakery she passes the entrance to the basketball pitch, a sandy clearing in the middle of the village, two large trees at either end serving as the goal posts with the basketball hoops and backboards hammered onto them.

By the time she arrives Rosa and Luis have already done good early-morning business and Luis, working bare-chested, has just put another batch of coco bread rolls, their best-sellers, into the ovens. The ovens are made from two old fifty-five-gallon drums laid on their sides and cemented into square concrete blocks. Luis feeds dried sticks of wood into the cavity beneath them – after years of practice he knows how much wood to burn to keep the ovens at exactly the right temperature. Luis's father had owned the bakery previously – Mariel had bought it from him after he'd had an accident damaging his arm so badly he could no longer work as a baker.

The delicious smell of the coconut bread fills the hut and despite the uncomfortable heat Mariel feels a deep sense of contentment, and of pride and satisfaction, arriving for work at her own business even if it is only a small 'mom-and-pop' local bakery.

"Morning, Mom. We've prepared a workspace for you, here. Are you happy if I leave you to it while I serve the customers? There're a couple of people waiting."

"Yes, sure, dear." Mariel looks at all the ingredients carefully laid out. "I've got everything I need."

She starts to beat together the butter and sugar. It feels strange making such a familiar recipe in such an unfamiliar location. She realises that she misses KL – the peacefulness of the house when everyone is out, and she can bake on her own in the kitchen. She doesn't miss Mrs Laura and her moods, even though things had been better in the run-up to her leaving, especially after she'd found a temporary maid. Mariel smiles at the thought that soon she'll no longer be tied to her employer – once her divorce is arranged and she's married Vijay, they can move back to the Philippines whenever they've had enough of serving other people. It's such a relief to finally have this option. She feels free.

But she's surprised by how much she misses Tilly and Aggie. Perhaps it's just the eagerness and joy with which they greet her cookies, but it'll be hard to leave them when she does go. And undoubtedly it will take time to get to know her own family, although already in the last two weeks she feels so much more connected with them. And she and little Gloria are already firm friends. She adds the egg and vanilla essence and starts to stir in the flour. It's hard work because the dough is thick, and the heat is sapping her strength. She worries a little that the lesser quality of the butter will mean the cookies don't taste as good, but there's nothing she can do about it and, for the moment, this is just an experiment – to see if people like these American cookies and are willing to buy them. Before adding the chocolate chips, she does her special trick of stirring in a little milk to stop the dough from being too dry. And then she starts to spoon out cookie-sized dollops onto the baking trays that Rosa has prepared for her.

"Luis, I've nearly finished with the preparation. Is the coco bread ready? Can I use the ovens?"

"Yes, no problem. I've just taken the bread out." He walks over to her, wiping the sweat from his neck and chest with a towel. "Do they bake at the same temperature as bread, or should I make the ovens hotter?"

"I think the same temperature should be fine."

"OK, good. We'll need to turn them halfway through 'cos the ovens don't bake evenly."

Mariel settles down at the table outside, in the shade, with a cup of coffee and a coco bun. As she breaks the coco bun in half the delicious warm coconut oozes out of its middle and she bites it quickly to stop it spilling. *Like the jeepneys*, she thinks, *another thing that really feels like home.*

After twenty minutes the cookies are done. She tries one while they're still warm, as she always does. She can taste the difference in the butter, but they're still delicious.

"What do you think?" she asks, handing one to Luis and then one across to Rosa at the counter. They're both silent as they eat, and she notes the professional manner they have as they taste.

"They're good, Mom," says Rosa, and Luis nods in agreement, "but we're going to have to charge quite a lot for them to pay for all that sugar. So, I'm just not sure they'll sell. People here aren't used to paying a lot for baked goods – remember, this is not fancy KL."

Luis lays them out on a clean tray and takes them over to the sales counter, setting them down next to the coco buns. The sight of them displayed like that makes Mariel smile with pleasure. Having spent so many years baking these cookies for children in her care, it's a new and thrilling sensation to be selling them.

"Well, I believe we can expand the range of things we sell here, so I want to give it a go. Let's break a few up for customers to taste and see what they say." She can tell from Rosa's facial expression that she's not at all happy hearing Mariel enforce her position as boss. But she concedes and indeed the next customer who comes along buys a couple of cookies, having tasted them.

*

It's the Saturday of Mariel's final weekend at home. On Wednesday she'll take the overnight bus back to Manila, see the lawyer about her divorce and then fly back to KL. As promised, Vito and Mila have returned for the weekend. Mariel is watering the vegetable patch while her mother and Mila are making the final preparations for a family dinner. The others are all watching the football in the house on the new TV. Or rather, Rosa is nursing the baby while the boys watch the match. Tensions between Mariel and Rosa gradually seem to be easing. After the entire batch of cookies had sold out by the end of the day, Rosa had had to agree that the plan to expand the bakery might in fact work.

Dreamily, Mariel's thinking that Vijay will oversee the vegetable patch when they move back. Looking at the many little green chillies hanging from the four bushes at the end of the row, she knows how happy he'll be that they grow well here. Her divorce feels so close now she can hardly believe it.

She's booked an appointment to see the lawyer in Manila, Mr De Borga, at eleven o'clock on Thursday morning. Mila had helped her find him. From the directory by the phone in the nurses' dormitory where she lives, she'd ripped out all the pages listing lawyers and sent them to Mariel in KL a few weeks before she'd left to come home. Mariel had wanted to be prepared well in advance – she only has the one day in Manila so she had to be sure she could get an appointment then. She'd looked through the adverts and picked the three that she thought might be the cheapest, and then had used up a great deal of her credit on her international phone card by ringing them. Mr De Borga was a lot more expensive than she'd been expecting to pay, but he was cheaper than the other two, so she'd booked a meeting.

The family dinner is a proper feast of everyone's favourites: *chicken adobo* with rice – Mariel's personal choice; Mariel's mother has made her special *Kare-Kare*, a rich beef stew, with a *bagoong*, a fermented seafood paste, to go with it; there's also Vito's favourite, sizzling *sisig*, chopped-up pig's face and brains with onions and chilli and a raw egg on top; and of course there's *pancit guisado*, stir-fried noodles with chicken and vegetables and kalamansi lime squeezed all over it. This last dish they always serve at large family gatherings, especially birthdays, as it's a symbol of long life.

There's a happy atmosphere – everyone enjoying their food. Little Gloria is showered with attention and is passed from one family member's knee to another. Looking around the table Mariel feels blessed. She prays that when Vijay joins the atmosphere will remain happy and that any initial tensions and resentments will soon melt away.

After dinner she asks Rosa, Mila and Vito to sit with her around the table for an important talk.

"My dears, as you know, this week I'm going to see a lawyer in Manila to start my divorce." She shifts nervously on the bench. "My passports are proof that I've been away for ten years, but please, it would be very helpful if you could all write a letter saying that you didn't see me during that time."

Rosa stands up abruptly. "I don't believe this! You abandon us for almost our entire childhood and now you want us to help you get this divorce. Well, I won't! I won't have anything to do with it."

Mariel wants to tell her that she too has endured much pain over the years, but she says nothing, and Rosa storms off into the house.

Leaning over, Vito puts an arm around his mother's shoulder. "It's OK, Mom, I'll do it. None of us liked you leaving us for such a long time. But it's done now, and it'd be a tragedy to waste it."

"Yes, Mom, me too. I think divorce should be allowed. And you shouldn't have to leave your family for ten years to get it." Mila's eyes well with tears.

Giving her a tissue from the box on the table, Mariel longs to comfort her. She gently pats her on the shoulder. "I don't think I've said this enough, but I am sorry. It was a terrible thing, but I didn't know what else to do."

The end

Mariel wakes with a start as the bus jolts to a halt at traffic lights. Her neck aches from the awkwardness of the night's sleep. They've arrived in Manila. Telegraph wires crisscross overhead – there are so many of them. The traffic is heavy and chaotic, motorbikes and *traysikels* vying for space at the junction, two sad-looking pigs heading to market in what would normally have been the passenger cab of a *traysikel*. She sees a street vendor setting out his produce for the day – cabbages, eggplant, water spinach, a huge mound of green chillies. She smiles, thinking of Vijay. Tomorrow she'll be home with him, the process of her divorce will have begun and they can start to plan their wedding properly.

She stretches as best she can within the confines of her seat and realises that her blouse, her best one, is now sweaty and crumpled from the night's journey. She attempts to smooth it out and rummages in her bag for her perfume. Her appointment with Mr De Borga is in three hours. She has left plenty of time to change buses at the bus terminal, to catch a local city one and find the lawyer's office on Chino Roces Avenue. For about the tenth time she fumbles in the side pocket of her handbag to check that her current passport and her old one are still in there. With them she can prove that between 1997 and 2007 she didn't enter the Philippines. She also has the letters from Vito and Mila. Rosa had eventually calmed down and they'd patched things up, but Mariel had felt it was better not to mention the letter again.

She closes her eyes and hums under her breath to settle her nerves, but it doesn't work. She unwraps a Werther's Original toffee, pops it in her mouth and sucks on it purposefully.

*

The lawyer's firm is in a run-down building, above a 7-Eleven. What did she expect? He was the cheapest. She waits on a chair in the corridor outside his office, her eyes drawn to the dirty linoleum floor and the peeling paint. Two men are also waiting – the young, good-looking one is bouncing his right leg over his left knee and fiddling with the laces of his fashionable trainers. The older one is less well dressed and looks as though he's carrying the cares of the world on his shoulders. A revolving fan perched on a rickety table provides little relief from the heat and humidity. Her blouse clings to her. She can smell her own sweat, her anxiety, filtering through, past her perfume.

Mr De Borga, ushering her into his office, offers her a seat. He's a friendly-looking round man – a round face and a large round belly that's straining to break free from his grey polyester suit trousers and his white short-sleeved shirt. Sweat patches under his arms are gradually creeping towards his stomach. An ancient air-con unit is rattling away.

Before she's even sat down Mariel starts to explain, nervously, that she's fulfilled the ten-year separation requirement and would now like to get a divorce. Mr De Borga looks at her. "I'm sorry, Mrs Ramos, I don't understand. What do you mean by 'the ten-year separation requirement'?"

She hands him her two passports and the letters from her children. "My passports and these letters prove that I've been separated from my husband, living in another country, for ten years. So now I'd like to apply for a divorce."

He glances at them, briefly, and sighs. "Mrs Ramos, Philippine law does not allow for divorce."

"But these are special circumstances, I had a meeting with a lawyer in Kuala Lumpur, he told me that if I didn't see my husband and children for ten years and didn't return to the Philippines then I could get a divorce." She pulls at her blouse again.

"I'm sorry, Mrs Ramos, but in the Philippines you *can't* get divorced under any circumstances." He speaks slowly, as though trying to ensure she understands every word.

He has, of course, just made a mistake. Why had she been so stupid to choose a cheap lawyer who clearly doesn't know about the different rules for special circumstances?

"But no, sir... you're wrong... if you're completely separated for ten years... then you can get a divorce. The KL lawyer told me..."

"I'm afraid he misinformed you." He looks pointedly

at his watch, but Mariel hardly notices.

"You don't understand…" Her voice starts to crack. "It's different if you're in another country. I was in Malaysia for the ten years. I didn't see my family…"

"It's possible that this ten-year rule applies if you're Malaysian, but it definitely doesn't apply if you're Filipino, whatever country you're in." His tone is softening.

"But there's been a mistake… I showed the lawyer my Filipino passport. Maybe… sir, you don't know about this rule for people abroad, sir? Because… why did he tell me that?"

"I fear he cheated you. I think he told you something you wanted to hear to ensure you'd pay his bill."

She gulps at the air, choking on the information he's just told her. And she places the palm of her hand against her heart as though trying to stop it from shattering. The rattling of the air-con unit grows to a sinister growl.

Leaning forward a little across his desk, he says gently, "As I'm sure you already know, Mrs Ramos, there are a lot of bad people in this world."

But Mariel's struggling to hear what he's saying. His voice seems muffled and distorted. And then she remembers Amy Perez, the famous TV presenter, and regains some of her composure.

"But what about the TV host, Amy Perez? I read in the papers that she's getting a divorce."

"Not a divorce – I believe she's applied for an annulment. That *is* another option for you." He smiles at her sympathetically. "I could help you apply for an annulment. Although, it's a long and expensive process –

it could take up to another ten years."

"Another ten years…?! How do I get this annulment?"

"I'm afraid you'd need to prove that your husband is suffering from 'psychological incapacity' – that he has a personality disorder. You may be required to show that *you* have a personality disorder as well."

"A personality disorder? What d'you mean?" Her confusion is overwhelming her. As though in slow motion, she watches the lawyer wipe the perspiration from his forehead with a dirty white handkerchief.

"I'll be honest with you, Mrs Ramos, it's very difficult to prove. And it will be *very* expensive. My initial fee alone will be US$2,000 and, if it takes many years, then the fees will build up and up."

Mariel gasps and again feels like she's choking on the stale air in the room. "But I can't afford that… "

"Then I'm afraid there's nothing more I can do for you."

*

She stumbles out of the building and wanders, trance-like, in the direction of the bus stop. Then the grief comes. It feels physical, as though the cords of her soul have been severed. The pain cuts across her body, just below her ribcage, and then creeps through her arms to her hands. She curls and uncurls her fingers, but there's no stopping it.

She slumps onto the narrow plastic bench. Wrapping her arms around her handbag, she hugs it to her chest, rocking gently back and forth. Sunlight shines through the narrow gap between the panels of the bus shelter and casts crooked, jagged shafts across her body. Traffic roars past, oblivious to her pain. Eventually, the bus comes.

*

Mariel wakes slowly, relishing the pleasure of having slept in her comfortable bed, and realises she's alone – Vijay is already up and out. Then, she remembers, and the pain smothers her. She throws off the sheet and rolls onto her side, curling into a foetal position. How can this have happened? Leaning over to open the window she listens – yes, Vijay's sweeping the leaves off the veranda. The swish of the broom, normally so comforting, seems to scrape across her heart.

She'd arrived back from Manila late the night before and told him what the lawyer had said. She'd had to explain three times and still he'd struggled to understand: "But ten years no visit, just like he say." And then a surging anger: "I kill that cheating lawyer! Tomorrow I go downtown, I find him, I kill him!" And then bewildered concern for the future: "If not married, what we do?"

Mariel had spent the whole flight back thinking about what they'd do. Hopefully they can go on as they are, living together until Mrs Laura and the family move back to England. She knows they've decided to stay for a couple more years. Mariel will of course do everything she can to make herself indispensable – Mrs Laura has already shown she can't manage without a maid. After that, she and Vijay could try to find another job in KL together, but it won't be easy to find new employers who are willing to hire a couple that aren't married. Or, they could go back to the old system and just see each other on Sundays. But she knows that after living together that would be torture. Either way, the problem will come when it's time to retire. They won't be legally allowed to stay in Malaysia and neither of them will be able to move to each other's countries unless they're married.

Her mind had been whirring so fast she hadn't been able to sleep on the plane despite her exhaustion after the overnight bus journey and such a traumatic day. Being in the window seat she'd wriggled onto her side, rested her head and gazed out at the blackness of the night sky. Her eyes were just starting to droop when she'd suddenly remembered Tala, a friend of Jenny's, who she'd met a few times at church, years ago. Tala had moved to England with her employers. Mariel remembered having coffee after church one day with Jenny and Faye, and Jenny telling them that Tala had written to say that she'd managed to get British residency because she'd lived in England for some time and had been sponsored by her employers.

After remembering this there was no chance of Mariel getting any sleep on the flight. She'd sat back up and smoothed out her blouse. If she and Vijay moved back to England with the family, they could live together even if they weren't married and then maybe one day, like Tala, get British residency. It was terrible to think she wouldn't be able to be with her children and little Gloria, especially after the lost ten years and all her dreams of moving home. Plus, she'd never wanted to live somewhere as far away as England. But, if it's the only way she and Vijay can stay together, then that's what they'll have to do. Then she'd wavered – could she bear being such a long way from her family? In truth, after all these years, they've all grown used to being apart and at least now she'll be able to visit.

So, she and Vijay will have to persuade Mrs Laura and Mr Peter to take them back to England with them. She'll have to convince Mrs Laura that she can't manage without them even back home. The children have told her that it's not normal to have a maid in England, but Mrs Laura is definitely getting more and more like a lazy boss – she used to help clear the table but now she just lets Mariel do everything. And Mariel has heard her say laughingly to her friends that she's forgotten how to cook. If they stay in Malaysia for a few more years then Mrs Laura will hopefully become more and more dependent on having full-time help. And for Vijay, Tilly and Aggie are always talking about their 'ginormous' garden in England, so they must need someone to help with that.

As the plane had started its descent, Mariel had felt the tightening in her chest loosen a little – she had a plan now. She always feels better once she has a plan. But when she'd got back and spoken to Vijay, he'd been so distressed by the lawyer's news he hadn't been able to see the possibilities of her plan. And this morning she senses its fragility and perhaps its impossibility.

She gets dressed and lets herself into the main house to prepare breakfast. Stacking the plates, glasses and cutlery on a tray, the tablecloth under her arm, she walks out to the veranda to set the table. Vijay is still sweeping even though the leaves are all long gone. The passionflower in full bloom, hanging from the trellis, seems to frame him. And for a fleeting moment he stops, rests on the broom and looks at her, his eyes and face awash with a profound sadness.

Back in the kitchen she slices up the fruit and arranges it on the platter with particular care, fanning out the mango the way that Aggie says is 'pwetty'. Through the window she sees the golden oriel performing its morning flight across the garden – a vibrant yellow, streaking across her peripheral vision and landing on its favourite branch of the jacaranda tree.

EPILOGUE

June – thirty-five years later

Gently, Mariel guides the bamboo straw between Laura's lips. Laura closes her lopsided mouth over it and sucks up the apple juice. A little stream escapes and runs down the side of her face. The two of them are sitting in the garden, under the shade of the big beech tree. The dappled sunlight is making patterns on the old cashmere blanket covering Laura's lap. She seems to keep losing interest in the apple juice and watches the patterns instead, transfixed by the light. There's a lovely smell of freshly cut grass – the self-driving electric tractor is mowing the extensive lawn. And in the distance Mariel can see the river winding its way out to the estuary. Vijay is hoeing one end of the long flowerbed and Peter is hoeing the other. Peter used to leave all the gardening to Vijay, but since Laura's stroke it seems that he likes to keep busy.

Mariel is waiting for Aggie and the boys to come round and for Aggie to take over caring for her mother for the afternoon. Laura's face always lights up at the sight of little Rory and Max. They're noisy and boisterous, but she seems to find comfort in the sight and sound of them charging around the garden and having fun. Mariel wishes that Tilly and her wife and daughter could be here more often – they came over soon after Laura had the stroke and spent time visiting her in hospital, but then they had to get back to Shanghai.

Mariel checks her phone-watch. It's nearly four. They'll be here soon. She wants to pop over to her house and do some invoicing. The little converted barn that she and Vijay live in is so close to the main house that she can easily nip back and forth when she needs to. Since Laura's been ill and in need of constant care, Mariel's catering business has not been getting the attention it requires. She'd set it up when Tilly and Aggie left school and went off to university. She mainly does dinner parties for people within about a twenty-mile radius and sometimes shooting lunches for the big estate in the next-door village. Being such a good cook, she'd built up her reputation in no time. Vijay does the waitering and helps her with the washing-up. She loves working with him – their routine is so finely tuned they barely communicate with words, just the occasional look or gentle touch. When Vijay serves the food and wine, he beams his beautiful smile at all the guests – they're immediately won over and Mariel feels proud that he's hers. When Tilly and Aggie were students, they'd often waitressed for her as well, and Mariel always felt a particular sense of satisfaction as she, the boss, paid them their wages. Now if she needs extra help, she uses a young girl in the village called Sam.

This afternoon, before it gets too late, Mariel needs to ring Rosa. In privacy she wants to tell her that because of Laura's stroke she and Vijay won't be coming home for their usual annual visit. She feels bad, partly because she won't be able to see all her family but mainly because, in truth, she's relieved not to be going home this year. It's such a long way and the flight is terribly expensive now that the carbon taxes are so high. She finds the trip very tiring both physically and emotionally. Even though her house in the Philippines has been greatly modernised over the years and now has air-con in every room and three proper bathrooms, she still finds staying there uncomfortable. She can no longer take the heat. Even Vijay struggles, and he's never liked the long flight.

These feelings of guilt snaking their way into her heart remind her of a while back when Rosa had managed to keep from her, for three years, the news that Vincente, Mariel's husband, had died. Mariel had been so confused when she'd finally found out (Mila had eventually decided it was wrong to keep it from her) and she'd asked, "But why, Rosa? Why didn't you tell me before?"

"I didn't want you to know you were free of him – in case you then stopped coming home."

"But I wasn't coming home because I was still married to your father. In fact, I don't *have* to come home at all – after all, I didn't for ten years – I come because I *want* to, because I want to see you."

Of course, she and Vijay were married the moment they found out Vincente had passed. Indeed, Mariel had wondered whether Rosa's continued mistrust of Vijay had been another reason for her deception. After their wedding they had considered moving back to the Philippines, but Mariel had just started the catering business and was enjoying it so much she hadn't wanted to give it up. That, plus the fact it was clear the community in her village, not to mention her family, were never going to truly accept Vijay. So, they'd stayed in England but visited the Philippines once a year. And when her son, Vito, had moved to Switzerland to be a vet they'd tried to visit him regularly as well.

Now, admitting to herself that she doesn't want to see her family enough to overcome the effort of making the trip home, she's almost overwhelmed by the guilt. *But then again*, she thinks, *I'm getting old*. Perhaps it's time to face the truth – she's been away from home for fifty-five years and although she's always loved her children and grandchildren and great-grandchildren, she's never really known any of them. As the joy of loving Vijay and growing old with him had strengthened, the sorrow of having to leave her family had passed – it had faded gradually, with a lingering glimmer, like the light at the end of an English summer's day.

Hearing the crunch of wheels on gravel, she looks up to see Aggie's car coming up the drive.

Acknowledgements

Thank you to:

Zoë Pagnamenta, for encouraging me to 'get on and write a novel'; Alan Higgs, for suggesting Faber Academy; Sue Gee, my mentor at Faber Academy, who guided me through my first draft, and my wonderful Faber Academy writing group, Betsy, Matt, Annett and Fiamma, who patiently read and gave feedback on each chapter as it emerged.

David Roberts, who encouraged me not to give up when my spirit was flagging and to write the next draft ensuring that some of the smoking guns in the plot were actually fired.

Screenwriter, Jonathan Wakeham, who was incredibly generous with his time, reading the manuscript and giving invaluable feedback as to how it could be improved.

Writer and editor, Justine Abigail Yu, a fierce advocate for anti-oppression and equity, whose critical feedback on the manuscript was hugely helpful and led to some fundamental changes.

Friends and family who've all been incredibly helpful and supportive, particularly Cecily Carey, Susan Wilmot and Julia Crozier who read my first draft and Lily Spicer who proofread the final draft.

Lastly, big love and thanks to my husband and daughters who have lived with this book for so many years and who have allowed snippets of their lives to be reimagined.